TO THE LAST DROP

TO THE LAST DROP

Sandra Balzo

This first world edition published 2016
in Great Britain and the USA by
SEVERN HOUSE PUBLISHERS LTD of
19 Cedar Road, Sutton, Surrey, England, SM2 5DA.
Trade paperback edition first published
in Great Britain and the USA 2016 by
SEVERN HOUSE PUBLISHERS LTD

British Library Cataloguing in Publication Data
A CIP catalogue record for this title is available from the British Library.

ISBN-13: 978-0-7278-8592-0 (cased)
ISBN-13: 978-1-84751-695-4 (trade paper)
ISBN-13: 978-1-78010-756-1 (e-book)

All Severn House titles are printed on acid-free paper.

Severn House Publishers support the Forest Stewardship Council™ [FSC™],
the leading international forest certification organisation.
All our titles that are printed on FSC certified paper carry the FSC logo.

Typeset by Palimpsest Book Production Ltd.,
Falkirk, Stirlingshire, Scotland.
Printed and bound in Great Britain by
TJ International, Padstow, Cornwall.

For Lisa and Mike,
the reason I'm here

ONE

'I didn't expect to inherit anything. I was just relieved he wasn't a terrorist.' I shivered, pulling the sleeves of my Uncommon Grounds T-shirt over my hands for the two-block walk. I should have grabbed my jacket – it was the second Friday in November, after all. And Wisconsin.

My partner in the coffeehouse, the normally unflappable Sarah Kingston, stopped dead on the sidewalk. 'You—'

A horn interrupted her. A silver BMW was trying to pull out of the parking lot that served both Uncommon Grounds and the historic Brookhills, Wisconsin train depot it was housed in.

Sarah stayed put. 'You thought your brother was a terrorist?'

'Not international. The home-grown kind that live in the woods.' I tugged my partner past the driveway so the car could turn onto Junction Road. 'You're going to get us killed, you know.'

Sarah shook me off. 'Yeah, I can see the headline now: "Coffeehouse owners mowed down by overly caffeinated Brookhills Barbie."'

I waved for the BMW to bump up and over the railroad tracks before we started across on foot. 'Keep your voice down – she might hear you.'

Sarah stopped again, one sensibly-shod foot on the wooden tie of the track, the other balanced on the metal rail. In her usual uniform of trousers and long baggy jacket, she didn't seem to be affected by the cold wind. 'Who, the Barbie? You're the one who called them that in the first place. Plastic, perfectly coifed and legs attached at their unnatural waists, remember?'

'I do, but they're also our customers, which Amy continues to pound into me.' Amy Caprese was our sole barista, who – despite henna tats, multiple piercings and rainbow-striped hair – had proven herself to be the most socially well adjusted and level-headed of the group.

Which didn't take much, given that Sarah was an irascible manic depressive and I just didn't give a shit.

'C'mon,' I said as a train whistle sounded from the east. 'That's the four p.m. from Milwaukee. Which, coincidentally, is the time of my appointment with Mary's sister.'

Mary Callahan was Brookhills' head librarian and my favorite gossipmonger. She also prepared taxes on the side and, when I'd asked Mary about the tax implications of my inheritance, she'd suggested talking to her sister, Lynne Swope. Lynne was a financial planner who had recently moved to Brookhills.

'And you know how I hate to be late,' I continued, waving my partner onward.

'I do,' Sarah said, considering that. 'Never quite made sense to me. You're cynical and occasionally uncaring, but always prompt.'

'I . . . well, thank you.' Take a compliment where you can get one, I figure. Even if it's riding the rump of an insult.

'So Mary has a sister,' Sarah said, starting out again. 'I don't think she's ever mentioned—'

'Stop!' I flung my arm out just in time to keep her from stepping in front of a Lincoln Navigator. 'You have to look before you cross.'

Sarah shook her head. Or maybe she was looking both ways. 'What's with all this traffic lately?'

'Traffic' was a relative term, but by our town's standards it was true the number of cars using Junction Road, an angled street just off Brookhill Road, the main east/west drag, had picked up. 'People are avoiding that damned roundabout.'

A traffic circle, or roundabout, had recently been installed to slow down drivers using Brookhill Road through town to access Interstate 94 into Milwaukee.

'You have a problem with roundabouts?' Sarah asked, allowing me to lead the way.

'They confuse people. Never a good thing, especially when they're driving two-ton SUVs like the one that just nearly flattened you.'

'Except when it makes those SUVs use Junction Road as a detour, bringing them right past our shop.'

Pollyanna.

Halfway down the block between an upscale resale shop and a designer shoe store was a plain plate-glass door stenciled

Swope Financial Planning. I stopped in front of it. 'This is the place.'

'Not very impressive,' Sarah said, pulling the door open. 'You sure you want to trust this woman with your money?'

My partner stepped into a small, dark hallway but I remained on the sidewalk. 'Where are you going?'

'To your appointment. Why else would I have walked here with you?'

'Honestly?' I said, following her in. 'I figured you wanted to avoid helping Amy serve the commuters from the four o'clock train.'

'Which is exactly what *you're* doing.' Sarah started up the steps. 'Are you telling me you don't want my advice?'

'Isn't that what I'm going to an advisor for?' I called up after her. 'Advice?'

'You're *welcome,*' Sarah said, not looking back.

'*Thank* you.' If you stick your tongue out at somebody in a stairwell and they don't see it, is it still passive-aggressive?

'How much are we talking about anyway?' Sarah asked as I joined her on the upper landing.

'A little under fifty thousand dollars.'

My partner whistled as she swung open the door in front of her, drawing a curious glance from the dark-haired woman at the front desk.

The woman set down her cell phone hastily like we'd caught her playing games or sexting on company time. 'Can I help you?'

I slid around Sarah. 'I'm Maggy Thorsen, to see Lynne Swope?'

'Well, you're seeing her.' The brunette stood up, gaining about ten inches on me.

'Whoa,' Sarah said.

'I think she means you're tall,' I automatically translated.

'Especially compared to that shrimp of a sister,' Sarah said. 'Mary might be what? Five foot nothing?'

'Five two.' Swope's shoulders almost imperceptibly rounded. 'Dad said I must have inherited his height to compensate for the fact Mary got his brains.'

'Ouch,' I said.

'Oh, he was right, as it turns out.' Swope smiled and pulled her shoulders back where they belonged. 'But like my husband says, hard work trumps pure horsepower any day. And I would add "having a plan" to the hard work. Which is why I love this job.' She turned the smile on Sarah. 'And you are?'

'Sarah Kingston.'

'My partner,' I explained.

'Oh, how nice,' Lynne said, her gaze swinging back and forth between the two of us.

'Not that kind of partner,' Sarah growled.

'We're business partners,' I said. 'In—'

'Uncommon Grounds. Of course.' Swope beckoned for us to follow her and opened a door to a sparsely furnished conference room. A box of tissues sat in the middle of the round wooden table, presumably for the recipients of the unhappy financial tidings that would be outlined on the yellow legal pads next to it. On one beige wall of the room a schoolroom clock ticked off the seconds audibly and, on another, leaned a stack of metal folding chairs.

Lynne gestured for us to take our choice of the four chairs already set up at the table, as she did the same. 'Are you planning on investing part of the inheritance in the business, Maggy?'

'God, *no*,' was out of my mouth before I could stop it. I glanced over at Sarah. 'Sorry.'

Sarah had already slipped into the chair diagonally across from our host. 'Maggy sank her life savings into Uncommon Grounds' first location. Now it's my turn, apparently.'

'All my divorce settlement and *most* of my life savings,' I corrected, taking the seat next to her. 'Sarah inherited the train depot, so when my first partner pulled out after the collapse of our first coffeehouse, I—'

'Wait, wait,' Swope interrupted, pulling a yellow pad from the stack. 'Did you and this partner file for bankruptcy?'

'No,' I said, a little confused. 'We had insurance. And, besides, we were leasing the space.'

Lynne had started scribbling; now she glanced up. 'Is there a reason you think this new location in the depot will work out better?'

'It has walls and a ceiling?' Sarah ventured.

Lynne Swope's turn to look baffled. 'I know this isn't what

you came here to talk about, but in order to advise you, I need to know if there's debt from the failed business.'

'Ohhhhh,' Sarah and I both said, tumbling in unison to what she meant.

I shook my head. 'Sorry, Lynne, we didn't make ourselves clear. It wasn't the business that collapsed.'

'It was the entire strip mall.' Sarah held one hand horizontally above the other, palms facing, and slapped the two together. 'Flat as a pancake.'

'Ahh.' Lynne leaned back in her chair. '*That* strip mall. The roof caved in just as we moved here. Benson Plaza, wasn't it? You were there. Not personally, of course, but your store—'

'No, we were there,' I said.

'About as personally as you can get without being dead,' Sarah agreed.

Lynne looked like she wanted to ask more, and who could blame her? But I was paying by the hour. 'You'll have to stop by the shop sometime and we'll tell you all about it.'

'I—'

'Maggy's right,' Sarah said. 'This is about her and the check that's burning a hole in her pocketbook.'

The financial advisor bowed her head. 'Of course. There's one thing I do need to mention before we go any further, Maggy, and I hope it's not a problem. Your ex-husband is Ted Thorsen.'

'Correct,' I said, though it hadn't been a question.

'I don't know if you're aware that my husband joined Thorsen Dental in May,' Lynne said. 'I'm hoping you don't see that as a conflict of interest on my part.'

I let out the breath I'd been holding, relieved there wasn't some sort of financial complication resulting from my divorce. Like I had to give my cheating ex half of my inheritance. 'Your husband is a dentist?'

'Oral surgeon. He had a four-person office in Louisville with an upmarket clientele.'

I wasn't sure what 'upmarket' meant in dentistry. They flossed more often? Rinsed but didn't spit?

'When our daughter Ginny received her acceptance letter from Quorum School of Business and Management,' Lynne Swope continued, 'it almost felt like a sign.'

'A sign?' I asked.

'You know – that we should be closer to her school.' She held up her hands. 'Oh, don't get me wrong. William felt awful leaving his partner in the lurch – down an oral surgeon and they were training a new office manager – but sometimes you need to do what's best for you and your family, right?'

She looked at me expectantly so I nodded. In truth, Ted would have committed hari-kari with a dental pick if he'd been left in a similar situation. In fact, when Michaela, his long-time office manager, had retired in April, Ted had been nearly inconsolable and largely incompetent. I'd helped find a replacement if only to make the whining stop.

Sarah was frowning. 'Isn't Quorum in Minneapolis?'

'I'm sure Lynne knows that.' I was hoping it was true. Though it wasn't unusual for people to make that geographical mistake regarding what they considered 'fly-over states.' Minnesota, Wisconsin. Minneapolis, Milwaukee. Potato, potahto.

You'd like to think, though, that a 'planner' would have gotten out a map of the upper Midwest before making the move. Especially a planner I was about to entrust with my entire inheritance. 'Is your daughter in the MBA program at Quorum?'

'Oh, we expect that Ginny will go for both her masters and PhD in Business, eventually, but for now she's in the undergraduate school. Since she'll be in Minneapolis for quite a while, we went ahead and bought a house here a couple miles east on Brookhill Road.'

'But why not Minneapolis or St Paul?' Sarah asked, still not understanding.

Which made two of us. The 'Twin Cities' were adjacent to each other, as the nickname implies, but a good five hours from Brookhills, even at the frightening speed I feared my son drove to make the trek in 'record time.'

'William had talked about that,' Lynne said. 'But when he and I met your ex-husband at a dental conference in Scottsdale, Ted said he was looking a partner here in Brookhills.'

'And, of course, your sister already lived here,' I said, starting to get it.

'Oh, yes.' The color rose in Lynne's cheeks. 'It's good to be near family. But, more importantly, Brookhills is halfway between

Louisville and Minneapolis, so it cut the drive to and from Ginny's school in half. That seemed about right, lest anybody mistake us for helicopter parents.'

'Parents who hover,' I told Sarah.

'I'm not dense, you know.' And then, under her breath, 'Though it sounds like that whirlybird has already sailed.'

'What about your work?' I asked the financial planner to cover Sarah's rudeness. 'Did you have your own firm in Louisville, as well?'

'I was William's office manager originally, but started Swope Financial about twelve years ago.'

'And moving the business hasn't been a problem?' I asked.

'Not really,' Lynne said. 'Where there's money, taxes and people there's always the need for advisors like me. I have to admit it's been a challenge to get up to speed on the different state laws, and I must say Wisconsin has its quirks. It's one of only a handful of community property states, for example, and—'

'But you are?' I interrupted a little uneasily. 'Up to speed, I mean?'

'Oh, yes – not to worry,' the head of Swope Financial Planning assured me. 'We moved just after tax time this spring, so I've had plenty of time to bone up.'

'I don't know if Ted told you,' I said, 'but our son Eric goes to the University of Minnesota, which, like Quorum, is in Minneapolis. The distance is perfect – far enough away that Eric feels independent but he can also come home for a weekend when he wants to.'

'Precisely.' Lynne was nodding. 'In fact, I got a text from Ginny just before you came in. She and Eric are en route as we speak.'

'Here? Together?' I'd known Eric was driving back for the weekend but he hadn't so much as mentioned his father's new partner. Nor that the man had a daughter who went to school nearby. Not that I pumped my son for information. Much. 'What a coincidence that the kids already knew each other.'

'They didn't, but since this is Ginny's first year in Minneapolis, Ted offered to put them in touch. She's still feeling a little lost, I'm afraid.'

'I wouldn't worry,' I said. 'Once Ginny makes a few friends at school she'll come to love the Twin Cities. Did she say what time they'll arrive? Eric drives—' I swallowed the 'too fast,' given the Swopes' daughter was along for the ride.

'Oh, it's Ginny who's driving. Eric had car trouble and she offered to bring him down.'

Odd to be hearing all this second-hand from a woman I'd just met. But then Eric was coming home for the christening of his half-sister, Mia – Ted and his current wife's new baby. It made sense that father and son had been in touch about the trouble with my old Dodge Caravan. Maybe that even meant Ted was going to pony up for the repairs.

Heartened by the thought, I said, 'What luck that Ginny was coming home, too.'

'It was spur of the moment, I think. But a nice surprise, of course.' Lynne didn't look all that happy, though.

'I hope she's not making a five-hour drive just to give Eric a ride.'

'Honestly, Ginny seemed to be looking for an excuse to come home anyway. And a long drive is always more fun with company.' She flashed a smile. 'Wouldn't it be something if they became a couple?'

'It certainly would.' Especially since Eric was gay.

'You didn't mention that Eric was coming home this weekend.' Sarah was looking grumpy.

Sheesh, my business partner might as well be my partner-partner. 'I did, too, remember? I told you I could work tomorrow morning but needed Sunday off because Eric was coming home for Mia's baptism.'

'Oh, yeah.' No apology, but she did make a conversational lane change from accusation to pleasantry. 'You going?'

'To the christening? Sure,' I said. 'The baby is Eric's half-sister. Divorce or not, we're still family.'

'More's the pity,' was Sarah's opinion. 'Is the lovely Rachel being sprung for the soiree?'

Rachel Slattery Thorsen was the hygienist who had stolen Ted's heart right out from under my nose. Using assorted body parts of her own, no doubt.

'No.' Unsure how much Lynne knew about Ted and the melo-drama surrounding his wife, I said, by way of partial explanation: 'Rachel is Ted's wife and she's . . . away.'

Twenty to life, as it turned out.

'Ted told us all about it,' Lynne said sympathetically. 'In fact, it's why he said he's decided to take on a partner. Solo practice is tough enough without being a single parent, for all intents and purposes.'

Though having money – even if it was courtesy of the Slatterys, his uppity in-laws and Southeastern Wisconsin's answer to the Hiltons – should help.

But speaking of money, the ticking of the clock on the conference room wall reminded me that twenty minutes of God-knew-how-expensive time had elapsed. 'I can't imagine how Ted and William being in business together could be a conflict, Lynne. I assume you wouldn't share information about a client with anybody, including your husband.'

'Of course not,' Lynne said solemnly and then cracked a grin. 'Even financial planners aren't hard up enough to use profit-and-loss statements as pillow talk.'

I smiled back and opened my bag, pulling out an envelope. 'Sarah and I need to get back to work, but I should give you this before I forget.'

'I understand. I need to send off an email myself before it's too late.' Lynne Swope took the envelope and slipped out a cashier's check. 'Forty-nine thousand, seven hundred and thirty-five dollars.' She looked up. 'Any ideas on what you'd like to do with it?'

'Not a clue. I was hoping you'd tell me.'

'How are you set for retirement?' Lynne leaned back in her folding chair and it creaked ominously.

'I have an Individual Retirement Account from my job at First Financial,' I said. 'But since I left there to start Uncommon Grounds, I haven't been able to contribute to it.'

'Just how much of that,' Sarah chin-gestured to the check in Swope's hand, 'is going to be left after taxes anyway?'

I swallowed my annoyance at my partner's interference. It was a good question, even if I thought I knew the answer. 'Mary said there are no estate or inheritance taxes here, right?'

'Correct,' Lynne said. 'Wisconsin is different in that way, too, to some other states. And you'd have to have a lot more than this,' she smoothed the check out on the table, 'for federal estate tax to kick in. But income tax could come into play. Do you know the source of the money?'

I used my fingernail to pick at an imaginary spot on the table. 'Not really.'

The financial planner seemed to sense my discomfort and tried to ease it. 'I only ask because if this was a distribution of pre-tax money, like from a retirement account, you'd be required to pay ordinary income tax on it.'

Ugh. But before I could respond, Lynne continued, 'On the plus side, though, if the funds are from the sale of securities or real estate *after* your brother's death, there might be a tax benefit to you.'

'Why is that?' Sarah nosed back into the conversation.

'For inherited stock or property, the cost basis is stepped up to its value at the time of death. That can mean a huge saving when Maggy goes to sell it because she'll be taxed on the increase in value since she inherited it, not since her brother bought it. Of course, if the money is the proceeds of either stock or real estate your brother sold himself, then—'

'It was cash,' I burst out. 'I found it in the chest freezer in the garage. Under a dressed-out deer carcass.'

Unlike the financial adviser, Sarah seemed to delight in my discomfort. 'Oh, perfect. *Please* tell me it was a male deer. You know, your brother hid his bucks under a buck?'

Lynne Swope acknowledged the pun with a pained smile and turned to me. 'It's not so unusual for folks to hide their money in a freezer or refrigerator, Maggy, thinking it'll be safe from fire. In reality, it's not much better than the proverbial mattress.'

But Sarah was squinting at me. 'Are you telling me you found nearly fifty grand in *cash*? Was Pavlik with you?'

Jake Pavlik was Brookhills county sheriff and my main squeeze, for want of another expression that didn't make us sound like horny sixteen-year-olds. Though since our return from a trip together to Fort Lauderdale a week ago, I'd seen very little of Pavlik – horny or otherwise. I assumed he was catching up on business, as was I. Or should be. Or intended to.

'I drove up there alone that July weekend, remember? You were ticked because you had to deal with the contractor here on your own.'

Sarah was usually irritated about something, though this time she'd probably had cause. We'd been just weeks away from the grand opening of Uncommon Grounds in its new location when our contractor had run into legal trouble. The new one had barely been in place before I made my unplanned trip north to deal with my brother's property in the Upper Peninsula of Michigan. The UP, as it's called, crouches on the northern border of Wisconsin, like a hat doffed by Michigan proper.

But my partner's problem at the moment didn't seem to be with my leaving. She held up one hand like a student waiting to be called on in class. 'So you're in this backwoods cabin, probably with no toilet or running water—'

'To be fair, it had both,' I said, remembering the chemical commode I'd used to get rid of the marijuana I'd also found in the freezer. 'Just not quite . . . up to code.'

'—and found this stash of cash?' Sarah continued unabated.

'Correct,' I said. 'So I called the estate lawyer—'

'Why in the world would you do that?' Sarah demanded. 'It's *cash.* You were alone with no witnesses. You could have taken it and nobody would have been the wiser. No probate, no income ta—' She seemed to remember Lynne Swope was there. 'Sorry.'

'Don't be,' said Lynne. 'I'm sure it's been done before. Once Maggy brought the attorney in, though, he'd have a fiduciary duty to include it—'

'Duty, schmoody,' I muttered. 'I was just glad the carcass it was hidden under was a deer.'

TWO

'You are such a goody two shoes,' Sarah said as she mounted the stairs to our coffeehouse's wraparound porch.

'Just because I like to follow the rules?' I protested, following. 'Do the right thing?'

'Sometimes the two aren't synonymous.'

Not wanting to argue more than we already had on the stroll

back, I turned my attention – and, I hoped, the subject – to the wrought-iron tables and chairs pushed close to the building. 'I suppose we should chain these up.'

'Afraid the patio furniture is going to make a run for it?'

'I'm *afraid* they're going to be stolen. We probably should be securing them every night, even during the nice weather for the winter.'

Sarah paused, her hand on the doorknob. 'Geez, louise – this is Brookhills. Who would scratch their Beemer or Lexus by loading our cheap-ass tables and chairs into them?'

'You have a point,' I said tightly. Being 'the responsible one' in running the coffeehouse was getting old fast. My first partner, Caron Egan, had filled that role originally, but now that Sarah had taken her place I felt like I had to be the grown-up by default.

And I wasn't very good at it.

'Oh, there you two are.' Amy Caprese pushed open the door, the sleigh bells dangling from it giving Sarah just enough warning to jump back. The barista put up her hand in apology. 'I was just sticking my head out to count the tables and chairs one last time before I ordered the tarps to cover them and cables to secure them for the winter.'

Them that can't do hire somebody who can.

'You are a gem,' I said, catching the door as the wind tried to take it. 'Thank you.'

Sarah preceded me into the store and looked around. 'Big crowd, I see.'

My partner was being sarcastic. Truth was there wasn't a customer in sight, though three tables remained strung together forming a long rectangle.

'Apparently there was a good-sized group here earlier, though.' I pulled back a chair and signaled for Sarah to take the other end of a table so we could move it back into place. 'Honestly, I don't know why people think they can rearrange our furniture and then walk out the door without—'

'Wait, wait!' Amy was holding up both hands, palms out. 'I just finished setting this up for the book club tonight.'

Still hunkered over the table, I cocked my head. 'The book club?'

'We talked about it before you left for Fort Lauderdale,

remember? We're hosting the Brookhills Library's book club at seven p.m. on the second and fourth Fridays of the month.'

I frowned as I straightened up. Truth was I didn't remember anything about a book club, but then I'd been pretty much fixated on what I'd expected to be a romantic weekend in South Florida with Pavlik.

Which just shows the wisdom of the saying, 'Be careful what you wish for.' It might bite you in the butt. Or, in this case, swallow you whole.

'But we *close* at seven,' I pointed out. 'Besides, why wouldn't the library book club meet at the library?'

'They used to but it closes at six now.' Amy shoved the table I'd dislodged back into place, the six gold rings lining her right earlobe tinkling. 'Budget cuts.'

'Well, we have a budget, too.' While grateful for our barista's initiative, it sometimes made me feel like a crappy boss. So, of course, I overcompensated. 'And with Tien on vacation, we don't have back-up.'

Tien Romano was the chef who worked out of our kitchen at night. The shared arrangement meant the freshest pastries and take-out items for us each morning and, for Tien, the workspace to launch her own catering business. Tien also jumped in when we needed an extra hand in the shop, but right now she and her father Luc were off exploring their family roots in Italy and Vietnam.

'Don't worry, Maggy,' Amy said. 'I joined the group so I'll do most of what needs to be done to close the shop before everybody arrives. And then finish up when they leave. You won't have to pay me for the extra time.'

I must have looked doubtful, because she added, 'I did talk to Sarah about this, and she said it would be all right.'

'I did,' my partner confirmed. 'And what are you being so negative about, Maggy? This could eventually mean a dozen or so additional customers every two weeks.'

'And *new* customers,' Amy added. 'Some of the book club members may never have been here and they'll bring in other people. It's good exposure for Uncommon Grounds.'

There was that damn level head again.

*   *   *

Amy and I were tidying up after the returning commuters from the 5:30 p.m. train when the front door opened, the wind sending napkins from the condiment cart sailing.

'Welcome to Uncommon Grounds,' Amy chirped, even as she chased down the napkins.

How could you not love – and simultaneously hate – somebody so unfailingly cheerful and efficient?

Determined to match our barista cheery for cheery, I ducked behind what had been the train station's marble-topped ticket counter to reappear at our service window. 'What can I get you today?' I called to the bundled-up woman who'd just entered.

But she just frowned as she approached, leaning what looked like a weathered fence board against our clean counter before stripping off a grubby blue knit hat and laying that, too, on the counter. 'This doesn't look like a dental office.'

I frowned back at her. 'Because it's not. Uncommon Grounds is a coffeehouse.' The scent of brewing coffee rather than the clove-y aroma of a dentist office might have been a tip-off, though I could personally attest that both odors attach themselves to clothes and hair and follow you home at night like stinky puppies.

The woman unbuttoned her coat, revealing a dingy white blouse fastened high at the throat. And probably a turtleneck under that. She was missing her right cuspid and the rest of her teeth looked like they'd benefit from a good cleaning.

'Well, that's inconvenient,' she said.

With an effort, I turned my frown upside down, managing to disgust even myself with my insincerity. 'Might you be looking for my ex-husband's office, Thorsen Dental?'

Limp dark hair swung forward from a high V on her forehead as the woman dug into her shoulder bag. I tried to gauge her age. Forty, maybe. Resisting the urge to scream 'Get the hair out of your face!' like my mother, I waited until she finally came up with a wrinkled printout. 'It says here it moved from Benson Plaza to this address on Junction Road.'

'The coffeehouse did,' I said. 'But the dental office is at 501 Brookhill Road – the 501 Building, it's called – and remains there.' I pointed out the window, noticing a gray-haired woman mounting the steps outside. 'I have a customer coming in, but you just take Junction Road out there to Civic, turn left and then make another quick left onto Brookhill Road.'

'Why don't you drive her over right away?' Sarah, who'd emerged from the storeroom, said in my ear as the front door opened.

Not on my – or preferably my partner's – life.

'Excuse me.' The new arrival popped her head around the information seeker and I recognized Ted's new office manager, Diane Laudon. She flashed me a smile. 'I just stopped over to pick up a pound of Kenyan AA for the office, but did I overhear you're looking for Thorsen Dental?'

The woman just nodded.

Diane pulled a card out of her shoulder bag and handed it to her. 'You really can't miss it. Our building is about a half mile down on Brookhill, just past Schultz's Market. It and the Morrison Hotel, which is a few blocks farther east, are taller than anything else in Brookhills. If you hit the roundabout you've gone too far.'

The woman looked at the card. 'So Thorsen Dental is in suite,' she glanced up, 'ten-oh-three?'

'Tenth floor,' I said over the sound of the coffee grinder. That 1003 was on the tenth floor probably didn't need clarifying; the woman *had* mistaken a coffeehouse for a dentist's office.

'Thank you.' She stuffed the card, her assorted junk and the printout back into her purse. 'And they're still open?'

Was I my ex-husband's keeper? But Diane fielded this one, too. 'Doctor Thorsen and Doctor Swope are both in, but I'm not sure either would have time to see you this afternoon. If you like, you can follow me over and I can see if we have an opening tomorrow morning.'

'It's Doctor Thorsen I want to see.'

'That'll be fine. He starts at nine.'

'Let me get that coffee for you,' I told Diane before the woman could ask yet another question. 'Do you want it grou—?'

'Of course not,' Sarah cut me off. 'The woman knows her coffee – grinds it fresh.' A brown sack of whole beans sailed over my head. 'There you go.'

'Perfect.' Diane caught the pound deftly and dropped it into her own handbag before fishing out her wallet.

'It's your free one,' Sarah told her.

A free pound of coffee? Apparently the book club wasn't the only change that had been put into place while I was gone. We had punch cards for drinks, of course – but beans?

'Thank you,' Diane said, stashing her wallet. She smiled at the other woman. 'Was there something you wanted to get before we leave?'

'Oh, no. I only drink coffee in the morning,' the woman said. 'But is there a restroom?'

There was, of course, and since it was shared with the public train depot I couldn't even make her purchase something to use it. Not that even *I* was cruel enough to deny a full bladder its relief. 'Right around the corner,' I said, hooking my thumb. 'Across from the side entrance.'

'Oh, thank you.' She leaned down to retrieve the fence board and when she hoisted it onto her shoulder I saw there was a placard attached to it.

'Cavity Searches Done Here,' I read aloud as she rounded the corner to the restroom.

THREE

'You're not going to take her in your car, are you?' I asked Diane when the woman had disappeared into the bathroom.

Ted's office manager blew an errant gray curl off her face. 'Why?'

'She's a stranger. And besides, she seems a little . . . off.' I could hear the sound of a toilet flushing down the hallway, followed by running water.

'Oh, honey,' Diane said with a flap of her hand. 'Between running interference between patients, creditors and high-and-mighty medical professionals—' She broke off. 'No offense, Maggy.'

'None taken.'

Sarah chipped in. 'Yeah, she divorced his high-and-mighty cheating ass. But you were saying?'

A suppressed grin at – or with – my partner. 'In truth, I was thinking more of Doctor Swope than Doctor Thorsen. The man won't even answer a phone, though it's true surgeons are a breed apart in the first place. The ones I've worked with over the years make the kids my hubby and me foster look like mature, stable individuals.'

'You're foster parents?' I asked.

'For twenty years, though my Manny died about five years back and that was the end of that. But we adopted two ourselves – a twin brother and sister I couldn't bear seeing separated.' She pulled out her cell phone and punched up a photo.

Holding hands, the twins looked to be about five or six. The girl's widow's peak and braids and the boy's striped shirt and stocky build reminded me of a blonde Wednesday and Pugsley Addams staring somberly at the camera.

'What cuties,' I lied.

Diane's eyes grew moist. 'They're all grown and gone now, too.'

Empty nest syndrome. I'd experienced it when Eric flew the coop but imagined it was more of an adjustment after having had a house full of kids.

I opened my mouth to ask how many children they'd fostered but our non-customer exited the bathroom and came toward us, the weathered sign dragging on the tiles behind her. As it snagged in a crack and she went to free it, I whispered to Diane, 'Separate cars.'

The office manager didn't answer me, but when she put her arm around the woman I did hear her say, 'You do have a car, don't you, dear? Because I'm afraid my Accent is full . . .'

The door closed behind them.

'So now we're giving away coffee beans?' Sarah and I were reorganizing the refrigerator wedged in the alcove between our office and storeroom.

Or *I* was reorganizing. My partner was leaning against a file cabinet watching me. 'No different than coffee drinks. Buy nine and your tenth is free.'

'But the beans are where we make money. They have a much higher profit margin than our drinks.'

'Which is exactly why it's good to give away a pound every

once in a while. Our cost is low and we shame them into grinding their own beans, so there's nearly no labor involved.'

I'd be damned if it didn't make sense. Which meant: 'Amy's idea?'

'Uh huh,' Sarah confirmed. 'Buy nine pounds, get the tenth free. Not only are the local businesses like Thorsen Dental stopping in regularly but even the commuters.'

'Buying for their offices on the way in to work, you mean?'

'Or for home, on the return trip.' Sarah cocked her head. 'Got to hand it to Amy. She's a marketing genius.'

'She is.' I set a gallon of non-fat milk on the desk to get it out of the way. 'Sometimes I feel inadequate.'

'Just sometimes?' Sarah slapped me on the back as she slipped past me to settle in the desk chair. 'Hey, did Diane know what that sign was about?'

'The cavity search one?' I asked. 'I didn't ask, but for the sake of Eric's college fund I hope it's not his father's new marketing slogan.' If so, Ted needed more help on the marketing front than I did.

'I like a good pun, but even to me "cavity search" has unpleasant connotations.' Rocking back in her chair, Sarah was picking at a fingernail.

You think? 'And it certainly wasn't a professionally made sign.' Satisfied with my reorganization, I turned to retrieve the gallon of milk. Sarah's crossed, coffee-flecked loafers were perched on the desk next to it. 'Do you mind?'

'No, go ahead.' Her feet stayed on the desk and her attention on the fingernail.

I didn't bother to roll my eyes. Sarah wouldn't notice and, besides, the plastic milk gallon was sealed. I slid it onto the refrigerator shelf and closed the door.

Sarah was gnawing at her nail now. 'Maybe she's an employee demonstrating for higher wages.'

'Did you see her teeth? Not exactly a walking advertisement for a dental office. Besides, I've never seen her before. She can't be a new hire because Diane has been working for Ted since April and she certainly didn't seem to know her either. Not to mention that the woman would know where her own office was located.' A new thought struck me. 'Do you think this has something to do with Rachel?'

'Rachel?' Sarah looked up.

'You know, cavity search? Like they do in prison? Which is where she is.'

'Interesting thought.' Apparently giving up on both the conversation and the fingernail, Sarah stretched and stood up. 'Time for me to leave. I'm opening tomorrow, right?'

'Right.' Which meant I could sleep in. And alone, since Frank would likely – please, God – choose my son's bed over mine for the next couple of nights.

I loved Eric and I'd come to love the sometimes smelly, always hairy sheepdog that he'd had left with me when he'd gone off to college. What I didn't care for was trying to worm myself out from under whatever furry body part the canine draped over me during the night.

The side door slammed. I stuck my head into the hallway to see a delivery man backing into it with three stacked boxes on a dollie.

'Our order from Wicker Place, thank God,' I said to Sarah. 'We should have started assembling the gift baskets a week ago.' And would have if I hadn't forgotten to place the order for the baskets.

Next year, Amy's job.

'Gift baskets?' Sarah was already shrugging into her coat.

'We make fifty percent of our annual profits between Thanksgiving and Christmas.' I stabbed a thumb over my shoulder toward the overstuffed storeroom. 'Haven't you noticed the extra inventory of beans and mugs and such? Which reminds me—'

'Maggy?' Amy called from the hallway. 'Do you want to check this order before I sign for it?'

'Go ahead and take care of it.' Sarah slipped past me. 'I'll see you tomorrow.'

'See ya,' I said before turning to the driver. 'It's quarter to seven. You're working late.'

'From now right through Christmas.'

''Tis the season, I guess.' I checked the delivery, meaning I made sure the outside of all three boxes read, 'Twenty-four wicker baskets.'

The driver handed me the signing screen. 'Winter is long enough. I don't see why people need to rush to get there.'

I, for one, was not in a hurry for the first snowfall – especially since the last one had been in May.

Yes, May.

And, though I imagined drivers earned overtime, it probably didn't make up for the long hours and the fact they didn't have time to so much as warm themselves on the holiday glow before it was extinguished under a barrage of shipped returns.

Speaking of warming . . . 'Aren't you freezing?'

'You bet.' He rubbed at the goose flesh on his thigh. 'No long pants until the day after Thanksgiving.'

'Is that company policy?' I asked, thinking it was just short of inhumane treatment here in the tundra.

'Nah, I'm the only idiot.' He waved at the autumn leaves Amy had made out of orange, yellow and brown construction paper and tacked up to our menu board. 'I'm glad to see you, at least, are still celebrating fall.'

I scribbled something resembling my signature and handed the screen back to him. 'We sell a lot of autumn drinks so we don't want to plunge right through pumpkin in order to get to peppermint.'

He pulled his gaze away from the menu board. 'You have pumpkin lattes?'

'Sure do.' Eggnog lattes were already on our menu, too, though I thought that might be too Christmassy for the principled, if goose-pimpled, driver. 'Would you like one?'

As the man left with his pumpkin latte the front door opened, sending a cold wind howling through the store.

Folding my arms over my chest for warmth, I rounded the corner to the front of the store and saw Lynne Swope.

'Lynne,' I said to the financial planner. 'Is something wrong?'

The check was bogus is what I was thinking, the UP attorney having absconded with my $50,000 in singles.

'Oh no, I'm just here for the book club.' Lynne draped her trench coat over the back of a chair at the long table. 'I meant to tell you I'd see you later but we were busy discussing your . . . brother.' She glanced over at our barista behind the counter.

'Not to worry,' I said, thinking the financial advisor was concerned about confidentiality. 'Amy knows where all my –

and now my brother's – skeletons are buried. Have the two of you met?'

'We have,' Amy said brightly, dumping milk from a gallon jug into the metal frothing pitcher. 'Your usual triple-shot, two-sugar latte, Lynne?'

'That would be wonderful. Thank you, Amy,' Lynne said. 'Are you staying for the meeting, Maggy? Mary practically forced me to come last time but I have to admit it's a great way to meet people.'

And build the business, as both Amy and Sarah had pointed out to me. But the last thing I wanted to do was spend more hours at the coffeehouse than I already did. 'I don't get much time to read these days,' I said a little sheepishly as the bells signaled another member had entered.

'It's only one book a month.' Lynne Swope held out a hard-cover of *Gone Girl*. 'Have you read it?'

'No,' I admitted, feeling obliged to take it and page through. Brookhills County Library was stamped inside the front cover.

'You're probably the only person on earth who hasn't?' Mary, the new arrival, offered. 'Or seen the movie?'

They weren't questions. Lynne's sister Mary had the habit of ending declarative sentences with an audible question mark. Kind of a Valley Girl? At thirty-something?

'Who else is in the group?' I didn't intend to join, I just wanted to get them off my back.

'Well, there's the three of us,' the librarian said, nodding at Amy and Lynne. 'And Laurel?'

'She'll be here.' Amy set the latte she'd just made in front of Lynne. 'And before you ask, Jacque is coming, too, so I did my part.'

Laurel Birmingham was Brookhills town clerk and Jacque Oui was the owner of Schultz's Market and Seafood. He was also Amy's boyfriend.

The tattooed, pierced barista and the pseudo-suave French storeowner/fishmonger were an unlikely couple. But then people probably said that about Pavlik and me, too.

'Your part?' I asked.

'We're trying to get more men involved?' Mary said. 'How about William, Lynne? Is he coming?'

'So he said.' Lynne took a sip of her latte and sighed in appreciation.

'Good, I'm looking forward to meeting him,' I said, meaning it. I was still amazed that the man had joined Ted's practice in May and this was the first I knew about it. Though it said something about the wisdom of hiring Diane in April and just in time to deal with the new partner. The woman was an organizational dream. And if that meant I was left out of the information loop, so be it. There was probably something healthy about *not* knowing everything that was happening in your ex-spouse's life.

The door opened again and a man with dark hair graying at the temples entered. He was wearing neatly pressed khakis and just a red golf shirt despite the blustery autumn weather. His face lit up when he saw Lynne. 'Hello, my love.'

Lynne turned her cheek to receive his kiss. 'William, I'd like you to meet Maggy. She's Ted's—'

'Former wife, of course,' William said, holding out his hand. 'Ted speaks highly of you.'

'That's because I didn't take his pension,' I said, extending my hand.

'Perhaps so.' William enveloped my paw in both of his like I was the meat in his hand sandwich. 'But he does nonetheless.'

I freed myself, ostensibly to point toward our barista by way of introductions. 'Have you met Amy Caprese?'

'I haven't had the pleasure.' Swope took her hand in the same two-fisted embrace. 'Caprese? Is that Italian?'

'On my dad's side,' Amy said, smiling up at him. 'Can I get you something to drink?'

I didn't hear his answer because a familiar voice rang out, 'Lucy, I'm home!'

Before I could fully turn I was caught up in a hug from my tall, sandy-haired son. Giving back as good as I got, I smiled past Eric's shoulder at the tall young woman coming up behind him. 'And you must be Ginny?'

'I am, Mrs Thorsen,' she said, peeking out from under a fringe of dark hair.

'Just call me Maggy,' I told her. 'You two have good timing. Your mother, father and aunt are all here, Ginny.' I tugged my son to one side so his new friend could see the table beyond.

Lynne was already hopping up, but William reached their daughter first with a bear hug that matched and raised Eric's.

Ginny just stood there, arms at her side, looking self-conscious at the display of parental affection. 'Hi.'

'You're embarrassing the girl?' Mary said, wiggling her fingers in greeting to her niece.

'How'd you know we were here?' Lynne asked, taking her turn.

'Eric wanted to show me his mom's coffee shop. I didn't know I'd see you two here.'

'I bet,' her father said with a wink. 'Did you drive the Lexus down?'

Ginny nodded. 'I told you Eric's van is in the shop.'

'Well, let's not talk about that now.' William squeezed his daughter's shoulder. 'We'll catch up later.'

'Can I get anybody else coffee?' Amy asked. 'Or a nice hot specialty drink like a pumpkin latte on this chilly autumn night?'

That's my girl, I thought. Push the higher profit espresso drinks.

'Black coffee would be terrific,' William said, settling into a chair.

'Regular or decaf?'

'High test.'

'You won't sleep,' his wife warned.

'I need to go back to the office tonight anyway,' the oral surgeon said as Amy set a white ceramic mug in front of him and then filled it with steaming coffee. 'I told you that, Lynne.'

Seeming to sense tension between her parents, Ginny cleared her throat. 'So, Dad – did you ever get that desk you wanted?'

'I did.' William seemed delighted his daughter was taking an interest in his new office. 'Come by after you've dropped Eric off at his dad's and I'll show you what I've done to the place.'

'But you said you'd stay for the book club.' Lynne's bottom lip was jutting out in a pout.

'I can't come now anyway,' Ginny said hastily. 'I'm going to Aunt Mary's for pizza with Caitlin.'

'Cousins' dinner. Don't you two get into any trouble,' Mary teased.

'Then we'll do it tomorrow.' Ignoring the cup handle, William picked up his coffee by circling his hands around it.

Like the sandwich handshake, it seemed a practiced move. I started to warn him about what his hands were apparently too manly to feel: coffee is hot. God knows we didn't need a McDonald's-type lawsuit for scalding somebody. Especially a surgeon, who presumably valued his hands.

But Swope just took a careful sip and then pulled back, wisely leaving the coffee to cool.

'I thought Ted was working this Saturday,' Lynne said.

'He is, but we have some personnel issues I want to discuss and it seemed a good time.' Another wink, this one directed at me. 'Your ex-hubby has agreed to let me take over the staffing.'

Lynne glanced sideways at him. 'Professionals or office personnel?'

'Well, some might argue that all should be considered professional, my dear. No one likes an elitist.'

Lynne's face reddened and she opened her mouth, but her husband gave her no opportunity to defend herself against the implication.

'I'd honestly like to go for a younger, trendier feel at Thorsen Dental. Dress up the place. Ted had already hired an office manager when I started, but—'

'Actually, I hired Diane,' I interrupted. The matronly office manager should apparently count her blessings she'd slipped in under the wire before William turned the place 'upmarket.' 'Is she too long in the tooth for you?'

A deprecating smile – probably one I deserved. 'A dental joke – very clever. But to Diane's credit, she's quite the worker and a technological marvel. Networked our computers and instituted document sharing. Computerized our prescription system. Even enhanced the music in the waiting room.'

Whatever it took to drown out the whine of the drill. And the screaming.

'My philosophy,' William went on to the group at large, 'is that clients are willing to pay a premium if the dental procedure is not only painless but even enjoyable from the time they are greeted until they leave with their—'

As I was contemplating what an 'enjoyable' dental procedure entailed, Eric touched me on the shoulder. 'Place looks good, Mom. And a book club is a great idea.'

'It was Amy's,' I admitted. But I was thinking about something William had said and, passive-aggressive person that I am, I backed into it. 'Frank is going to be delirious to see you. How long will you be home? Until Monday?'

'Yeah, but,' Eric shifted feet, 'I kind of promised Dad I'd stay with him this trip. You know, get to know the baby and all.'

Unreasonably, I felt tears rise. It made perfect sense that Eric would bunk at Ted's place this weekend, but it hadn't even occurred to me until William mentioned Ginny dropping Eric off at his dad's. 'Of course. That'll be great.'

'You're so transparent,' my son said, giving me a kiss on the cheek. 'I'll stop by and see you and Frank tomorrow, OK?'

'Sounds good,' I said. 'I'm working nine to noon and then I'm off the rest of the weekend.'

Which I thought I'd be spending with my son. Wah, wah, wah.

Get over it, Maggy. 'Are you and Ginny heading out now?' I asked. 'I can make you something for the road. Pumpkin lattes? Or we have chai and matcha, if you prefer tea.'

I knew I was trying too hard but Eric just smiled and pulled out his phone. 'Nah, we're good. I just want to text Dad first and make sure he's home.'

'Your father was still at the office when I left about half an hour ago,' William volunteered, getting up to go to the condiment cart.

'Do you have a key for your dad's house?' I asked Eric.

'No, but I can stop by the—'

I assumed he was going to say the office but it wasn't necessary as the door opened yet again and his father walked in. 'You son of a bitch!'

We all froze.

My ex-husband had never been abusive, verbally or physically. But there was something dangerous in Ted's tone now.

The words, though, weren't directed at Eric or me. They were meant for the man by the condiment cart. One William Swope.

FOUR

The sugar packet dangling between William Swope's thumb and index finger slipped out and landed on top of the condiment cart.

'Maybe we should go,' I heard Eric whisper to Ginny.

I caught my son's eye and head-gestured toward the side door. Eric nodded and whisked Ginny down the hallway as her mother, seemingly frozen, watched Ted and William from the table.

'Is there a problem?' William asked lightly.

Ted didn't answer but I could see a vein pulsing in his temple.

Recognizing that particular vessel, I tried to defuse the situation with the mundane. 'Oh, a patient stopped by here earlier, mistaking it for your office, Ted. Did she find you?'

'Rita Pahlke, you mean? She stopped me on my way out of the building. Though it wasn't me she wanted to talk about any more than it was me Clay Tartare wanted to talk to when he called.'

William Swope cocked his head, puzzled. 'My ex-partner telephoned? Am I supposed to call him back?'

'From the sound of it he's wanted you to do that for over a week now.'

But William had pulled his cell out of the pocket of his khakis and was punching buttons. 'I don't see any missed calls.'

My ex didn't take his green eyes off his new partner. 'You don't have to call him now. But *we* need to talk, Swope. Outside.'

For his part, William didn't seem at all troubled by either Ted's tone or his suggestion they step out into the cold. 'Sure.'

He scooped up a fresh sugar packet and slipped it and his phone into his back pocket before crossing to the table to claim his mug. 'Lynne, honey – why don't you get Ted a cup and bring it outside. We'll be on the porch.'

I thought Ted was going to slug him. Whatever this Rita Pahlke or Clay Tartare had said, it had certainly pissed off my ex. And what kind of name was Tartare for a dentist, anyway?

But to his credit, Ted just responded with a tight, 'No, thanks,' before swinging open the door and allowing his new partner to precede him.

The door slammed shut behind Ted whether by his hand or a sudden burst of wind, sending the bells crashing against the plate glass.

Lynne Swope cleared her throat. 'My, it's nearly seven. Where can everybody be?'

I was straining to hear the men on the porch when the side door opened and a burst of voices dashed my hopes of eavesdropping on the conversation.

'Hey, Maggy,' Laurel Birmingham, a statuesque redhead called. 'We just ran into Eric in the parking lot.'

'With zee very tall, very pretty girl,' the dapper man behind her added, unwinding a burgundy scarf from around his neck.

'Jacque!' Amy leaned back across the counter to replace the carafe on the warmer and turned to him. 'Thank you for coming.'

'A pleasure,' Jacque said, kissing her.

Jacque Oui wasn't my cup of tea – or even French press coffee – but he seemed to adore Amy.

'Jacque,' the barista said, 'I don't think you've met Lynne Swope. She and her husband moved here this spring and the girl you saw with Eric is their daughter.'

Lynne stuck out her hand.

Jacque kissed it. '*Enchante*.'

I wanted to gag but Lynne seemed to favor smooth, as evidenced by her choice of William as her mate. 'How charming.'

'Zee mother is as lovely as zee daughter.'

'*The* mother,' I wanted to scream. But there was nothing to be gained. Jacque's accent had thickened to almost comical over his two decades in the US. He sure wasn't about to drop the shtick now. After all, it had helped make him fishmonger to the rich – if not famous – of Brookhills.

All that charm stopped short of me, for some reason, my last shopping expedition having ended with Jacque refusing to sell me a piece of halibut because, 'You vill ruin eet, do you hear me? One second too long, eet will be zee cat food!'

'I'm going home,' I said, even now my face warming at the memory. 'Enjoy your meeting.'

Ducking back into the office, I snatched up my purse and coat. Though my Ford Escape was parked in the lot behind the depot, making the side door the more direct route, I had no intention of missing whatever was transpiring between Ted and William on the front porch.

But, alas, the fireworks seemed over. As I pushed open the door, my ex-husband was pounding down the steps. '. . . Told Diane to cancel your appointments. Pack up your crap tonight and get out. You can leave your keys on her desk.'

By the light coming through the shop window, I could see

William's shadowy figure. He was sitting on a chair slid away from the huddle of furniture by the building, coffee mug on the floor beside him.

'God damn!'

I swiveled to see Ted pointing keys at his midnight-blue Miata parked on the street.

'He's trying to open the car with the office keys.' Swope seemed curiously detached.

'Should we tell him?'

A 'bleep-bleep' signaled that Ted had figured it out, so I turned back to the man sitting on my porch.

'Are you all right?'

'Oh, yes, certainly.' A car door slammed and the Miata's engine fired up. 'I'm sorry . . . it's Maggy, correct?'

I nodded.

'A simple misunderstanding that I'm sure we'll work out.' The dentist got to his feet a little unsteadily, rubbing at his lower back. 'College lacrosse injury,' he said with a wry smile. 'I think I'll take a cue from you and skip the meeting.'

A burst of laughter from inside made us both look through the window to the brightly lit tableau inside Uncommon Grounds. Jacque was seated in William's vacated chair, apparently being *très* amusing.

'Don't mind Jacque,' I said as Ted's Miata accelerated away from the curb. 'He's dating our barista but seems to think flirting is required of any Frenchman. It's harmless.'

'Is it?' William Swope started down the porch steps. 'I wonder.'

FIVE

I was feeling as blue as the stucco walls of my living room as I parked the Escape in front of the garage and mounted my porch steps. The forecast for the night was miserable – a cold rain that could freeze on the streets and sidewalks if the temperature dropped any further – but my mood had nothing to do with that or even Ted and William's quarrel. In fact, the fight had actually cheered me a bit, given I was petty and required payback for Ted hosting our son instead of me.

Which brings us, of course, to why I was moping. No Eric, and I purposely hadn't made plans with Pavlik, who'd been non-stop busy anyway, since we'd gotten back from Fort Lauderdale.

As for me, I was alone and contemplating having a bowl of cereal for supper. Maybe watching an old movie before I turned in. Early, naturally.

Spinsterhood, here I come. Hell, I'd get a cat if I didn't think Frank would eat it.

Which reminded me. 'Frank?' I called as I stepped into the house.

Normally the sheepdog would be snuffling at the door as I unlocked it, whining plaintively and barely allowing me to get out of the way before exploding out onto the porch and down the steps into the yard.

Now I felt a stir of anxiety as I looked around the front room. 'Frank? Are you all ri—'

That's when I registered the scent of roasting pepperoni in the air. That, along with Frank's absence at the door, could mean only one thing. 'Eric?'

'In the kitchen.'

I found my son with his head ducked into the oven, Frank nearly cemented to his right leg so as not to miss anything that fell.

'I see you discovered the pizzas.'

'Yup,' Eric said, closing the oven door. 'How many of these things do you go through? I don't think I've come home from school when there weren't at least three in the freezer.'

Because I bought them for him, of course. Dad might have the fancy house but Mom kept a freezer full of pizza and ice cream, a fridge full of soda and a house full of sheepdog.

I mean, which would you rather come home to?

'I thought Ginny was dropping you at your dad's.' I dumped my purse and coat on a chair and, yielding to the seductive aroma of browning cheese, took two plates out of the cupboard. Nudging Eric's cell phone to one side, I set them on the counter.

My son tilted his head, as if considering, and then opened the freezer door to pull out a second pizza. Wise boy. 'I don't have a key, remember? I just had Ginny drop me off here. I figure Dad'll call or text when he's through with Doctor Swope.'

I had an inkling Ted was through with Dr Swope in more ways than one. 'Ginny didn't want to stay for dinner?' I asked, taking our second course from him to strip the cellophane and cardboard off it.

'I didn't think to offer.' Eric looked surprised. 'Should I have?'

Further proof my son was gay, God bless him. Let the gorgeous co-ed eat by herself.

'Anyway,' Eric continued, 'Ginny said she was going to her cousin's house for dinner, didn't she?'

Of course. In all the excitement, I'd forgotten Ginny planned to visit Mary's daughter Caitlin, who had been two years behind Eric in school. 'After the long drive, I'm sure she's happy to just kick back with family.'

'Long is right. Cool car, but I could have shaved thirty minutes off the trip if I'd been behind the wheel.'

'But overall, Ginny's a good driver?' I was thinking this ride-sharing agreement might be a good idea, given my son's lead foot.

Eric shrugged. 'I guess. Talks a lot, though.'

Opening the oven door, I slid the new pizza in, pulling the one on the shelf above it out and onto the cutting board. 'This done enough for you?'

'It's going to have to be – I'm starving.' He took a cleaver to the pizza, pressing down. Given the satisfying 'crack' the crust gave between each of the six slices I was thinking it was done. Or overdone, by most people's standards.

But we Thorsens weren't most people. In my family, we preferred our bacon extra crispy, our ribs falling off the bones and our Thanksgiving turkey roasted to an inch of its edible life, thank you very much.

Eric put two slices of pizza on each of our plates as I considered whether I should tell him that his father was likely home by now. Given Ted's mood, though, maybe Eric was better off here while his dad cooled down.

Oh, hell, who was I kidding? My reluctance had nothing to do with Ted's temper tantrum. I just wanted Eric home. In fact . . .

I eyed my son's phone on the kitchen counter. Would it be childish to turn off the ringer while we ate dinner?

Of course it would.

'Could you grab a bottle of wine out of the pantry?' I asked, pointing to the cabinet behind him.

Eric rolled his eyes but turned to obey. 'You're getting to be a wino, you know.'

'I have one glass a night.' Feeling defensive – and therefore justified – I flicked the switch on his phone to the silent position with my fingernail while his back was turned to the counter.

A growl of far-away thunder sounded outside the window.

'Sorry,' I whispered.

'You don't have to apologize to me, it's your liver.' Eric held a bottle of wine in each hand. He lifted the one in his right. 'Red or,' he looked at the bottle in his left, 'red?'

The liver comment hurt. And was probably justified a year or so ago. Blame me, blame Ted, blame the divorce. But now that I'd cut back to a single glass a night, I made sure it was a wine I loved. Which meant red, though even the best-structured was barely drinkable by day four. Not that I didn't persevere anyway. 'One is a blend, the other a cabernet. I'll take the blend. Right hand.'

Putting the cab away, he brought the other bottle to the counter. 'You want me to open this?'

'You know how?' I asked, sliding the junk drawer out to retrieve the corkscrew.

He took it. 'Of course. I'm in college, you know.'

I should probably have been relieved he hadn't gained the skill from watching me. 'You're also underage. You won't be twenty-one until your senior year.'

He removed the foil from the bottle. 'Lucky for you and your Zin/Petite Sirah blend, I have older friends who enjoy wine.'

I was a little unnerved by the expertise with which my nineteen-year-old was setting about opening the bottle.

Plunk. Cork out, Eric took a glass from the rack over the sink. 'Want me to pour shallow so it can breathe?'

'Umm, sure,' I said as he tipped an inch of deep red liquid into the stemmed glass and slid it to me. The kid had learned something about wine. From somebody. 'So these older friends. Are they . . . nice?'

Eric told me he was gay during his freshman year of college. I knew he'd been stressed about something, so it was a relief to know exactly what. Now out to everybody, the subject of Eric's sexuality didn't come up much anymore.

Don't get me wrong, I was as curious as any mother about my offspring's life but I did draw the line at asking Eric whether he was seeing somebody. It had been an annoying question when I was in college and probably was no less so now. Gay or straight.

'Nice? Sure.' He opened the refrigerator. 'No beer?'

I'd taken a sip of the wine and choked on it.

Eric was laughing at me. 'Just kidding. And while I might have had a drink once or twice, my friends *are* nice and I'm being careful. You don't have to worry about me. OK?'

'OK.' Like I'd ever stop.

We downloaded the first *Jurassic Park* movie and ate pizza on tables in front of the TV. The meteorologist on the *Ten O'Clock News* was predicting that the storm, when it finally broke, would be in the form of rain rather than sleet when a phone rang.

Eric grabbed his empty plate and made for the kitchen. I followed with mine and arrived to see him retrieve his cell from the counter. All credit to the quality of the movie and quantity of the pizza that Eric had forgotten to take the phone into the living room with him. 'Not me,' he said, holding it up.

Which I could have told him, even if the ringing hadn't been coming from under my coat on the kitchen chair. Setting down the plate, I dug my bag out from under my coat and the phone from my purse. By the time I finally had it in my hand, the thing had stopped ringing.

'Damn,' I said, pulling up the missed call: 10:09 p.m., but . . . 'I don't recognize the number.'

Eric was frowning at his own phone. 'Why'd I turn the ringer off?'

Outside the window there was a white flash of lightning – this time with a simultaneous *crack* of thunder overhead. The heavens finally opened, pelting rain against the glass.

Ignoring the escalating celestial reprimand, I tried to look innocent. 'Did Dad call?'

'Nope, nothing yet.'

See? I mouthed skyward as my son set the cell face down on the counter. As if in answer, my own phone dinged that a voice-mail had been left.

I punched in to listen and the voice was not God's but Lynne Swope's. 'Hi, Maggy? Sorry to bother you but I'm looking for William and he's not answering his phone. If you have Ted's cell, could you call me with it? I think they might be together.'

'Not much chance of that,' I said after replaying the message for Eric.

'Yeah, Dad seemed really ticked. Did he say why?'

'Not really. It sounded to me like it had something to do with Louisville, where the Swopes came from. Dad told Doctor Swope to clear out his office.' Though not quite in those words.

Eric stood his plate in the dishwasher rack and straightened up to get mine. 'That's kind of brutal.'

I agreed, but tried not to criticize Ted to Eric. Ever. So I just said, 'I wonder if Mrs Swope tried the office.'

'You need Dad's cell number to give her?'

'No, I have it, unless it's changed.' I'd been about to call Lynne back but looked up and smiled at our son. 'Your dad and I do talk, you know.'

'Cool.' He slid the rack into the dishwasher, closed and latched it.

I mentally shrugged as I waited for Lynne to answer. Eric had taken the divorce in his stride – siding with neither Ted nor me but supporting us both. He was so even-keeled that sometimes I worried it was a front. 'Lynne?'

'Oh, Maggy – thanks for calling me back. Hang on a second.' To someone in the background, presumably Ginny, I heard her say, 'Did you get something to eat?' The girl's voice answered and then Lynne was back on the line. 'Anyway, could I get Ted's number from you? I'm sure they've mended their fences and are just off having a drink. Don't you think?'

I didn't. 'Have you called the office?'

'Yes, but the after-hours recording is on. And when I drove past on the way home the building was dark so I just assumed William would be here.'

'Maybe he did go out for a drink but I doubt Ted is with

him. I . . . well, there's no easy way to say this: I overheard Ted tell William to pack up his office and leave.' Another paraphrase.

Silence on the other end. Then, 'Mom? What's wrong?' in the background.

'Lynne?' I said into the phone, tugging her in the other direction.

Another offstage whisper and then, 'I'm here, Maggy – just a little worried.'

I checked the clock on the microwave, feeling guilty for having added to that worry. 'It's just barely ten-fifteen. Ted hasn't called Eric to come over to the house so maybe I'm wrong and they did work things out.' I dictated Ted's number into the phone.

'Thanks. I'm sure you're right.' She didn't sound sure. 'Should I tell Ted to call Eric?'

I glanced at my son's back at the sink. 'Nah, don't bother.'

SIX

Hanging up the phone, I probably should have been concerned about William. And even Ted.

But no, I was wondering what in the world was wrong with me. A grown woman sabotaging her son's phone and plotting to keep a father and son – and baby half-sister – apart.

Reprehensible.

But . . . shouldn't Ted remember to come and get Eric or at least call him without Lynne Swope reminding him?

And if Eric didn't pick up, shouldn't his father be smart enough to call me? I glanced at the phone still in my hand and slid my fingernail close to the ringer control.

'Mom?'

'Yes, dear?' I returned the phone to my purse. After all, Eric had turned his own ringer back on so the belt and suspenders of turning mine off would be merely belt. Or was it suspenders?

'Is everything all right? Think I should call Ginny? Or maybe Dad?' He reached for his phone.

'No!'

Eric pulled his hand back and frowned at me.

'Mrs Swope is calling him right now. You don't want to make him miss the call.'

'Dad has call waiting.'

So did I, though every time it signaled a second call coming in I went into a panic trying to figure out how to get to it. And back again. 'Just give him a couple minutes, though, to talk with Mrs Swope. Your dad was so angry earlier I'm not sure you want to get in the middle of it. Maybe let him cool down.'

Eric seemed to see the sense in that. 'I guess so. I wish he'd call, though – it's been a long day.'

My son had probably had classes this morning, then jumped into the car for a five-plus hour drive. He had every reason to feel tired. And I to be ashamed. 'You want to text your dad? I can always drive you over—'

A ring and vibration *sprrrung* from the phone on the counter. Eric picked it up. 'It's him,' he said as he pushed to answer it. 'Hi, Dad. Did Mrs Swope get hold of you?'

Not able to hear Ted's half of the conversation, I edged closer. Eric hit 'speaker.' What a good son.

'I told her that the last I saw of Doctor Swope he was heading to the office to clean out his crap.' Ted still sounded angry and, unlike me, wasn't candy-coating it for Eric's benefit. Nor would he have, I feared, for Lynne.

'Where are you now?' I asked, and Eric threw me an irritated look.

'Maggy?' Ted's voice asked. 'I guess I should have known you'd be listening.'

Well, yeah. 'So what's going on? What did William's ex-partner say? And what's with the woman with the picket sign?' Figured I might as well get my money's worth.

'Picket sign?' Eric repeated.

I held up a finger, indicating I'd fill him in.

'I don't have time to go into it all with you now, Maggy,' Ted said. 'Even if it *were* your business.'

That seemed a little unfair, given he'd stormed into my coffee-house and made a scene. Happily, though, Ted was still talking: 'As for your first question, I'm on the way to the Slatterys to pick up the baby.'

The Slatterys being Rachel's parents and, of course, Mia's grandparents. 'Didn't they move out to some big place in Mequon?' Mequon was about fifteen miles north of Milwaukee, while Brookhills was about the same distance west. It might not be my business but I did have an agenda. 'What about Eric? He can stay overnight here if that would help.'

I glanced at my son and he nodded.

'That would be great,' Ted said, sounding relieved. 'I'll swing by and get him in the morning but it's really starting to come down out here and I'd rather drive straight home once I pick up Mia in case it turns to sleet.'

Fate settled, Eric pulled a carton of mint chocolate-chip ice cream out of the freezer and claimed a soup spoon from the silverware drawer.

I smiled and said into the phone, 'You have office hours tomorrow morning, right? How about I drop Eric off before I go in to work?'

'If you don't mind, that would be perfect. I won't be in until nine, though Diane will be there by eight-thirty.'

'Perfect,' I said. 'Sarah's opening so Eric can sleep in and I'll bring him by at nine.'

'Wish Mia would let me sleep in. I'll be up late on the computer. Doing research.'

Right. That was what all guys did on their computers late into the night.

But it was Eric who asked the question: 'Research into what?'

A sigh at Ted's end. 'Doctor Swope. And how to dissolve a partnership.'

'I assume Doctor Swope has gone,' I said to Eric as we drove to Ted's office the next morning. 'I hope he locked the door behind him.' Though one could argue that a disgruntled former partner could do more damage to the office than somebody who wandered in off the street. And up ten stories.

While the rain had stopped overnight, the sky was still overcast and my son's mood seemed equally as bright, probably due to the carton of ice cream he'd consumed before going to sleep.

Getting only a burp in reply, I gave up on the conversation and turned left off Brookhill Road onto Silver Maple. Waiting for a lanky man headed toward the front of the building to pass by, I nosed an immediate left into the entrance of Thorsen Dental's parking lot, then made a U-turn so I could let Eric out on the street next to the office and head back in the direction of Uncommon Grounds.

As we pulled up to the curb, the Escape's right front tire splashed into a puddle, earning me a glare from a figure on the sidewalk. It took me a second to realize it was the same woman who'd come into Uncommon Grounds. Rita Pahlke, according to Ted.

Granted, the sign in her hand and the blue knit cap now on her head against the damp morning chill should have been a dead giveaway.

I held up a hand to the woman in apology but she just shook her sign and disappeared through a gap in the six-foot-high hedge on the side of the office building.

Eric squinted after her. 'Is she the one you told Dad about?'

'Yup, but where did she go?' I was craning my neck. 'Your dad needs to trim those bushes. They're getting way out of hand.'

Ted owned the building and he and I had done the planting ourselves with the same type of arbor vitae we'd used to screen the building's parking lot from Silver Maple Drive. It seemed a very long time ago.

'Who is that lady, anyway?' our son asked. 'You said you'd tell me about her after you got off the phone with Dad last night.'

'I don't know all that much more. She came into Uncommon Grounds thinking it was your dad's office.'

'Why would she think that?'

'Googled "Thorsen" and came up with both of us? You're better at this stuff than I am, but—'

An eardrum-piercing screech interrupted me as Pahlke came bolting out of the bushes, tugging up her jeans as she went.

Eric perked up. 'Cool! Bet she went back there to pee and a snake got her. Or a rat.'

'Ugh.' I wrinkled my nose. 'Your father hates rodents. That's why we planted the hedge a few feet away from the foundation. He was convinced animals would nest in it and find their way into the building otherwise.' I leaned down to look across Eric and out the passenger-side window. 'She really is in a panic. Maybe we should see if we can help.'

'Cool,' Eric said again, yanking on the door handle to hop out.

I turned off the engine and joined him and the frightened woman on the sidewalk. 'I'm Maggy from the coffee shop – remember me? Are you hurt?'

'No.' The woman's lips were white and trembling. 'Dead. I touched . . .' Her hand was shaky as she pointed beyond the shrubbery.

'Well, if it's dead it can't hurt you, right?' I said, ever the voice of reason.

But she just shook her head, her eyes huge.

Shrugging, I started toward the gap in the hedge. Eric had said snake or rat but I was thinking the 'dead' thing might be a bird that had flown into the mirrored side of the office building.

But Eric had gotten ahead of me and stopped short just past the shrub line. 'Holy shit.'

'What is it?' I dodged my head around my son and saw a green compressed air cylinder by the bushes. An oxygen tank, like the ones used in Ted's office – maybe thirty inches long and four inches in diameter. *Had* somebody broken in? Or had William Swope trashed the place? 'How in the world did that get—'

'No, Mom! Look.'

I followed my son's finger. A figure lay crumpled face down on the gravel depression next to the building. A man's body clad in a red golf shirt, the edge of a sugar packet peeking out of the back pocket of his no-longer-neatly-pressed khakis.

SEVEN

'It's Doctor Swope.' I pushed past Eric as I pulled out my cell phone.

'Is he dead, like she said?'

I handed the phone to my son. 'I don't know. Dial nine-one-one.'

As I went to kneel next to Swope, Eric called out a warning. 'Careful, Mom – glass.'

Seeing what he had, I shifted to avoid the shards and knelt.

William Swope's face was over-rotated toward me and away from the building. His eyes were open but clouded over, the pupils huge.

I felt for a pulse and found none, which was what I'd expected. There was a bloody dent the size of a silver dollar to his forehead and the unnatural angle of his head seemed to indicate his neck had been broken.

I rocked back to touch one of the arms thrown up over his head. Cold and stiffening, the backs of William's forearms and lower biceps were turning dusky.

'Oh my God – it is him.'

I turned to see Diane Laudon, hand to her mouth. Behind the office manager was the tall man we'd seen a few minutes earlier.

The phone in Eric's hand squawked, 'Nine-one-one, what is your emergency?'

'What should I tell them?' he whispered.

I took the phone. 'We're at 501 E. Brookhill Road. There's a body – male – in the bushes on the Silver Maple side of the building.'

'Can you tell if he's de—'

I'd learned from Pavlik to be precise and objective, giving only the facts as I knew them. 'I can't find a pulse and there are signs of blood pooling and rigor mortis. Dilated pupils.' A raindrop fell on the back of Swope's shirt, leaving a crimson circle. Then another. 'It's starting to rain again. You might want to tell them to hurry.'

'We had an earlier report, so responders are already en route,' the dispatcher said.

I glanced toward Diane, who nodded in answer to my unspoken question.

'Do you know who it is?' the dispatcher was asking.

'William Swope,' I said. 'He's an oral surgeon in the building.'

'And your name?' the dispatcher asked. He seemed impressed that I knew the procedure. When I gave him my name, he seemed less impressed.

'We called it in from upstairs,' Diane confirmed as I clicked off the phone.

'So you saw it happen?' Eric's eyes were wide.

'Happen?' The man with Diane repeated. 'What *did* happen?'
I was confused. 'Are you a patient?'

'No, I'm Clay Tartare. A friend of William's.' Tartare stuck out his hand to shake mine. 'Stopped by to see him this morning but when Ms Laudon called back there was no answer.'

Ahh, the ex-partner who'd fueled Ted's rage last night. Had the man been so desperate to get hold of Swope that he'd flown here? 'Was William in the office this morning, Diane?'

'Yes, well, I assumed so.' Diane dragged her eyes away from the body on the ground. 'Doctor Swope's car was in the parking lot when I pulled in and the office door was unlocked so I assumed there must have been a change in plans from what Doctor Thorsen told me last night.'

So Ted had told Diane that William would be leaving, if not necessarily why.

'It was only when I went back to fetch Doctor Swope for Doctor Tartare,' Diane continued, 'that I heard screaming and saw the window pane was broken. I looked out and, and . . .' She let it trail off.

Clay Tartare put a reassuring hand on her shoulder. 'Poor woman had quite a shock. I came running and called nine-one-one.'

The rain and wind was picking up and I beckoned them closer to the building, careful to avoid the area around the body. Not that it helped much, anyway, since there was no roof overhang to protect us.

'Could you see it was Doctor Swope on the ground?' Eric asked, oblivious to the raindrops. 'Though I guess it kind of had to be him, right?'

Diane was shaking her head, but more in the 'I can't believe it' way rather than the affirmative. 'I suppose it did, but . . . it's just so surreal. A body? Somebody I actually know? I couldn't quite put it all together.' She turned her head to me. 'Do you know what I mean?'

Sadly, I did. A number of times over.

Naturally, Pavlik showed up without my having to call him. Diane and Tartare had gone into the building with the deputies but Eric and I were standing under an orange and red-striped golf umbrella. I didn't play golf, but Ted did and had left behind the gaudier of his collection. Rachel probably hadn't allowed them in the house.

The sheriff's hat was pulled down and his jacket collar turned up against the rain. He didn't say, 'Funny meeting you here,' because, frankly, it wasn't so funny anymore. To either of us. And it also probably didn't improve Pavlik's mood that the rain was damaging his scene.

Still, I'd have liked a warmer greeting after not seeing each other for a week.

'Good to see you, Eric,' Pavlik said, shaking hands with my son. 'When did you get home?'

'Just last night,' Eric said.

'I was dropping him off at his dad's office,' I said, answering the question that hadn't been asked, 'when we . . . um, came across this.' I gestured toward the crime-scene tape strung up ahead of the hedge and the makeshift tarpaulin tenting beyond it.

'What were you doing in the bushes?'

'We weren't. There was a woman named Rita Pahlke here picketing and—'

'She's the one who went into the bushes,' Eric chimed in. 'I'm figuring she had to pee. Came back out still tugging her pants up, screaming about something being dead.'

'Where is Ms Pahlke now?' Pavlik glanced around, his gaze finally landing on the knot of Saturday morning gawkers gathered under a bus shelter on the corner. 'Don't tell me she's with that group.'

'No, I think one of your deputies took her into the building,' Eric said, pointing toward the front entrance. 'Along with Mrs Laudon and Mr Tartare.'

'Doctor,' I automatically corrected.

'Another dentist in the practice?' Pavlik asked.

A dentist, but not with Thorsen Dental. Clay Tartare is William Swope's former partner from Louisville. According to what I gathered from Ted, William was dodging Tartare's phone calls so he flew here to see William. When Diane went back to William's office this morning—'

Pavlik interrupted. 'Diane?'

'Diane Laudon, Ted's office manager. She found the window broken in William's office and Tartare called nine-one-one.'

Thankfully I hadn't been the first one who'd stumbled over the body this time. Eric and I were, in fact, numbers four and five – after Diane, Tartare and Rita Pahlke, who nearly had quite literally.

'Mom touched the body,' my stool-pigeon son revealed nonetheless. He saw my expression. 'What? Don't you want to account for your fingerprints on the body?'

'I was checking to see if he was still alive,' I told Pavlik in my own defense. 'And, besides, I think the picketer said she touched him, too.' So there.

But Pavlik just asked, 'Any idea what Ms Pahlke is protesting about?'

'Her sign said something about cavity searches,' Eric said. 'Kind of clever, it being a dental office and all.'

'So her target was Thorsen Dental, not another business in the building?' Pavlik slipped a notebook out of his pocket.

'Definitely,' I said. 'She came into the coffeehouse yesterday looking for the office.'

'But you didn't know her?' Pavlik was ready to make a note.

I shook my head. 'Nope and she didn't introduce herself, just asked directions. When I mentioned it to Ted last night, though, he told me her name and that she'd stopped him on his way out of the building.'

Pavlik looked up sharply. 'Did Doctor Swope know this Pahlke woman?'

'I'm not sure but Ted said something about neither of them – Pahlke or Tartare – looking for him, despite the fact he talked to both of them.'

'And by "him" and "he" you mean Doctor Thorsen?' Pavlik was being patient.

It made me nervous, somehow. 'Yes, so I just assumed their business must be with William. But you should ask Ted.'

Pavlik slid the pad into his jacket pocket. 'Doctor Thorsen is in his office?' While between us, Pavlik might refer to my ex as 'Ted,' he was all business now.

'Not yet, I don't think. Though he said he'd be here by nine and it's just past—' Eric nudged me and I twisted around to see Ted's Miata just turning off Brookhill Road. 'There he is now.'

The Miata slowed to a stop opposite my Escape and the window lowered. 'What's going on?'

Eric opened his mouth to reply but Pavlik held up a hand. Remarkably, my son obeyed.

'If you'll just park, Doctor Thorsen,' Pavlik said, 'I'll fill you in.'

Ted nodded and pulled the car into the parking lot. As Pavlik went to meet him, Eric said, 'Uh oh.'

'What?' I followed the direction of his gaze.

'That's Ginny's car.' He gestured toward the black Lexus that was sliding to a stop where Ted's Miata had been just a minute ago.

Cool car, indeed, as Eric had said the day before. And it was still rolling as the passenger door swung open.

'Oh my God, oh my God,' Lynne Swope was saying as she emerged from the car, her trench coat flapping. 'Is it William? Maggy, is it William?'

'I—'

'He never came home last night.' She was headed for the taped-off area. 'Is he—'

Out of the corner of my eye I could see Pavlik approaching from the parking lot with Ted just behind him. They wouldn't make it in time to stop her.

As Lynne ducked under the tape I started for her, but a female deputy appeared in the gap between the bushes and held up a hand. 'You are, ma'am?'

Lynne stopped like she'd hit the wall of the building, me just behind her. The question seemed to throw the financial planner. 'You mean my name? I'm Lynne Swope. I'm—' She gestured toward where I could see the blue tarp covering the body. 'I think – I mean, my husband is missing.'

'And your husband's name is?' It wasn't asked unkindly.

'William Swope.' Lynne seemed to be gulping for air. 'Is it him? Is it?'

'Mrs Swope, I'm sorry to inform you that your husband is dead.'

'But how?' Lynne asked. 'Did he—'

'Mom?' a girl's voice called.

I glanced back and saw that Ginny had left the car where it stood on the street.

She pushed past me to reach her mother. 'What's going on?'

'Don't look, sweetie. Don't look.' As she pulled her daughter toward her, Lynne caught sight of Ted coming up the sidewalk with Pavlik.

'You *bastard*!' she screamed. 'You killed him!'

EIGHT

I wasn't sure who to tend to first. My ex-husband, who had just been accused of killing somebody or our son who . . . well, this might not be the first time one of his parents had been accused of something, but it's never fun.

Then there were Brookhills newcomers Lynne and Ginny Swope, whose husband and father's broken body was under the tarp.

Pavlik settled it. 'Maggy, we're going to ask Mrs Swope to formally identify her husband's body. Then will you and Eric take her and her daughter somewhere private and sit with them while we sort things out?'

'Of course. I assume you don't want us in the dental office?'

'Correct.'

Uncommon Grounds would be full of Saturday morning customers, so when Lynne returned looking more shaken than ever, I suggested we go to her office.

'But shouldn't I stay here? I can't just leave William lying . . . there.' She flapped her hand toward where the technicians were working.

'We'll take care of Doctor Swope now,' Pavlik said gently. 'You go with Ms Thorsen and the detectives will come to you in an hour or so. Your office address is?'

A deer caught in the headlights didn't quite capture it. Lynne looked like she'd been hit and then backed up over a couple of times.

'It's the old Waverly building,' I told Pavlik. 'You know, in the block just the other side of the tracks from Uncommon Grounds. It says Swope Financial Planning on the door.'

Taking Lynne's arm, I steered her toward my car. Ginny's Lexus was still sitting in the middle of the street, the doors open. As we got closer I realized its engine was running.

'Ginny?' I said, turning to the girl and Eric who were trailing us. 'Do you want Eric to pull your car into the lot and we can ride together to your mom's office?'

'No.' She seemed to gather herself and touched my son's sleeve. 'Will you come with me if I drive the Lexus?'

She seemed to assume her mother was riding with me, which was fine. I unlocked the door for Lynne as the kids continued on to the Lexus. Circling to the driver's side, I took the opportunity to look up at the side of the building.

The mirrored glass reflected the vista to the east, including the skyline of downtown Milwaukee in the distance. But it wasn't a reflection I was looking for, it was the absence of one.

The gaping black hole in the glass of the tenth floor.

The rain had let up, so we parked both vehicles behind Uncommon Grounds. Being Saturday, the gravel lot was only about a quarter full without the usual contingent of commuters leaving their cars there to board trains to jobs in downtown Milwaukee.

'Why don't you and Ginny get us some coffee?' I suggested to Eric as the two joined us next to the Escape.

Although Ginny seemed the more together of the two Swope women, she was still as white as the proverbial sheet. I thought having a mission might do her more good than staying with us.

Eric nodded and they headed into Uncommon Grounds while Lynne and I crossed the tracks to her building and climbed the dark stairs in silence.

Since the only furniture in the outer room of Lynne's office was the reception desk, I suggested we sit in the conference room.

She stepped inside the doorway but just stood under the tick-tocking clock, her shoulders slumped.

Stripping off my soggy jacket, I hung it on the back of a chair and held out my hand for hers.

When she didn't respond, I said, 'Can I take your coat?'

Startling like she'd forgotten I was there, Lynne shrugged out of the trench coat. I draped it over a second chair and gestured for her to take a seat in one of the two remaining.

She ignored me. 'I don't understand – how could he do this?'
I sat. 'Ted?'

She pressed the heel of her hand to her forehead. 'Ted?'

'My ex-husband? William's partner?' The person you just accused of murder in front of his son?

But Lynne's eyes were bewildered. 'I was talking about William.' She finally slipped into the chair, seeming . . . what? Angry? Sad? Scared?

All of the above?

As for me, I was confused. 'So you think he jumped then.'

The headache must have been getting worse because Lynne leaned forward, her elbows on the table, fingers massaging her temples. 'What else?'

Murder was always my first thought, quite honestly, and some of what I'd observed at the scene had bolstered that view.

What was William Swope doing in the office this morning? Or had he never left, at least by the door?

And then there was the mysterious appearance of William's ex-partner. I had no idea what Clay Tartare needed to discuss with William Swope that was so important he'd gotten on a plane to do it. Apparently Ted did and he'd likely tell Pavlik. I was hoping one of them would share it with me.

But presumably whatever trouble might have been dogging William was serious enough for the oral surgeon to take his own life. The supposed 'easy way out.' To me, falling ten stories didn't sound that easy. 'Just minutes ago you said that Ted had killed William. What did you mean by that?'

'That it was Ted's fault.' Lynne's raised hands grabbed clumps of hair like a deranged Pippi Longstocking. 'Oh, I know that's not fair. But if what you said last night is true and he told William to clear out his things that could have pushed William to the edge.' As she realized what she'd said her hands slipped down to cover her eyes. 'Oh, God. William, of all people, suicidal? I never thought he'd do something like this.'

'He didn't have a history of depression or anything?' I asked after a moment.

Her hands came down and her eyes met mine. 'You met him. My husband always acted like he was on top of the world.'

'*Was* it an act?'

'Oh, everybody has downs, I suppose. But one of the things that attracted me to William was how he finds . . . found,' she sniffled, 'the bright spot at even the darkest times.'

I handed her a tissue from the box on the table, wondering about the 'darkest times' and the Swopes' move from Kentucky. 'Lynne, why is Clay Tartare here? Were there problems at the practice in Louisville?'

Lynne looked up, startled. 'Clay is in Brookhills?'

I bobbed my head. 'He came to see William this morning at the office.'

'So they spoke?'

I was watching her. 'No. William was already dead.'

Lynne shook her head. 'But I don't understand. How can you know that? Maybe he pushed William out the window.'

I wasn't delving into things like body temp and lividity with her at a time like this, with the exception of, 'I saw Tartare walking toward the front entrance a few minutes before William's body was found. And it . . . he, had been dead for a while.'

'But—'

'Besides,' I continued, 'Diane was with him in the office. In fact, he was the one who called nine-one-one when she discovered the broken window and William . . . gone.'

Lynne looked like she was going to be sick.

'Do you know why Clay wanted so badly to talk to William? And why William wasn't returning his calls?'

She mopped at her eyes. 'No.'

I cocked my head. 'So Tartare never tried to get hold of you?' It certainly wouldn't have been difficult. Even if the former partner didn't have Lynne's cell number he could have done a quick internet search for Swope Financial Planning.

She didn't meet my eyes. 'He may have called a few times but I told him that he needed to talk to William. The last thing I wanted to do was get in the middle of something between those two.'

Sounded like this wasn't the first argument between the partners. 'Ted was certainly riled up and it seemed to have to do with something Tartare and this Rita Pahlke told him. Do you know anything about her?'

'Only from William.' Lynne seemed as puzzled as I was. 'I had no idea she'd followed us here.'

'From Louisville, too?'

'Yes.' Finished with the eyes, Lynne blew her nose and set aside the tissue. 'Oh, she's just a harmless nutcase from what he said. You know, one of those government conspiracy people. Thinks dentists are implanting tracking devices in people's teeth. That fluoride is a mind-control drug.'

'Planting tracking devices for whom?'

'Washington? Mars? Who knows?' Lynne rolled her eyes. 'She wanted money to "keep quiet," can you imagine? William just laughed.'

I could almost see the thought that William would never laugh again cross her face.

But Lynne swallowed and kept going. 'I honestly can't see why Ted would be so upset. Every dentist has heard this kind of nonsense and the woman was a nuisance, nothing more. William could have no way of knowing she'd come here.'

My ex-husband, admittedly, had endured a tough year that ended with a wife in prison and a new baby who'd been born there. By bringing in a partner Ted had certainly meant to lighten the load, not open the door to new crazy-ass problems.

'Maybe it wasn't Rita, but whatever brought Clay Tartare here that set Ted off then.'

Lynne just lifted her shoulders and let them fall, her eyes on the empty table in front of her.

'William did say it was just a misunderstanding that he and Ted would work out,' I said, feeling bad for pressing the woman. William's death was her loss, not mine. As was the cause of it.

But she glanced up at my words. 'When was this?'

'Last night on the porch as he was leaving.'

'To throw himself out a window.' She sniffled, but didn't ask anything further.

'I'm so sorry, Lynne,' I said after a minute. 'Do you want me to call Mary for you?'

Why hadn't I thought of it the moment Pavlik asked me to sit with the Swopes? Of course, Lynne and Ginny should be with family at a time like this.

Or not.

'No,' Lynne said sharply and then softened. 'I'll phone her myself after I talk to the police.'

I glanced at the clock. It was just past ten, so we'd left Pavlik less than a half hour ago. 'It may be a while before they get here to interview you. They'll want to talk with Rita Pahlke, of course, and—'

'But why would the investigators talk to her?'

More than one reason, from what Lynne had just told me. For one, the fact the woman had followed them all the way from Kentucky and tried to extort money from the deceased, regardless of the whacky allegations. But most important, for now: 'Pahlke found the bod— Umm, William.'

Lynne sat up straighter. 'That's odd, don't you think?'

'Coincidental at the very least,' I concurred. 'But then again, she was hanging around the building with her picket sign.'

'Are you suggesting she might have seen something?'

I hadn't been, but it was a good thought. 'I suppose she might have, but—'

A duet of young voices interrupted as the outer office door swung open.

'Got lattes,' Eric said, bringing in a cardboard drink carrier and setting it with a flourish on the conference room table.

'Like "got milk."' Ginny's mascara had slid beneath her eyes – evidence that she'd been crying – but she seemed to be trying to pull it together for her mother's sake. 'Get it, Mom?'

'I do.' Lynne Swope smiled up at her daughter. 'How're you doing, kiddo?'

'I'm OK.' Ginny freed a drink from its cardboard trap and frowned at the scribbling on the side of the medium to-go cup. 'Does this say "profit reform lat?"'

'That's probably my non-fat, no-foam latte,' I explained, reaching for it. 'Sarah has her own form of shorthand.'

'I think this "3lat 2sug" is yours then, Mom.' Ginny set the cup in front of her mother. 'Triple shot latte with two sugars, right?'

'Thank you, dear.' But Lynne didn't touch it.

'*Drink.*' Daughter was brooking no resistance from mother. 'It was the first of the four she made so it should have cooled down by now.'

Lynne cautiously went to take a sip, but when there was a rap at the outer door she nearly spit it out.

The door creaked open and a familiar voice called, 'Hello?'

'It's OK,' I said to the group in the conference room. 'It's just Pavlik.'

'That's the sheriff,' Eric explained to Ginny.

'The sheriff?' the girl repeated. 'Why is that OK?'

'He's . . . umm, a friend,' I said.

As I went to greet Pavlik, I heard my son add in a whisper, 'With privileges.'

Now didn't seem to be the time to explain there was a difference between a meaningful relationship and a close friendship with sex. Though, come to think of it, I wasn't sure I could.

But my meaningful relationship wasn't alone in the outer office. I recognized one of the two men with him. A stocky, shaved-head New Yorker with an icy stare, Al Taylor had joined the sheriff's department last year. The other man – taller and thinner, with graying hair and a mustache – was unfamiliar to me.

'You remember Detective Taylor from Homicide,' Pavlik said, then hiked a finger at the tall man. 'And this is Detective Hallonquist, Violent Crimes.'

'Homicide?' I heard Lynne repeat from the conference room, nearly in tandem with Ginny's audible intake of breath.

I nodded at the two men as they passed by me to enter the other room. Hallonquist gave me a polite nod back while Taylor gave more of a smirk.

Pavlik remained in the outer office and I did the same, wanting to talk to him.

'No need to be alarmed, Mrs Swope.' The voice sounded Midwest, carrying none of the swagger I knew Taylor to project. Must be Hallonquist. 'Standard procedure in a death like this.'

I glanced in to see the man shake Lynne's hand as Taylor unfolded one of the spare chairs from against the wall. 'May we sit down?'

I looked at Pavlik and whispered, 'Homicide and Violent Crimes. So you don't believe he jumped either?'

Pavlik's eyes narrowed. 'Like Hallonquist said, it's standard procedure. Violent unattended death is investigated as a crime until it's proven otherwise.'

'Well, I saw something that might help to prove that,' I said, pulling him further out of earshot. 'Or it would have if the rain hadn't started again. It was the first drop, though, that made me realize.'

Accustomed to my occasional incoherence, Pavlik just said, 'Realize what?'

'William Swope's shirt was dry. I told you I touched him to see if he was dead. As I did, the first drop of rain fell directly onto the back of his red shirt and I realized that the surrounding material was dry.'

'It's a good observation,' Pavlik said. 'But don't read too much into it. It rained from a little after ten to about three this morning.'

Leave it to Pavlik to know when the rain ceased, if not desisted. The sheriff pulled out his notebook and jotted down something anyway.

'But if William's back was dry,' I said, thinking out loud, 'does that mean he went out the window after the rain stopped at three a.m.? If so, what was he doing all that time in an empty office?'

'You're assuming he was there. Do you know when Doctor Swope arrived? There are no security cameras in the lobby or elevators.'

His tone added, *Believe it or not.* I could believe it. Ted was cheap and this was safe little Brookhills.

'I don't, really,' I admitted. 'Though my impression was that he was going there directly from Uncommon Grounds last night.'

'What time?'

'A little after seven. Did you interview Rita Pahlke?'

'We did,' was all I got.

'Lynne thought she might have seen something,' I prodded.

'So Mrs Swope knows her?'

'Only that William said she's some kind of government conspiracy theorist and wanted William to pay for her silence.'

Pavlik's forehead wrinkled. 'About what?'

'Dentists putting tracking devices in teeth, for one thing,' I said like I knew what I was talking about. 'Pahlke didn't tell you why she was there?'

'According to the Louisville police she's been in and out of shelters. She told Taylor and Hallonquist she was simply exercising her civil rights.'

'Including dropping her drawers in the bushes?'

Lines next to Pavlik's eyes crinkled, signaling I'd amused him. 'She did admit that, once Hallonquist assured her he wouldn't cite her.'

I guess you had to feel sorry for the woman. 'What I don't understand is why she didn't see the body right off when she went behind the hedge.'

'Apparently Ms Pahlke was desperate to relieve herself and thought the man was a drunk sleeping off a Friday night bender.'

Not likely in Brookhills. Most of our drunks slept in their comfortable beds in their highly priced homes.

'She kept an eye on him as she squatted,' Pavlik continued. 'It was only when she'd finished up that she realized something was wrong.'

Feeling I'd plumbed the depths of Pavlik's knowledge of Rita Pahlke, I moved on. 'What about Clay Tartare? Did he say why he was so hot to talk to—'

'Want me to go?' The sound of my son's voice caused me to close my own mouth and tune back in on the conversation inside the conference room.

'Just who are you again?' Taylor asked.

I could feel my eyes narrow. I'd never liked the man and I sure didn't like him talking to my son that way. Or any way, for that matter.

Pavlik put a hand on my arm. 'Eric is nineteen. He can handle himself.'

I stayed put.

'Eric Thorsen. My mom and I called in the body.' I swore I actually heard him swallow. 'I mean, Doctor Swope.'

Taylor snorted. 'Following in your mom's footsteps?'

I shot a look at Pavlik and he shrugged.

'We weren't the first ones,' Eric said defensively.

'The decedent worked at Thorsen Dental,' Taylor said. 'That's your dad's office, correct?'

'Correct,' I heard Eric say, the word managing to convey both preciseness and uncertainty.

'When was the last time you were there?'

'Before today?' I could hear surprise in Eric's voice. 'Maybe August?'

'That's a long time.' This voice was kinder – Hallonquist. 'Away at school?'

'Yes, in the Twin Cities. We just drove back from Minneapolis last night.'

'We?' The violent crimes' detective continued the questioning.

'Ginny and me.'

'That would be you, young lady?' A pause. 'Virginia Swope?'

'It would.' Ginny's voice sounded sullen.

'When was the last time you saw your dad, Ginny?'

'Last night. Eric took me to see his mom's coffee shop and my mom and dad were there for some book club.'

'How did he seem?'

'My dad? Fine.' Ginny sounded more forthcoming now, though her voice still held an edge. 'He said he'd see me later and we left. I dropped Eric off at his mom's house and went over to my cousin's for pizza.'

'So neither of you saw Doctor Swope after that? Did you maybe stop by Thorsen Dental on the way?'

The 'no,' was a vehement chorus.

'And even if we had,' Ginny continued, 'my dad was at the coffee shop when we left, remember?'

'Good point,' Hallonquist said. 'Why don't you two wait in the outer office? We'll want to get fingerprints for elimination purposes and may have some follow-up questions after we've finished talking with Mrs—'

'I'm staying with my mother,' Ginny's voice interrupted.

'Suit yourself,' Taylor said as Eric came out, not having to be told twice.

My son hovered just outside the conference room door uncertainly but Pavlik gestured for him to move away and took his place there.

'Why doesn't he just go in?' Eric asked me in a low voice.

'Pavlik?' With a glance at the sheriff's back I beckoned my son to the desk where we could sit and still hear – even partially see – the proceedings. 'I assume he doesn't want to undermine his detectives or overwhelm Ginny and her mother.'

'Ginny's got *cojones*, huh?' Eric said as he settled his rump on the top of the desk next to me.

I nodded. From our vantage point we could see Hallonquist

seated across from Lynne and Ginny. Taylor was next to him, his arms crossed. The bald homicide detective had pushed his metal folding chair back a bit from the table, as if distancing himself from the conversation.

Hallonquist looked up from what I assumed was a notepad on the table in front of him. 'Mrs Swope, when was the last time *you* saw your husband?'

'At the book club meeting.' Lynne's voice came out wispy and she cleared her throat. The next words were stronger, the tone more like her daughter's. 'Just before seven.'

'And this was at Uncommon Grounds. But Ginny didn't stay, correct?' Hallonquist was apparently playing the good cop to Taylor's bad. Not that it took much. Just their comparative voices and demeanors painted different pictures.

'I told you,' Ginny said before her mother could answer, 'I took Eric home.'

Hallonquist made a note. 'When did the meeting finish up?'

'A quarter past nine, I think,' Lynne answered.

'You texted me about then,' Ginny confirmed. 'To say you were leaving.'

'Is that when Doctor Swope left as well?'

This one Lynne fielded. 'William didn't stay for the meeting.'

Hallonquist looked up. 'Why not?'

The financial advisor shifted uncomfortably. 'He didn't really say but I know he planned to go back to the office anyway.'

'So Doctor Swope never intended to stay for the meeting in the first place. Did he just stop in to say hello?' Hallonquist's face projected open and encouraging.

Lynne shot an uneasy glance out the door and caught my eye before answering. 'No, he came to stay but there was a bit of a disagreement beforehand. I assumed then that's why he decided to leave but I don't know that for sure.'

The detective registered surprise, though I had to assume he'd already been briefed on the dust-up with Ted. 'This disagreement was between your husband and somebody else at the meeting?'

The guy was good. And maybe more dangerous – or effective might be the better word, assuming you were on the right side of both the table and the law – than the more abrasive Taylor.

'Not exactly at the meeting,' Lynne said. Another glance at Eric and me. 'It was before, as I said—'

'Oh my God,' Ginny interrupted. 'Who do you think you're protecting? Just *tell* them.'

She turned to Hallonquist. 'Doctor Thorsen came in, ready to rip my dad a new one.'

Taylor reentered the conversational circle, the metal chair squealing as he scooted it forward. 'About what?'

'William had just joined Thorsen Dental this spring,' Lynne said.

I couldn't be sure, but Hallonquist's eyes seemed to narrow at the non-answer.

Taylor kept his gaze on Ginny. 'Do you know why Doctor Thorsen was so mad at your dad?'

The girl shrugged. 'No idea. Eric suggested we head out and we did.'

'So your friend was expecting trouble.'

Both Eric and I opened our mouths. Pavlik, seeming to sense it, threw us a warning glance over his shoulder.

'I'm sure he didn't want to hear parents bickering,' Lynne Swope said. 'What young person does? Besides, Eric was probably eager to get home.'

'The Thorsens are divorced,' Taylor said. 'Which home did you take him to, Ginny?'

This time Pavlik didn't have to warn us.

'His mom's, up on the corner of Poplar Creek Road and Elm, I think it was. It's a tiny place that's kind of run-down. I'm not sure it's even in Brookhills.'

Ouch. The spoiled brat could take her Lexus and shove—

Eric elbowed me. This was the downside of being close to your kid. He can read your nasty little mind. With a smile, my son held a finger to his lips.

'I didn't say anything,' I whispered.

'You didn't have to.'

'. . . Key to his father's place,' Ginny was saying.

Hallonquist raised his head after penning another note. 'So you dropped Eric off on Poplar Creek and then went directly to your cousin's house. Can you give me his or her name?

'Her. And it's Caitlin Callahan.'

'And Caitlin's address?'

'No clue. But it's on Silver Maple Drive.' Ginny looked to her mother for confirmation and Lynne nodded.

'But isn't that . . .' Hallonquist flipped back in the notebook, '. . . yes, that's the same street Thorsen Dental is on. The corner of Brookhill and Silver Maple.'

Again, something Hallonquist would have known without checking his notes. He'd just come from that location and Brookhills wasn't a large place. 'So you must have gone past the 501 Building where your dad's office is, even if you didn't stop.'

Ginny was shaking her head. 'I didn't have to go that far south. Caitlin's house is north of Brookhill Road, like Mrs Thorsen's.' She wrinkled her nose. 'Nicer neighborhood, though.'

I scooted sideways out of elbow range.

'And what time did you leave your cousin's house?'

'Around ten maybe?' Ginny said. 'And before you ask, I drove south on Silver Maple to Brookhill Road because my mom and dad live about two miles east on it.'

'That means you passed the parking lot and east side of the office building. Did you notice anything? Lights, maybe, or—'

'Nothing,' Ginny said. 'Thank God.'

'Why do you say that?' Hallonquist asked.

'I knew my dad would have wanted me to stop if he was there. But I was tired and . . . and, I just didn't want to get into it.'

I couldn't judge whether the hitch in Ginny's voice was regret or something else altogether.

Hallonquist was bobbing his head. 'Problems with Dad, huh?'

'Fine. You got me.' I could imagine the teenage roll of the eyes. 'My grades weren't good and I was afraid he would take away my car.'

'Ginny!' Lynne said.

'Layoff, Mom, OK? Dad's dead? Maybe there are more important things than my grades right now?'

Aunt Mary's uptick on the end of what should be a sentence might be hereditary. Though it sounded a lot more normal coming from a teenager.

Lynne sniffled.

Taylor jumped back in. 'Let's get back to this argument at the coffee shop, Mrs Swope. Can you tell me exactly what was said?'

'I didn't hear much,' Lynne said. 'Ted burst in just as we were all sitting down and called my husband a . . .'

'Son of a bitch,' Ginny supplied.

'And?' Taylor encouraged as Hallonquist wrote notes.

Lynne shrugged. 'That's about it. Ted said Clay Tartare – that's William's partner in Louisville – had called and that this Rita Pahlke person had also talked to him. He seemed upset and said that he and William needed to discuss it.'

'Rita Pahlke,' Hallonquist repeated. 'Isn't that the woman who first discovered Doctor Swope's body?' Again, I was sure he knew the answer to his own question.

'That's what Maggy told me,' Lynne said.

'Do you know Ms Pahlke?'

'I know of her,' Lynne said. 'She made a nuisance of herself outside William's Louisville office, spouting crazy anti-government things.'

'Is that why you moved?' Hallonquist asked.

'Oh, no. No, we wanted to be closer to Ginny's school. But,' she seemed to be giving the question more thought, 'I do think William was glad to be away from the unpleasantness.'

'Do you think it's possible Doctor Swope didn't tell Doctor Thorsen about the . . . unpleasantness?' Hallonquist asked.

'Perhaps.' Lynne put both hands on the seat of her chair and pushed up, seeming to resettle herself. 'But William couldn't have had any way of knowing she'd follow us. It's quite . . . well, unpleasant.'

My kingdom for a thesaurus.

'Assuming Ms Pahlke's appearance was the reason for the argument,' Hallonquist continued, 'do you have any idea what the outcome was?'

'Outcome?'

Hallonquist shrugged. 'Outcome, resolution. How did Doctor Swope and Doctor Thorsen leave it?'

'Well, I only know what Maggy told me later.'

Taylor's eyes flitted my direction just enough for me to notice and then back. 'And what was that?'

'That she overheard Ted tell William to pack up his office and get out.'

I had to admit Lynne was a good witness. That was pretty much word for word what I'd told her.

'But you didn't ask your husband about it yourself?' Hallonquist asked.

'No.' There were tears in her voice. 'William didn't come back in so I . . . I didn't get to talk to him again.'

Ginny reached over and took her mother's hand.

'I'm confused, Mrs Swope. Where exactly was this argument? You said your husband,' Hallonquist with the notes again, '"didn't come back in," but my impression was that this all took place in the coffeehouse.'

Lynne shook her head. 'Ted suggested they step outside.'

'Like a fight?' The question was from Ginny. She hadn't witnessed this part and seemed more intrigued than distressed now.

'No, of course not. Just to talk privately,' her mother assured her.

'Which explains why you didn't hear the rest of the conversation,' Hallonquist said. 'But Mrs Thorsen did? How?'

'Maggy was leaving for the day and went out that door so she passed them.'

'Where do I register my surprise?' Taylor muttered.

Hallonquist might be wilier but I still much preferred him over Taylor, the macho jerk.

'And Mrs Thorsen overheard the part about him packing up his office,' Hallonquist continued. 'Where were the men at this point, as far as you know?'

'Still on the porch, I assume,' Lynne said. 'But, again, I have no independent knowledge of all this. I'm just repeating what Maggy told me.'

Who needed a bus when Lynne could throw me under the porch?

'Oh my God. Why don't you just ask *her*?' Ginny asked, flinging an arm in the direction of where Eric and I were sitting. 'Mrs Thorsen is right out there. And, for that matter, *Doctor* Thorsen should be around somewhere and he should have a *real* good memory of what he said that made my father kill himself.'

'Ginny!' Another reprimand from Lynne.

'That's fine, Mrs Swope,' Detective Hallonquist said. 'Ginny is asking a good question. And the answer is that we interview multiple people because recollections of an event can differ. Having two or more versions helps, especially in a case like this where people are afraid they're responsible for what happened. They tend to . . .'

'Bullshit,' Taylor supplied.

'I was thinking sugarcoat.' Hallonquist's head was bobbing again. 'But the fact is, Ginny, that we're not trying to assign blame. We're looking for a precipitating event that we can document. Something that led to the outcome. It makes everybody's life easier.'

'Except for the guy who jumped out of the building,' Ginny snapped.

'Listen, missy.' This was Taylor. And though his tone was straightforward it surprisingly wasn't unkind. 'I've worked a lot of suicides and every one of them leaves a torn-up family behind. People spend the rest of their lifetimes beating themselves up, wondering what they should or could have done or said different. Don't do it.'

'I'm not—' Ginny started.

Taylor held up a finger. 'I mean it. Don't do it to yourself, don't let other people do it to you and don't *you* do it to other people.' He stood up. 'There are some questions that just don't have answers. Not answers we'll ever be privy to, anyway.'

NINE

'So the bad cop isn't so bad after all?' Sarah asked. I'd arrived at the shop two hours late, much to my partner's displeasure. When I relayed the events of the morning, though, she perked right up.

'I still think Taylor's a jerk but maybe buried under the swagger there's a human being.' I slipped a copy of *Gone Girl*, left over from the book club meeting the night before, onto our bookshelf next to the condiment cart. 'I'm sorry I wasn't here to help with the Saturday morning rush.'

'Yeah, yeah, yeah – you said that. Sit down and talk to me.'

Since it was still half an hour before lunch and the place was empty, I obeyed and took the chair across from my partner. She had a coffee mug in her hand and a sticky bun in front of her.

She unrolled a coil of the roll and dangled a five-inch length of gooey deliciousness in front of my face. 'Want some?'

I was tempted for a second, but as the melted sugar and spice started to rappel off the pastry toward the table top, I shook my head. 'You're going to get that all over the place.'

'Your loss.' She tipped her head back and, holding the coil overhead, lowered it into her mouth like a sword swallower with a limp, sticky . . . sword.

Forcing my eyes away, I said, 'I must say I was also impressed by Taylor's use of the word "privy."'

'As in john?' Sarah swallowed. 'Porta-potty?'

She was mocking me.

'Privy, as in "aware of." Nobody uses words like that anymore.'

'Oh, for the good old days of verbiage,' Sarah said, swiping at her sticky cheek. 'So what else happened?'

'Nothing.' I handed her a napkin. 'When I retrieved my jacket from the conference room the detectives were wrapping up and Lynne was about to call her sister.'

And understandably wanted some privacy to do so. I'd headed across the tracks to work and Eric had taken the car in search of his father.

Sarah dunked the corner of the napkin in her coffee and rubbed at her face. 'So why do you think Swope took his swan dive?'

'Good question. The good doctor has some bucks, judging by the Lexus his daughter drives and the supposed "upmarket clientele" he served. If Pahlke was a pest, why not hire a lawyer or get an injunction to keep her away?' Two things I'd have tried before jumping off a ten-story building.

'From what you've said, Swope wasn't all that worried. It was Ted who went ape-shit.'

I winced at the memory, given the aftermath. 'At both that and whatever Clay Tartare told him on the phone.'

'Which was?'

'I don't know.'

'Bet that makes you crazy.'

I frowned at her. 'No, it doesn't – why should it? Besides, Pavlik or Ted will tell me.' Eventually.

'What I do know,' I continued, 'is that no matter how angry Ted or anybody else got at me, I sure wouldn't jump out of a window over it.'

'You're not a guy.'

'So what?'

'Four times as many men commit suicide in the US as women.'

'They don't get help?' I guessed.

'Maybe that's part of it, but the statistics are also skewed because guys are better at it.' Sarah tossed the soggy, crumpled napkin on the table and took a sip of her coffee. 'More women try, you understand – we just use less certain methods like pills. Guys go for the big guns.'

'Guns? Literally?'

'You bet – like half of all suicides in the US are committed with firearms.'

Lovely. And my bipolar friend owned a gun. 'You don't ever have thoughts, do you?'

'Sure, but I don't act on them. You're right to worry, though – ninety percent of suicides have a diagnosable mental disorder of some sort. And here's another fun fact,' Sarah said, getting up with her plate and cup.

Fun fact? I was still reeling from the stats she'd already cited.

'In the UK,' she continued, 'where you can't own a gun, hanging and suffocation is at the top at fifty-two percent and firearms way down at two percent. Their rates overall are lower than ours anyway – apparently the English are a cheerier lot than they appear.'

'How in the world do you know all this?' I asked, worried.

'I read.' Her back was toward me as she set her dirty dishes on the counter. 'Don't you?'

'Yes, but not necessarily studies on suicide.'

'Not just on suicide.' She turned to face me. 'For example, did you know that bipolar disorder can run in families?'

If Sarah hadn't already had my full attention, she did now. 'Are you saying that one of your parents, or—'

'I don't want to talk about it.'

Now she didn't want to talk. But the fact was that Sarah never said much about her family. Apparently there was a reason for that.

But I knew my partner well enough not to pursue it. At least for now. 'Anyway, we don't know that William committed suicide.'

Sarah leaned her back against the cabinet, her arms folded. 'Please don't tell me you're going to try to make a homicide out of this.'

'Some things don't add up. Like William's shirt was dry.'

'So? You said he landed next to the building. The overhang probably kept the rain off him.'

'The 501 Building has a flat roof. No eaves, no overhang.'

'Even so, if the wind was blowing from the west couldn't the building have sheltered the body on the east?'

'Yet when the rain started up again, it *was* hitting William's shirt. That's when I realized it had been dry in the first place.'

But Sarah wasn't buying it. 'Winds shift. What did Pavlik say when you showed him?'

'That's just the problem. I told him about it but couldn't actually show him because it started to rain while I was still on the phone to nine-one-one. They only have my word that the shirt was dry.'

'And Pavlik thinks you're lying?'

'No, of course not. But he does seem to be discounting it. Says that William could have jumped after the rain stopped early this morning.'

Sarah shifted and braced her hands behind her to protect her back from the jutting edge of the counter. 'Cheer up. In support of your original theory he also could have been *murdered* after the rain stopped. Happy now?'

'It's not that I want the man to have been murdered.' Especially given that the suspect who had access to the building and had just argued with William was the father of my son. 'It's just—'

I broke off as hurried footsteps sounded on the wooden front steps. Before I could get up from the table the door was swung open and slammed back into the condiment cart.

'I'm so glad you're here,' Lynne Swope said. 'I really need to talk.'

Standing to pull the door closed behind her, I said, 'I thought you were with your sister.'

'This isn't really something I could discuss with Mary. Oh,' she held up a mug, 'this was on the porch.'

William's coffee mug from the night before, though I thought it best not to remind her.

'Thank you,' I said, taking it. 'Can I get you a coffee? Or something to eat?'

'No, thank you,' Lynne said. 'What I do need you to do, though, is help me prove that Rita Pahlke killed my husband.'

TEN

'But you seemed so sure William's death was suicide,' I said, setting the mug of cold coffee aside.

'I know.' Lynne Swope was unbuttoning her coat. 'I guess I just assumed William jumped, given the circumstances.'

I pulled out the chair across from Sarah for her. 'What changed your mind?'

'The fact that Rita Pahlke is here in Brookhills.' Lynne sat but didn't quite meet my eyes as I came around the table to take the seat next to my partner. 'We already know she was stalking him. Maybe she snuck up to his office last night and pushed him out the window.'

Sarah frowned. 'But didn't you tell Maggy that Pahlke was just a harmless nutcase and William just laughed her off?'

Lynne's eyes flashed toward me like she'd caught me sharing confidences. 'Those were William's words. I also told Maggy the woman demanded money.'

'And William gave it to her?' Sarah asked.

'Of course not,' Lynne snapped. 'He said she was—'

'A harmless nutcase,' I finished for her, with just a tinge of satisfaction. 'What makes you think now that William was wrong about her?'

She jerked up her head and met my eyes squarely. 'He's dead, isn't he?'

'I'm sure the sheriff's department is looking into all the possibilities.' I realized I must sound like Pavlik when I ran one of my theories past him. 'Including, to be honest, Clay Tartare. I noticed you didn't tell the investigators that he'd been trying to get hold of William and, like Pahlke, had just showed up here.'

She flushed. 'I told you, Maggy, whatever Clay wanted was between him and William.'

'Who, as you've pointed out, is dead,' said Sarah.

If my partner hadn't vocalized it I would have, because I sure was thinking it. 'You're telling us that you never asked William what it was all about?'

'I didn't want to know.'

'Don't ask questions you don't want answers to.' It was one of my favorite mantras. 'But it had to be important. The guy flew all the way here.'

'Maggy's right,' Sarah said. 'That's gotta involve at least one change of planes.'

Lynne's color got deeper. 'When I was their office manager I was stuck in the middle between those two gigantic egos. Once I became William's wife I said no more.'

There was something she wasn't saying. 'Did you have more than a professional relationship with Tartare?'

Lynne's chin went up. 'We might have gone out, once or twice. But that was before William and me.'

Ah, so a romance gone bad. No wonder she didn't want to talk to the ex-boyfriend. Yet Swope and Tartare had remained partners. 'Did William know that you and Clay had dated?'

'Of course.'

'And it didn't bother him?'

'Why would it bother William?' Lynne said coolly. 'He'd won.'

It wasn't affection I heard in her tone. 'And Clay?'

Lynne shrugged. 'They stayed in the practice together, didn't they? Nearly fifteen years.'

Sarah snorted. 'Long time to be at each other's throats.'

'Oh, they actually seemed to enjoy the power struggle. And I was quite happy to leave them to it.' Lynne turned to me. 'Which is why this can't be suicide. William was a fighter. He loved competing. I can't *tell* you how out of character it would be for him to take his own life.'

'And yet here you are, telling us just that,' Sarah said.

Lynne looked sideways at my partner, confused.

But apparently even the financial planner's short exposure to Sarah had taught her to ignore and plunge on. 'Maggy, you heard what Detective Hallonquist said about finding a "precipitating event" to put in their report. I'm afraid the police are going to settle for the obvious solution and move on.'

'"Obvious" is sometimes right,' Sarah said, glancing at me with a 'keep your mouth shut and don't get involved' expression on her face. 'In fact, it's usually right. Which is why it's obvious, if you get my drift.'

'I don't believe William killed himself,' the widow said stubbornly, tears welling in her eyes. 'And I think you can help me prove it. My sister says you're the Jessica Fletcher of Brookhills, Maggy.'

I felt myself flush. 'Well, maybe so. But younger.'

'And bitchier,' Sarah added.

I plunged on this time. 'Sarah's right about one thing, Lynne. Sometimes things really are as they appear.'

The woman's chin went higher. 'So how do you explain the glass on the ground? If William jumped wouldn't he have opened the window first?'

The office building was built in the sixties with fixed floor-to-ceiling glass panes fronted by low heating/AC registers. Supposedly office workers with a fear of heights would be reassured by the foot-high separation between them and the nothingness outside. It hadn't done much for me.

But one thing I did know: 'Those windows don't open. William would have *had* to break the glass to jump.'

'Do we know for sure that he went out the tenth floor?' Sarah asked. 'Maybe he swan-dived off the roof and the broken glass is from him bouncing off the building on the way down.'

Lynne's head dropped and she let out a strangled sob.

I glared at my partner, whose 'don't get involved' strategy

apparently didn't include herself. Or maybe her plan was to traumatize Lynne so badly she left.

But Sarah just shrugged. 'I'm brainstorming – you know, providing a fresh perspective?'

'It's all right,' Lynne said. 'I know you're both trying to help.'

I wasn't so sure of that.

'One pane of glass on the tenth floor was broken out,' I said, 'so that's probably where William . . . exited the building.'

When Lynne didn't flinch this time, I continued, 'And I did notice the oxygen tank on the ground near William's body.'

'You think it was used to break the glass?' Lynne asked.

'Possibly,' I said, glancing toward Sarah.

But my partner was busy studying our guest. 'Suicide clause?' she asked.

Lynne sat up straight. 'What?'

I didn't understand where Sarah's brainstorming had taken her, either, so I kept my mouth shut.

'Maggy says that a couple of hours ago you were convinced your husband killed himself. You already knew about the two visitors from home. Something else had to have changed. Maybe you pulled out your husband's life insurance policy and found it had a suicide clause?'

'I just had a chance to think,' Lynne Swope protested. 'And I'm astounded, quite honestly, that you don't see it. Rita Pahlke is an extortionist who followed us here and then, ever so conveniently, found William's body. You don't call that suspicious?'

The woman was spinning the story to her benefit, but she had a point. 'Of course. But you have to admit you've done a complete one-eighty from suicide to murder in a very short amount of time.'

'Yes, but—' Lynne broke off and dove into her purse, murmuring something I couldn't quite catch.

'I'm sorry. Did you say something about Ginny?' I asked when she surfaced with a tissue.

The financial planner dabbed at her nose. 'Ginny told those detectives it was her fault.'

'She did? When?'

'After you left. I was on the phone with Mary and I heard Ginny talking to the detective.'

'Hallonquist?' Sarah guessed.

'No, the other one. The one who was talking about people having regrets.'

Taylor's moment of humanity. 'I was surprised, honestly, that he was so caring.'

'Caring?' Lynne half-snorted, leaving a string of snot dangling that wasn't nearly as appetizing as Sarah's sticky bun had been. 'I think he's the one who put the idea in her head.'

'Umm, you have something . . .' I swiped at my own left nostril.

She wiped.

'What idea did he put in Ginny's head?' I asked now that I could look at the woman without gagging.

'That my daughter should blame herself for her father's decision.'

I didn't like Taylor but I also knew that wasn't what he'd said. 'I think what the detective was saying was that survivors of people who commit suicide *shouldn't* blame themselves.'

'Exactly. And you know how perverse teenagers are. It's like sex. Tell them about contraception and they think you're giving them permission to do it.'

'Oh, please.' Sarah seemed at the end of both her patience and her brainstorming. 'Give kids a little credit, will you?' As the guardian of two teenagers herself, my partner figured she had some experience.

Before the two women took it out back over sex education, I steered us in the direction of our subject. 'What exactly did Ginny say to Detective Taylor?'

Lynne sniffed and shot an uncertain glance at Sarah. 'That it was her fault that William killed himself.'

'How could it possibly have anything to do with Ginny? She and Eric had just arrived in town.' Then I remembered what Ginny had told the detectives. 'You mean her grades? How bad can they be? This is still the first semester of classes.'

'Yes, her grades,' Lynne said. 'I had no idea but apparently she'd told William.'

'Told him what?'

'That she's been,' she looked around like she was afraid somebody would hear, 'expelled.'

ELEVEN

'People don't commit suicide because their kid flunks out of school.'

Lynne Swope had long departed and Sarah was wiping tables dirtied by the lunch crowd.

'But William was a guuuuy,' I said, mimicking my partner from the employee side of the service counter.

'If he killed himself over this, he's an idiot. Be a man – take the Lexus away.'

I didn't disagree. 'You heard Lynne. The car was contingent on Ginny keeping up her grades.'

'Then *she* should have been the one to kill herself.' Sarah tossed the dishrag she'd been using across the counter toward the sink. She missed.

'Nice.' I leaned down to pick up the rag. 'But that doesn't change the way Ginny feels. Quorum is expensive enough in the first place. Then add the fact that William bought her the Lexus as a reward for getting in. And that he and Lynne moved all the way here—'

'Not the daughter's fault,' Sarah reminded me. 'That was the "helicopter parents of the year's" choice.'

'Regardless, from Ginny's perspective, she'd already let her dad down. And now there was this blow-up with Ted.'

'I thought you said she wasn't here for that.'

'She and Eric arrived just in time for Ted to burst in and call her dad a son of a bitch. I'm sure she heard the rest of the story last night from Lynne when William didn't come home.'

'Or from Pavlik and his guys this morning.' Sarah rubbed her chin. 'So the kid *should* feel guilty.'

'She should not,' I started indignantly. 'Didn't you just say—'

'Oh, settle down.' My partner was grinning. 'Just trying to get a rise out of you. Ginny's obviously not responsible for her father's freefall.'

'Now convince her of that.' I squinted at the table where the three of us had sat. Sarah had already scrubbed it once but I'd be damned if there weren't still sticky smudges where she'd sat. I tossed her the rag. 'Go over that table again.'

'It's interesting, though,' my partner said as she re-cleaned her tacky mess, 'that Lynne has suddenly decided it's not suicide. She can say all she wants that her change of heart is because Pahlke's appearance here is suspicious, or she doesn't want the kid to feel responsible, but I like my theory about the life insurance policy better.' She sent the damp cloth back airmail.

I caught it. 'You mean that she's discovered there's no payout on William's life insurance policy in case of suicide? But he's been dead for less than twenty-four hours – there's no death certificate yet and it's a Saturday to boot. Could she even have filed a claim?'

'No, but how long does it take to go home, pull out the policy and a magnifying glass and read the fine print?'

About as long as the interval between my leaving Lynne at her office and her showing up at Uncommon Grounds. 'She *is* a planner, I guess, by her own admission.'

'And she's planning on using *you* to turn this into a homicide investigation. And I might point out that if that happens, your ex will be on the list of suspects right behind Crazy Rita and the grieving widow.'

'Don't forget Clay Tartare. Though Rita is my fave for now. So tidy,' I waved the dishrag, 'when the person who finds the body is also the killer.'

'You're usually that person,' she reminded me.

There was that. 'At least this time I had a witness with me.'

'Your son would lie for you in a heartbeat.'

'I'd like to think so,' I said with motherly pride. 'If you believe I'll let Lynne manipulate me, relax. The medical examiner will find for suicide and the case will be closed.' I chewed on the inside of my cheek.

'But . . .' Sarah prompted.

'There was a blow to William's forehead, did I tell you that?'

'Happens when you hit the ground with it.' Sarah's expression changed. 'Could we be missing something here?'

'Like what?'

'What we were talking about earlier – the obvious. Maybe William Swope just leaned against the glass and it broke.'

The windows *were* over fifty years old. 'That could put a dent in Eric's college fund.'

'What are you talking about?' Sarah didn't seem to know if I was entertaining her suggestion or dismissing it.

'If somebody can lean on the window and fall out, there might be a liability issue. I hope Ted's insurance policy is up to date.' Ted now owned the building alone thanks to the divorce-settlement gods.

'Even if the building itself isn't,' Sarah said, 'I do know building codes were different back then. I remember a kid in my kindergarten class falling through a pane of glass at our school.'

'Oh my God – was he or she hurt?'

'Nah, she was fine. A few scratches. You've such a bleeding heart.'

'The girl was *five*,' I said, turning on the water to rinse the dishcloth.

'And now she's forty-five. Not such a big deal anymore, is it?'

How do you answer that?

So I didn't. 'There's something else that's been bothering me. I'm nearly certain I saw lividity on the backs of William's arms.'

'You're the corpse-whisperer, but isn't that normal?'

Squeezing the last bit of water out of the rag, I hung it over the edge of the sink before I turned. 'Blood starts to pool after a couple hours.'

'So does that give you a time of death?'

I was back to chewing on my cheek. 'Not really. The rain stopped at three a.m., according to Pavlik, so if William died even at six or seven in the morning there was still time for the discoloration to start before I saw the body around nine. Obviously the medical examiner will know better but—'

Sarah interrupted. 'This "blood pooling" happens whether he jumped, fell or was pushed, right? What's your point?'

Honestly, my friend made thinking out loud feel like a contact sport. 'My point is that I *saw* it.'

Sarah was looking at me like she wouldn't mind committing a murder of her own.

'After death, blood settles in the lower parts of the body,' I explained. 'Meaning the parts underneath. How come I was able to see it on the backs of his arms?'

'Because . . .'

'Because, I think the body might have been moved. *After* lividity set in.'

TWELVE

While Sarah had seemed at least somewhat impressed with my theory about William Swope's body being moved, Pavlik appeared less so.

I was seated in one of the two leather guest chairs in front of his massive mahogany desk in the Brookhills County Sheriff's Office. The sheriff's office, in turn, was situated in the county complex that also housed the Brookhills' courthouse, administrative offices, sheriff's department and juvenile and adult jails.

My stomach growled. Having arrived at Uncommon Grounds late for my shift, I'd not only passed on Sarah's cinnamon roll and skipped lunch, but offered to work the afternoon. Before Sarah was to leave at three, though, I took a break and walked rather than drove to Pavlik's office as penance for all the pizza the night before.

At the sound of my stomach rumbling, the sheriff pulled open his right-hand desk drawer. 'Granola bar? Or an orange?' He picked up the orange. 'Well, maybe not. It's fuzzy. But I think the granola bar is still good.'

I started to refuse until I noticed it was peanut butter chocolate chip. If God had wanted us to skip lunch he wouldn't have made peanut butter.

A visit to Pavlik's office – high ceilings, wood paneling, marble floors, massive wooden desk and credenza – always reminded me that I was doing the sheriff, so it was good to know that even he stashed food – including rotting fruit, apparently – in his desk drawers.

'Thanks,' I said, taking the granola bar.

Pavlik could pull rank on occasion, sometimes with words and sometimes just with eyes that turned from sunny blue to stormy gray in an instant. But for now his eyes were neutral blue and he didn't seem inclined to kick me out of his office. Still, something just seemed . . . off. I missed the intimacy of our first long weekend away together. Here we were, back to real life. And, in Pavlik's case, his official role.

'We need to see what the ME has to say on the lividity.' The sheriff pushed his wheeled chair back from his desk. 'And by "we," I mean my detectives and me. Not you.'

Message received, if ignored. 'But don't you think the lividity, along with the fact the back of his shirt was dry, points to the body being moved? I know you just have my word to go on about the shirt . . .' I remembered something. 'His cell phone was gone.'

'Gone from where?'

'William's khakis. He slipped it and a packet of sugar into his back pocket before he went out onto the porch to talk to Ted. The sugar was still there this morning but I didn't see the phone.'

'Because we found it on his desk.'

So William had gone to his office – obvious, since that was where he'd fallen from, but also had been there long enough to settle in a bit before his fall. Take his phone out of his pocket. Maybe make a call?

I asked Pavlik.

'I don't have that information.'

Hearing the 'police spokesperson' in his tone, I tried another angle. 'I suppose when he pulled out his phone the sugar came partially with it, which is why I could see it poking out.'

'And this is remarkable for some reason?'

'Only because the paper wasn't soaked. Just like the shirt was dry until that first drop of rain fell on it.' OK, maybe I was hammering my point, but I thought it was important.

'Completely dry?' Pavlik asked. 'Or could it have partially dried in the five or six hours between the rain stopping and you seeing the body?'

'I—'

The sheriff leaned forward. 'If I put you on a witness stand, Maggy, could you swear that the shirt was totally dry?'

'Swear?' I was thinking back. The falling rain had made darker drops on the red shirt but that didn't mean it had been utterly dry. In fact, I was willing to bet the front half of the shirt was wet so it couldn't possibly be described as 'totally dry.' 'No, I guess I couldn't swear to it. But—'

'And lots of things can affect lividity patterns,' Pavlik continued. 'Tissue damage, for one thing.'

'You mean maybe he broke his arms in the fall.' I was remembering the 'flying superman' pose of William's arms above his body. Had the man broken the glass with the chair and performed an actual swan dive, head first? The very sight of the ground approaching had to be horrifying. And while falling ten stories might take mere seconds, it was certainly time enough to reconsider.

I shivered. 'I don't suppose anybody heard anything?'

Pavlik shook his head. 'No, but that's not surprising. Nothing but the parking lot and train tracks behind the office building and Schultz's Market next door. The rest of the area is office park until you get to the Morrison.'

True. And Schultz's market closed at eight p.m. 'Too bad, since we still don't know the time of death.'

'The ME's report should give us some idea on that.'

All roads dead-ended at the medical examiner's office for now. 'His neck sure looked broken. Did you see the head wound?'

'Hitting the ground from that height can do a lot of damage,' Pavlik said, echoing Sarah's comments on the same subject. But from Pavlik it felt like another info-block.

'I saw the broken window on the tenth floor from the street but I can't remember if that would be an exam room or an office these days.'

'It's Doctor Swope's office,' Pavlik confirmed. 'And before you ask: yes, that's where he exited the building.'

I was struck by Pavlik's 'exited' – the same term I'd used talking to Sarah and Lynne. Jumped, fell, was pushed – all might imply facts that had yet to be proven.

Elvis has, indeed, left the building. We're just not sure how.

'Was the air tank on the ground used to break the glass?' I asked.

'I don't have that information,' Pavlik said.

Argh. 'OK, would you let me know when the ME report comes back?' I stood.

'Don't leave yet,' Pavlik said, holding up a hand. 'Sit.'

I sat.

'How well do you know Lynne Swope?'

I was surprised by the question. 'We met just yesterday when I hired her as my financial advisor. You know, for my inheritance from my brother.'

For once Pavlik looked disappointed that I wasn't more involved.

'You could talk to Mary Callahan at the library,' I offered for having come up short. 'Mary and Lynne are sisters.'

'I'd like to keep this line of inquiry quiet for now.'

And no one trusted Mary to keep a secret, including the sheriff. 'Do you suspect Lynne had something to do with William's death?'

'Taylor thinks she's hiding something.' Pavlik pulled a folder over and flipped it open. 'Did you know that the daughter, Virginia, is Lynne Swope's child from a previous marriage?'

'I didn't,' I said. 'They seemed so close – Ginny and William, I mean.'

'Not so surprising. The girl was a toddler when her father was killed in an accident and only six when her mother remarried.'

'What kind of accident?'

Another check of the notes. 'The father had a blood alcohol level of .23 and ran off the road head-on into a tree. Virginia was strapped into a car seat in the back, which is the only reason she survived.'

No wonder Lynne was protective of Ginny. And vice versa. 'I'm not sure what Taylor thinks Lynne might be hiding but I do know she's worried about Ginny feeling responsible.'

Pavlik looked up, puzzled. He must have missed his homicide detective's post-interrogation chat with Ginny, just as I had. 'What does the girl have to feel responsible for?'

I waved away his sudden suspicion. 'William killing himself. That's still the most likely scenario, right?'

'We can't rule anything out.'

Another enlightening answer. 'Well, Ginny flunked out of her school up in the Twin Cities and thinks that, along with

William losing his job here, it might have pushed him over the edge.'

'From what I can see, his stepdaughter's grades were the least of his worries.'

Ah ha. Finally, an opportunity to find out more. 'You mean his practice in Louisville?'

'What about it?'

Pavlik was certainly playing it close to the vest today. 'I was hoping you'd tell me. Clay Tartare had been trying to get hold of him. Why?'

'Time will tell.'

Argh, squared. 'Well, what about Rita Pahlke and the extortion?'

'For putting GPS devices in patients' teeth?' Pavlik shrugged.

'Well, if Pahlke was camped out overnight, maybe she heard something.' Glass breaking. William screaming.

'No camp-out. Ms Pahlke stayed at the Morrison last night.'

A bit of information at last. 'The hotel confirms that?'

'Checked in yesterday afternoon and bought a large coffee from the restaurant at seven this morning.'

That explained the need to pee. 'Lynne thinks Pahlke might have killed William. Though I guess if Lynne is a suspect, as you seem to think, she'd be trying to deflect blame.'

Pavlik didn't bite. 'Even in a suicide, family members look for alternative explanations. People can't get their heads around the idea their loved ones voluntarily left them.'

'Sarah said maybe there's a suicide exemption in William's life insurance policy.'

'Entirely possible.' It was Pavlik who stood up this time. 'Like I said, we're looking into everything, but first we need—'

'—the ME's report.'

When Amy arrived to relieve me at five, Sarah was at the desk in the office.

'What are you doing here?' I asked, hanging my apron on one of the wooden pegs by the door. 'Your shift was over two hours ago.'

'I came back.' Sarah laced her fingers together over her head and stretched. 'Thought you might be up for Chinese takeout tonight.'

'That's a great idea – thanks.' The granola bar was long gone and I was starving again.

'You place the order,' I continued, 'and I'll just run home quick and let Frank out. I should be at your place by the time the food arrives.' I was already pulling on my jacket.

'I thought we'd do it at your house.'

I paused, one arm in the sleeve. '*My* house?'

'Courtney is having friends over tonight.' Sarah picked up her own jacket. 'Four sixteen-year-old girls chattering, one voice more piercing than the next.'

Courtney and her brother Sam had come to live with Sarah after their mother's death. My partner was an unlikely guardian, but not half bad at it.

'So you're inviting yourself to dinner.' I started down the hall, not even bothering to hope she wouldn't follow.

'Not only that but you're both ordering and paying.' Sarah pushed past me to open the door to the boarding platform and lead the way down the steps to the back parking lot.

'Goodness,' I said, following, 'why the largesse? I mean on my part?'

'Because you owe me.'

'Why's that?'

'I'm giving you a ride home.' Sarah pulled her car keys out of her jacket pocket. 'Eric has your car, remember?'

Oh, yeah.

THIRTEEN

E ric might have my car but he hadn't driven it home. At least, not home to my house.

'Honest to God,' Sarah said, wiping the glass-topped coffee table with a napkin so she could set down her wine glass. 'How do you stand it?'

'Stand what?' Having ordered our food, I set my phone on a dry area of the table.

'The drool, the dog hair, the—'

'Sheepdogs don't shed,' I said, picking up my own glass. 'Right, Frank?'

The dog raised his head and smiled, or so I imagined. But then I imagined many things. Being richer. Younger. Nicer.

Frank was lying on the hearth. The fireplace, like the flat screen above it and the sheepdog below, was far too big for the living room. What was left of the floor space was occupied by the coffee table, a couch and an overstuffed armchair. I was sitting on the chair; Sarah was on the couch.

She stuck a hand down into the space between the cushions and came up furry. 'Oh, yeah?'

I cringed. 'That's probably from when I brushed him.'

'Inside the house?'

'It's November. He shivers.'

'The dog's a walking parka.' She sniffed. 'Though I have to admit he doesn't smell nearly as bad as usual.'

'I know,' I said, nodding and smiling like some proud, lunatic doggy-mother. 'I think it's because I don't let him have onions on his pizza anymore. Did you know they're bad for dogs? Somebody told me I could have killed him.'

'And yet,' Sarah stuffed the handful of Frank back where it had been, 'you didn't.'

Now truth be told, there was a time when I'd have agreed with Sarah's opinion of Frank. But that was before Ted left me less than twenty-four hours after he and I had moved Eric into the dorms in Minneapolis.

Alone in the house, it was my son and his left-behind sheepdog Frank who kept me sane. Though away at school, Eric had promptly replied to every text message from me, occasionally even answering the phone when I called. Two years later he was back to being a normal college student, meaning he got in touch when he needed something. But Frank, bless his co-dependent canine soul, still dogged my every step and hung on my every word. Everybody needs a Frank in their life.

The bell rang and the sheepdog made a beeline for the front door, as eager as I was for our food delivery.

'Coming,' I called, picking up the bills I'd laid on the coffee table and following. Blocking the dog with my body, I cracked open the door. 'That was fast—'

But instead of our delivery guy, Lynne Swope stood in front of me.

If I was disappointed, Frank was devastated. He gave a pathetic little whimper more appropriate for a shih tzu than a sheepdog and collapsed like one of those fainting goats you see on *Animal Planet*.

'Oh my God,' Lynne said. 'Is it dead?'

'No. Though he'd like you to think he will be if the food doesn't get here soon.'

'Oh, I'm sorry. I didn't mean to interrupt your dinner.' Despite her words and my less-than-subtle hint, she stepped into the foyer and shrugged out of her coat.

'You're not interrupting dinner,' Sarah said, sticking her head around the corner from the living room as I reluctantly took the coat. 'Yet.'

Badly as I might feel for Lynne, I'd just met the woman yesterday. Wasn't calling her husband's body into 911 this morning and sitting with her while the police investigated enough of a commitment for such a new relationship?

Now, not only had she come to Uncommon Grounds this afternoon but here she was tracking me down at home.

At dinnertime.

'Wine?' Sarah was holding up her own glass.

'Oh, I'd love it.' Lynne sank gratefully onto the couch as I hung her coat in the closet.

'Is everything OK?' I asked as Sarah poured what was left of the blend I'd opened the night before into Lynne's glass. When I realized how stupid the question was I shifted to, 'How is Ginny doing?'

Lynne took the wine. 'She and Eric spent the afternoon at Ted's place watching the baby, which I'm sure helped get her mind off things. They got home just before I left.'

That explained where my car was.

'Eric is being so kind to Ginny,' Lynne continued with a wan smile. 'Wouldn't it be nice if something good came out of all this and the two of them—'

My stomach growled. 'Eric is gay.'

'Oh.' She took a careful sip of the wine. 'I'm sorry.'

'Why?' I said, readying for a fight. 'I'm not.'

Lynne blushed. 'No, I didn't mean I'm sorry he's gay, just that I hoped—' She broke off and took a bigger swallow of wine. 'Never mind.'

'Maggy knows what you mean,' Sarah said, throwing me a look as she sat down next to the woman.

I didn't necessarily know what Lynne meant. But if there was anything that could make me feel guilty it was Sarah being nicer than me. I reclaimed the chair, tucking my feet up under me, and said, 'So is there something we can do for you?' I tried again.

Lynne drained the remaining wine in her glass and set it on the table. 'Eric said you and the sheriff are . . . well, a couple.'

'We are.' I was wondering what was coming.

'It's just that I thought perhaps he'd told you what they'd found.'

'Found?' Other than that nobody had heard or seen anything and all roads led to the medical examiner, Pavlik had been extraordinarily stingy with information. Besides, what he *did* tell me I'd learned not to blather. Especially to somebody his detectives suspected was hiding something. 'I'm afraid not.'

'Oh.' Lynne sat back, looking disappointed.

'You can call him,' I told her. 'Or, better yet, one of the two detectives. I'm sure they gave you their cards, right?' It was standard procedure.

'Oh, yes, they did.' She opened her purse and started digging through it as if she planned to make the call right then and there.

Frank, having recovered, chose that moment to stalk back into the room and, eyeing Lynne on the couch next to Sarah, gave it as wide berth as the room allowed and harrumphed himself down on the floor in front of me. I checked the clock on the mantle. The food was late and Frank had decided Lynne was to blame.

The culprit came up with three business cards. 'I have each detective's card and one from the medical examiner's office, too. The detective said if I called tomorrow they might be able to tell me when William's body will be released.'

Sarah stirred next to her. 'Do you have a funeral home?'

'Brookhills Funeral Home and Cremation. The lady – I think her name was Mimi – said she'd take care of it from there, once the medical examiner says it's all right.'

'So your husband did have life insurance?' Sarah asked. 'You'll be able to pay for the funeral and all?'

Smooth.

But if Sarah's motive for the question was transparent Lynne didn't seem to notice. 'That's very kind of you to ask but I think I'll be able to cover the initial costs from our joint account.'

Sarah's brow furrowed. I wasn't sure if it was because she still hadn't gotten an answer to her question or because she realized that Lynne had taken it as a loan offer.

I suppressed a grin and said to the widow, 'It sounds like you have things covered. At least as much as possible for now.' When she didn't answer – or leave – I tried again. 'Is there anything else we can do?'

'No. I mean, yes.' She flushed. 'I was wondering what they'd found in William's office.'

I assumed she meant his cell phone. 'His cell was on his desk, though I'm not sure if you'll be able to get it back immediately. But, like I said, ask the detectives.'

'Thing is,' she said, fingering the card in her hand, 'it's not the phone I'm concerned about, it's something else. And if they haven't come across it I don't necessarily want to bring it to their attention.'

I frowned. 'Why not?'

'Maybe that's not your business, Maggy,' said Sarah.

'I appreciate your input, Sarah,' I said measuredly. 'But Lynne came here to *my* house, asking for *my* help. I think I have a right to know why.'

Lynne jumped up. 'I'm so sorry. I didn't mean—'

The doorbell rang. Frank looked at me expectantly.

'I'll get it,' Sarah said. 'Where's the money?'

I should have known that even in her new, kinder persona, my partner stopped short of paying. 'Table next to the door.' I turned back to Lynne. 'Sit down, there's plenty for the four of us.'

'The four of us?' she said uncertainly as Sarah came in carrying a brown paper bag, Frank on her heels. 'Your dog eats Chinese?'

'Turnabout's fair play,' Sarah shot over her shoulder as she unpacked the contents of the bag on the coffee table.

Lynne didn't seem to get it and I wasn't about to explain. Especially over dinner. 'I don't mean to be rude, Lynne. I know this has been a horrible day but you can't ask me to use my sources,' or source, singular, 'and not tell me why.'

'Don't say a word until I get back,' Sarah cautioned Lynne.

I eyed my partner. 'What are you, her lawyer?'

Sarah snorted. 'Of course not. I don't want to miss anything.'

That was more like it. My partner disappeared into the kitchen. I grabbed a domed container from the coffee table and followed.

'Dinner, Frank,' I said, cracking off the top and setting the black plastic tray on the floor.

'So onions are bad for dogs, but egg foo yung is OK?'

Frank sniffed and then swallowed the patty in one gulp.

'I guess we'll find out,' I said. 'Seemed like the safest item on the menu.'

Frank burped and sat down.

'He looks like he's waiting for the entrée.'

I rustled in the cabinet and found a box of dog treats. 'Dessert, Frank?'

He got to his four feet and stalked out.

'I try,' I said, putting the treats away.

'I know you do. That's what scares me.' Sarah pulled three plates out of the cabinet. 'Get the silverware.'

I obeyed. 'There's more wine in the pantry. Grab the cabernet.' There went my 'one glass per night.'

Sarah claimed the bottle and started for the living room. Being a good wingman, I remembered the corkscrew and followed.

'Help yourself,' I said, handing Lynne her silverware.

She opened a carton and peered in. 'Umm, beef something?'

'Mongolian beef.' I stuck a serving spoon into the carton, almost taking off her nose. 'There should also be Kung Pao chicken and broccoli with garlic sauce. And rice, of course.'

Sarah had the second bottle of wine open. 'Refills?'

'Please.' I dug out rice and ladled Mongolian beef on top of it, adding a dollop of the Kung Pao for variety. 'Now, where were we?'

'You were interrogating the prisoner.' Sarah refilled Lynne's wine glass.

'That's right. And Lynne, you were going to tell us what you're afraid the investigators will find in William's office.'

Lynne had touched neither her food nor her second glass of wine, but she swallowed anyway. 'Divorce papers.'

FOURTEEN

'Happy family's not so happy, huh?' Having finished pouring wine all around, Sarah waved to the Chinese takeout cartons. 'Appropriate, no?'

More appropriate than my partner ever was.

'No,' I said, but I was thinking about the apparent strain between William and Lynne at the book club. 'As for the divorce, who was serving whom?'

Lynne looked surprised at my question. 'I was divorcing William. Why? Did he say something to Ted?'

That Ted, in turn, blabbed to me? Fat chance. I didn't even know he had a partner until Lynne had told me. 'No, he didn't. Do you have reason to think William planned to divorce you?'

'That *would* put a whole new spin on things,' Sarah said, serving herself rice and Kung Pao chicken. 'And a pre-emptive strike is always a nice move.'

Lynne blinked. 'I'm sorry?'

'I think she means if you filed for divorce because you knew William was and wanted to beat him to it.' Sarah was right. If William had planned to file for divorce, Lynne solidified her position at the front of the suspect pack.

But the widow was shaking her head. 'No, I'm nearly certain William wasn't contemplating divorce.'

'Then why did you bring it up?' Sarah said, starting on her food.

'I didn't,' the financial planner said, 'or at least I didn't mean to. It just took me by surprise when Maggy asked who was bringing the action.'

'You see, it was Ted who served me with notice that he'd filed for divorce,' I explained. 'I had no idea until that moment that he was fooling around with his dental hygienist and wanted to marry her.'

'That's honorable, at least,' Lynne said.

From Rachel's perspective, maybe. But that was dirty bathwater down the drain. Which reminded me – the baptism was tomorrow. 'Did Eric say anything about bringing my car back tonight?'

'No, but we didn't really talk. I was on the phone to my divorce lawyer when they came in, so I went into my bedroom to continue the conversation.'

'Which was about what?' I'd set down my plate at Lynne's mention of the divorce and now picked it back up. A girl's gotta eat, startling revelation or not.

Tears were rising in Lynne's eyes. 'I was checking on the papers.'

'When were they served?' I asked.

'Yesterday.' The tears spilled over. 'When Ginny texted me that she was driving Eric home I immediately called my divorce lawyer and left a message. In fact, I was ending the call when you arrived for your appointment.'

'You wanted to hold off?'

'Of course. There was no reason for Ginny to be caught in the middle of this. I followed up with an email, just to be safe, saying we'd wait until Ginny was back at school.'

'Didn't she say the kid flunked out?' Sarah asked me.

'I didn't know that then,' Lynne said testily through the tears. 'Or that the idiot Milwaukee divorce lawyer I hired doesn't check his messages.'

'But when was the notice served?' I asked. 'William didn't act like a man who was being sued for divorce when he arrived at Uncommon Grounds. Unless he's a really good actor.'

'Oh, he is,' Lynne said. 'Or was. But no, I'm told the papers were served to William outside his office last night.'

Before William sailed out the tenth-floor window.

'Looking good for a finding of suicide,' Sarah said. 'So when you checked his life insurance, *was* there a suicide exemption?'

Lynne blinked but she didn't deny Sarah's assumption. 'It may have expired.'

'You should check that,' Sarah said, shooting a triumphant glance toward me.

Seeing as my partner had led us to the subject, I might as well pursue it. 'The exemptions expire?'

'It depends on the policy,' Lynne said. 'Sometimes they won't pay out if the policyholder commits suicide within a certain length of time. That way somebody can't buy a policy solely to support their family after they take their own life.'

Sarah picked up her glass. 'Or somebody takes it for them.'

But then that wouldn't be suicide, would it? 'How did the process server know William would be at his office? If it weren't for the argument with Ted he would have stayed for the book club.'

'The server would have waited until he got back to the office. I'm certainly paying enough.'

'But that doesn't answer Maggy's real question,' Sarah said. 'Somebody had to tell the server your husband was going to be at the office late last night.'

'Yes.' Lynne shifted on the couch, unnecessarily adjusting and then plumping the pillow next to her. 'I've . . . well, I've been having William followed since we moved here. It was the same company – Brookhills Investigations and Process Serving.'

Sarah grinned. 'One-stop shopping. I like it. Kind of like a burger joint having a cardiac unit.'

'You obviously suspected something,' I said to Lynne. 'What?'

Swope seemed to be considering and then apparently came to a decision. 'William's been cheating on me. For years, apparently.'

'In Louisville?'

'And every city that hosted a dental conference, most likely.'

I knew how that went. I was just surprised William and my ex hadn't met on the circuit earlier. Though Ted and Rachel probably hadn't left their hotel room long enough to socialize. 'How did you find out?'

'A text message that seemed to be setting up a liaison, among other things,' Lynne said. 'That's why I started going along to conferences like the one where we met Ted. I thought he'd try to talk me out of it when I first suggested it.'

I'd finished my plate of food and wanted seconds, but not badly enough to interrupt the flow of information. 'And did he?'

She shook her head with a wry smile. 'Damned if he didn't act like he was thrilled.'

'Yet you believe—'

'I honestly doubted myself. Until his office manager knocked on my front door in late March, confirming everything I'd suspected for years.'

'She ratted on him?' Sarah asked. 'Good for her.'

I frowned. 'You said that William's Louisville office was training a new manager. Was that a replacement for – what was her name?' I looked to Lynne for the answer.

'Bethany,' she supplied with a sigh. 'Young, blonde and beautiful, like most of William's hires.'

Which explained what the oral surgeon meant by 'dressing up' Thorsen Dental, though he'd never had the chance. 'Bethany left the practice around the time she came to see you?'

'Exactly,' Lynne said. 'And she didn't rat on William, as Sarah put it, so much as confess.'

'Bethany and William were having an affair,' I said.

'Indeed they were. She even showed me the cell phone pictures he'd sent her.' A brittle smile.

The widow had my partner's attention. 'Please don't tell me they were weenie shots – you'll ruin my appetite.'

It's true that the male penis is not the most photogenic of body parts.

'I'm afraid so,' Lynne confirmed. 'And I'd know William's anywhere. He had a little . . . bump.'

Moving on. 'But you'd already suspected, correct?'

'There was the text message, of course.' Lynne was tapping her fingernails on the wine glass. 'And that every employee William hired was female and drop-dead gorgeous. He said it was good for business so I tried not to let it bother me. After all, they all seemed to be happily married. We'd even go out with them and their husbands to dinner or the theater at William's suggestion.'

'And Clay Tartare,' I asked, 'and his wife or girlfriend?'

Lynne glanced quickly at me and away. 'No, William and Clay didn't socialize much.'

I noticed she didn't say if there was a woman in her former boyfriend's life. 'Dangerous,' I said, earning me another startled look from the financial planner. 'I mean, dangerous for William to set up double dates with his affairees and their spouses.'

'I think the danger, as you put it, gave him a rush. But he also was very careful to choose women who had as much to lose as he did.'

'Meaning their marriages,' I said. 'But wouldn't Clay have picked up on something at the office?'

Lynne snorted. 'Clay could be very obtuse – or maybe naïve is a fairer word. And if he *did* suspect William was having an affair he certainly didn't tell me.'

'Man code.' Having apparently recovered her appetite, Sarah was helping herself to broccoli. 'You having any Kung Pao?'

'No, go ahead.' Lynne still hadn't touched the food, but I grabbed another spoonful of the spicy chicken before Sarah could empty the carton on her plate.

'My husband could be very charming and attentive.' Lynne was looking off into the distance. Which, in my living room, was the stucco wall eight feet away.

'I'm sure he told them how smart and beautiful and funny they were,' she continued, 'all the while being respectful and perfectly honest about the fact that he was married. He loved his wife, he'd say, and had no intention of leaving her. Before they knew it they'd practically be begging him to make love to them.'

There was something in the woman's expression . . .

'You were one of them,' I said.

Lynne's eyes flew wide. 'What?'

'You had an affair with William yourself.' I was guessing but, given Lynne's reaction, I must have nailed it. 'When you were the office manager *and* dating Clay?'

If the financial planner's face had been flushed earlier, it was on fire now. 'That was different. I was widowed and didn't realize he was married. At first.'

'And once you did you liked the challenge,' I guessed. 'The adrenaline rush, just like William did. Who wouldn't have chosen the charming, married Doctor Swope over the "obtuse," available Doctor Tartare.'

'Anybody in their right mind,' Sarah muttered. 'So who blabbed to Swope's wife? Tartare?'

'Clay never would. He's too honorable.' A wistful look crossed Lynne's face. 'She just . . . found out.'

'Right,' Sarah said. 'Anonymous note or email? It was probably pre-text message so you couldn't plant one of those, right?'

'We loved each other,' Lynne said. 'He chose *me* over her.'

'And you chose him over Clay.'

'And everybody lived happily ever after.' Sarah rolled her eyes. 'Or not. Guess it explains why Doctor Nookie started fishing for young married women. He didn't want to repeat past mistakes.'

The past mistake in the room started to protest but I held up a hand. 'Let's get back to Bethany. What did she tell you?'

'That she,' Lynne used finger quotes, '"fell in love" and would have done anything for him.'

'What about *her* husband?' I asked.

'Apparently I wasn't William's only "mistake."' A nod toward Sarah. 'Bethany's husband had recently died, though apparently she hadn't shared that newsflash with William. Once he realized he told her the relationship was just a flirtation on his part. As he thought it was on hers.'

Guess that explained William's comment that flirting wasn't harmless. Though his definition of flirtation was a little different to mine.

And apparently Sarah's. She put her already empty plate on the coffee table. 'So wait. Were they still sexting or had they gotten down to playing hide the sausage?'

Leave it to my partner to stab right to the heart of the matter.

'The,' Lynne hesitated as Frank padded into the room, 'sausage.'

The sheepdog cocked his head at the word and sniffed the air. Then probably deciding the woman was nothing more than a tease, he wedged himself back into the floor space between my chair and the coffee table.

I set my plate down and gave him a scratch. 'What did William say when you confronted him?'

'I didn't tell William.'

I looked at Sarah and she said what we both were thinking. 'Why the hell not?'

'Because I needed to think. To plan.'

This time I tried *not* to meet Sarah's eyes. Might Lynne Swope have calmly set out to kill her husband? Maybe William wasn't the only one who was a good actor.

'I know what you're thinking,' Lynne said, proving she did. 'I didn't kill William. I left the book club and drove by the office but I didn't see any lights. When he wasn't home I tried his cell, the office and eventually you.'

So she'd said, but was it all for show, including tonight's dinner interruptus?

'Besides,' Lynne continued, 'would I have filed for divorce if I intended to kill him?'

'Good point.' Unless she was some sort of evil genius. And I was not one to taunt an evil genius. 'The jilted lover, then? Clay Tartare?'

'But how many years has it been?' Sarah asked.

'Twelve?' Lynne supplied, her expression blank. 'And Clay obviously got over me fast or he wouldn't have stayed in the practice.'

'Maybe the guy needed a job more than he needed you or his self-respect.'

Lynne shrugged but I was wondering if perhaps Tartare had stayed on in the practice to be close to his lost love. Maybe he hadn't given up in twelve long years.

A romantic notion. Right up to the murder part. 'But what about Bethany? If we're looking for a jilted lover, shouldn't we start there?'

'Do we know where she is?' Sarah asked. 'Maybe Bethany and this Rita person are one and the same.'

'You saw her. Rita Pahlke is maybe in her forties with dark hair. And Bethany is young and blonde, Lynne?'

The financial planner frowned. 'Perky little blonde with Reese Witherspoon bangs.'

'So? You've never heard of makeup and hair dye?' Sarah asked. 'The woman's in disguise.'

'I've never seen Pahlke close up,' Lynne said, 'but I'm certain she's not Bethany.'

Sarah just hated to be shot down. 'Why's that?' she demanded.

'Because Bethany's dead.'

FIFTEEN

O h.
        Instinctively I tried to scoot my chair back to distance
        myself from Lynne but only succeeded in digging my
toe into Frank's side.

He jumped up with a grunt and eyed me accusatorily.

'Sorry. Foot slipped.'

Sarah, for her part, seemed energized by the turn of events.
'How exactly did Bethany die?'

'She drowned,' Lynne said. 'William didn't say how or where.'

And his wife didn't ask. There seemed to be a lot of things
Lynne preferred not to know. 'But weren't you curious?'

'Of course. And I did Google her name but there was just the
obituary.'

'*When* did she die?' I asked.

Lynne scrunched her nose, thinking. 'It was before we moved,
I know.'

'And *after* she came to see you, obviously,' Sarah said. 'Just
to help narrow the time frame.'

Lynne colored up at the 'duh' in Sarah's tone. 'Maybe early
April?'

'How old was she?' I asked.

'Early twenties?' Lynne picked up her glass. 'Like I said,
William liked them young.'

William's preferences aside, it seemed *awfully* young to die.
And to be a widow. 'Did Bethany seem depressed when she
came to see you?'

Lynne thought about that. 'More angry, I'd have said.'

'But if Bethany . . . I'm sorry, what was her last name?'

Lynne took a sip and set the glass down. 'Wheeler.'

'So if Bethany Wheeler expected you to confront William, she
was probably disappointed when the blow-up didn't happen.'

'I see where you're going, Maggy,' Sarah said. 'Suicide *is* like
the leading cause of death in that age group.'

I looked at her. 'Again with the statistics.'

'No need to lose hope, Miss Marple.' Sarah picked up her own wine. 'Homicide is second.'

I opened my mouth and then closed it. Sarah would tell me in her own good time. Or not.

'. . . Now that I think about it,' Lynne was saying, 'I believe you may be right.'

'Right about what?' Pick a theory, any theory.

'Bethany perhaps committing suicide. As I told you, she was a young widow. That alone must have been such a burden. And then being let go—'

'Let go, as in fired?' I asked. 'How did William get away with that?'

'Yeah.' Sarah used her tongue to recapture a rivulet that had escaped down the side of the glass when she poured. 'Employer humped employee. He's the one who should have been out of a job.'

'From what I understand, somebody caught Bethany helping herself to the nitrous oxide,' Lynne said.

'Nitrous oxide?' Sarah was wearing her best confused face.

'That's the chemical name for laughing gas,' Lynne explained. 'It's administered before a dental procedure to relax the patient.'

My partner nodded but I was thinking furiously. Nitrous oxide was combined with oxygen when it was administered. Oxygen in a green tank like I'd seen by the bushes near William's body.

'It provides a short-term high,' Lynne was saying. 'Since it's readily available in a dental office and not nearly as tightly regulated as painkillers, it's tempting for the staff.'

'Cool,' Sarah said. 'What do they do? Kick back after hours and talk like ducks?'

Now it was Lynne who looked bewildered. 'You must be thinking of helium, which is used in balloons?'

Sarah was nodding. 'Like the Hindenburg. Gotcha.'

I glared at my partner.

But Lynne didn't know Sarah as well as I did. 'I think that was hydrogen. Though you're right that the Zeppelin was originally outfitted for—'

Somebody please kill me. 'No matter,' I cut in. 'We know the Hindenburg didn't use nitrous oxide.'

'Too bad.' Sarah cocked her head. 'At least they would have died lau—'

'Don't you *dare* say it,' I warned. 'Shame on you, Sarah Kingston.'

My partner, when thwarted, or bored, or tipsy – honestly, pretty much anytime – loved shocking people.

Having succeeded, Sarah grinned. 'So abuse of nitrous oxide would be grounds to fire Bethany?'

Lynne lobbed her own curveball. 'Or William's excuse.'

'Either way, why would Bethany have gone quietly?' I asked.

Lynne shrugged. 'I honestly don't know. Maybe my husband had more on her than she did on him.'

'And now they're both dead,' Sarah said. 'What do you think, Maggy? Murder-suicide?'

I sat back in the chair. 'You mean William killed Bethany and then himself? But you said Bethany drowned in April, right?'

Lynne took a forkful of cold Mongolian beef out of the carton. 'Uh huh.'

'Seven months is a pretty long delay between the murder and the suicide,' I said. 'Besides, what reason would William have for killing Bethany anyway? She'd already done her worst by squealing to you.'

'But William didn't know that,' Lynne reminded me.

'True.' Sarah picked up the wine bottle and, seeing it was empty, set it back down again.

'With all your suspicions,' I asked Lynne, 'you never said anything to William – not even that you were divorcing him?'

'Yeah,' Sarah said. 'What were you going to do after he was served on Friday night? Go home and share a bed like nothing had happened?'

'No, of course not. I had a reservation at the Morrison for last night. Though Ginny's visit put the whole thing on hold. Or at least so I thought. Damn!'

'What?'

'I forgot to cancel the reservation. I'm sure they've charged it to my card.'

This woman was not much of a linear storyteller. But at least now I understood why Lynne had looked less than thrilled yesterday about Ginny's surprise visit.

Sarah was regarding our uninvited dinner guest with a frown. 'But here's the good news: you won't have to divorce your husband because he *apparently* did himself in. Problem solved and you'll have plenty of money to pay your hotel bill.'

'I know it looks convenient,' Lynne said. 'Which is exactly what I'm afraid the police investigators will think. Especially that unpleasant homicide detective.'

'The spouse is always suspect number one,' Sarah said. 'Don't you always say that, Maggy?'

'But I was *divorcing* him,' Lynne protested. 'Again, why would I kill him?'

Sarah shrugged. 'Cheaper?'

'True.' Swope thought about it. 'Nobody comes out ahead in a divorce, though at least Wisconsin is a community property state, so marital property is split fifty-fifty, but not necessarily what you have going into the marriage.'

I was regretting sharing our Mongolian beef. 'So why are you here again?'

'I told you. To find out – or ask you to find out – if the divorce papers were found in the office. According to the process server, he gave them to William outside the front entrance between seven and seven-thirty that evening and William took them into the building with him. I'd assume to his office but the police haven't said anything.'

'And you're wondering how to play it?' I guessed.

Lynne hesitated and then said, 'I know it sounds awful but I don't know if they found the papers and are waiting for me to say something or—'

'Or William disposed of them on the way up to the office and you don't have to say anything at all,' I finished for her.

'Well, yes. I mean, why raise the subject if he ripped up the envelope and tossed it in the lobby wastebasket?'

'But if William was served, that means the papers were already filed with the court. Done deal.' I knew this from experience. 'The copy served on William was just his notice of that.'

'Meaning Pavlik and his troops will find out anyway.' Sarah was taking the serving spoons out of the containers and laying them across Lynne's cast-off plate. Either my partner was tired of the conversation or trying to signal to our visitor that the evening was over. Or both.

'Assuming the investigators know to look.' I stacked my plate and Sarah's under Lynne's.

Our guest didn't lend a hand. 'But that's just it. The detectives don't need to know. Nobody ever needs to know.'

'Even Ginny?' I asked.

'*Especially* Ginny. Why would I tell her now?'

'Maybe to give her a reason her father jumped out the window?' Sarah suggested. 'Beyond her own bad grades, I mean. Isn't that what you were worried about supposedly?'

'Regardless of what you decide to say to Ginny,' I said when Lynne didn't answer, 'you need to tell the detectives the divorce notice was served. They're going to find out anyway.'

'But won't they ask why I didn't say anything earlier?'

Frank stirred at my feet. 'Tell them that Ginny was in the room when you were talking to the detectives and you didn't want her to know.'

'That's genius, Maggy,' Lynne said. 'And also the truth.'

Though not the whole truth and nothing but the truth.

The financial planner was going through her purse for the cards again. 'Would you mind if I called from here? I know it's after business hours, but—'

The front door burst open.

'Mom!' Eric yelled as his sheepdog danced delightedly around his feet. 'You have to come quick. Ginny's been arrested!'

SIXTEEN

'But I don't understand,' Lynne Swope said from the back seat of the Escape. 'Why in the world would they arrest Ginny?'

'I don't know.' Having left both Lynne's Toyota and Sarah parked at my house, we were stopped at the light at the corner of Brookhill and Poplar Creek Road. Eric was driving, given the wine Lynne and I had consumed. 'Are you sure they didn't just bring her in for questioning, Eric?'

My son seemed to think that was a distinction without a difference. 'Got me. They didn't read her rights if that's what you mean. Or handcuff her. They just rang the Swopes' doorbell and when Ginny answered they asked her to get her coat and come with them. Just like on TV.'

'Can she be questioned without my being there?' Lynne asked.

'Is she eighteen?' I asked.

'Just this past July.'

I didn't need to turn to know she was close to tears. 'Who was it who came to the door, Eric?'

'Both detectives,' Eric said. 'That Taylor and Hallonquist.'

'But not Pavlik.' I'd tried the sheriff's cell before we'd left but been bounced to voicemail. I'd left a message asking him to call as soon as possible but not giving any details.

Eric shook his head as the light turned green. The car behind us beeped.

'One vehicle on Brookhill Road and it has to be behind us,' I said as my cell phone rang. 'Let's hope this is the sheriff.'

It was. 'Maggy?'

Eric pulled the Escape over to the shoulder to let the impatient driver pass. And listen in on the conversation with the sheriff, no doubt.

I put it on speaker. 'Thanks for calling back. Eric says that Taylor and Hallonquist have picked up Ginny.'

'Yes?' Pavlik said, managing to neither confirm nor deny.

Acutely aware of the two sets of eyes watching expectantly, I pursued it. 'Do you know why?'

Pavlik didn't answer that either. 'Is Lynne Swope with you?'

'Yes.' I glanced sideways at Lynne, who was signaling she wanted the phone. 'I think she'd like to talk to you.'

Not bothering to wait for another noncommittal answer, I handed the phone to Lynne in the back seat. In the transfer, one of us must have accidentally turned off the speaker because Eric and I had to make do with hearing only the Lynne half of the conversation.

'Discrepancy?' Lynne said. 'What kind of—' She listened. 'But, I don't have a lawyer here. I mean that kind—' She looked at me. 'Yes, I can ask Maggy. Where—' She listened again before handing me back the phone.

'Hello, Pavlik?' I said into it.

'I just told Mrs Swope you could help her find a lawyer for her daughter. Start with Bernie Egan. He's corporate but he should be able to refer her to somebody.'

'You're talking about a criminal defense attorney?' I tried not to look at Lynne. 'Why—'

Pavlik interrupted. 'No arrest warrant has been issued but the girl wants a lawyer present before any further questioning.'

Curiouser and curiouser. Maybe I did need a scorecard for both Lynne *and* her daughter.

'. . . In interrogation, for now,' Pavlik was saying. 'Have Mrs Swope and her attorney go there.'

I nodded, even if he couldn't see me. 'And where are you?'

A hesitation, and I could almost see the heavenward glance that accompanied it. 'In my office. And would it do any good to ask you *not* to come up?'

'No, but I'll call Bernie and we'll drop Lynne off downstairs first. Deal?'

A weary, 'Deal.'

'Ginny's not been arrested,' I said for Eric's benefit as I clicked off, since I assumed Pavlik would already have told Lynne that. I turned back to her. 'The sheriff suggested I call an attorney friend for a referral to a criminal defense specialist. Unless you want to try your divo—'

'I think the sheriff's suggestion makes sense,' Lynne interrupted, her eyes shooting a warning toward Eric's back.

Of course. She didn't want the divorce mentioned in front of him. I scrolled through the contacts on my phone for Caron Egan. Bernie's wife had been a friend for a good fifteen years and my partner in Uncommon Grounds for a bad one, but I'd be damned if I could remember her number at the moment.

'Ginny asked for a lawyer, huh?' Eric asked. 'Told you she had *cojones*.'

I hit 'call.' 'Again with the *cojones*?'

'You'd rather I said "b—"'

'Hush!' A voice picked up on the other end. Luckily I'd gotten Bernie instead of Caron and, if he wasn't a man of few words, they were fewer than those of his wife. Once I'd explained the situation I handed over the phone to Lynne again.

As she and the trademark attorney spoke, Eric maneuvered the car back onto the road and drove the remaining way to the county complex.

The call ended just as Eric turned the Escape into the complex. I directed him to bypass the courthouse parking and circle counter-clockwise to the lot serving both the sheriff's department and the jail.

'What did Bernie say?' I asked as Eric pulled my little SUV into a spot.

'He was very kind and offered to get hold of one of his partners for me. A criminal defense attorney, like you said. He—' Lynne's voice broke as she handed me back my cell. 'He'll have her call.'

I held up the phone. 'On this line?'

'Oh, dear,' Lynne said. 'I didn't think to give him my number.'

'Not a problem,' I said, returning the cell to her. 'You can keep it for now.'

Lynne took it and sat staring past me out the front windshield toward the lighted façade of the building. Eight-inch-high letters spelled out Brookfield County Sheriff's Department across the top of the entrance. 'How in the world did we get here?'

I knew she wasn't talking navigation and couldn't help but feel sorry for her. New to town and alone . . . but she wasn't really, was she? Lynne had family right here in Brookhills. 'Shouldn't you call Mary? In fact, she might have some ideas on a lawyer before you decide who to hire.'

She shook her head. 'I think I'll stick with your friend's recommendation. He sounded like a good guy.'

Bernie was not only a good guy but a great guy, yet I couldn't help but want to unload at least some of the responsibility on Lynne's sister. Family is family. And mere acquaintances were . . . well, us. Despite appearances to the contrary over the last twenty-four hours.

I climbed out of the car and swung open the back door for Lynne to get out. 'I'll take you in and then see what I can find out from Pavlik.'

She just nodded.

'Will you stay with Mrs Swope?' I asked Eric as he joined us on the sidewalk.

'Sure,' he said, handing me back my car keys. 'You'll probably get more out of Pavlik if I'm not there.'

I didn't raise a dumb kid.

Leaving Lynne and Eric on vinyl-cushioned chairs to wait for the detectives, I crossed to a counter on the other side of the lobby. For the second time that day I signed in with the deputy, waited for clearance and a visitor's badge and took the elevator to the third floor.

Given the hour, nobody was at the desk in the outer office, so I went through and knocked on the frame of Pavlik's open door. 'It's me, the one you don't want to talk to.'

'I told them to let you up, didn't I?' The sheriff, his shirt-sleeves rolled up on forearms tanned in the Florida sun, leaned back in his chair. 'And I don't mind talking to you. I just don't want to be interrogated by you.'

'I promise not to,' I said, sitting where I had that afternoon. 'Or to try not to.'

'And I appreciate the attempt at honesty.' He shifted in the chair, flexing his shoulders forward and back like he'd been sitting too long in one position. 'But I'm afraid you're wasting your time. There's nothing I can tell you.'

'No worries.' I set my purse down next to me. 'I drove Lynne so I have to be here anyway.'

'I thought you barely knew the Swopes. Why so solicitous?'

Good question. 'Honestly, I'm not sure. Lynne just showed up at my house and ended up staying for dinner.' I didn't mention the reason for the visit, figuring that was for Lynne to tell. 'We were just finishing up when Eric came home saying Ginny had been arrested—'

'She was asked to come in and answer a few questions.'

'I know. I'm just repeating what Eric said at the time. But why question Ginny, of all people? What could she know?'

If William Swope *had* been murdered there were certainly better suspects than his stepdaughter. Lynne, Clay Tartare, Rita Pahlke, Ted. Heck, even Bethany Wheeler, assuming she'd managed to fake her own death.

OK, that might be pushing it. But it had been a long day with many twists and turns. And theories. So very many theories.

'Taylor and Hallonquist just want to ask Virginia about a discrepancy in her story.'

I frowned. 'Story? She and Eric just got into town last night and saw Lynne and William at Uncommon Grounds. End of story.'

'And the girl never went to Thorsen Dental?'

'Not last night.' I stopped. 'Are you implying she did?'

'I'm not implying anything.' Pavlik pulled a manila file folder toward him and flicked it open. 'Crime scene found her fingerprints.'

I knew the sheriff well enough to realize he didn't offer information without intending to get some in return.

Unfortunately, all I could do was wrinkle my nose. 'So? She was probably there on another visit home. Or over the summer. Besides, there must be tons of fingerprints.'

'There were, of course,' Pavlik said, settling back in his chair again. But not with pepperoni grease on them.'

SEVENTEEN

Ginny had gone to her cousin's house for pizza, she'd said. Like Eric and me, apparently they favored pepperoni. 'But Ginny said she didn't go to her father's office,' I said again to the sheriff. 'How can her prints be there?'

'You'd have to ask her.' He didn't take his nose out of the file on his desk. 'And if she answers, let us know.'

I noticed the name on folder wasn't Ginny's. Was I being dismissed? 'You said Ginny lawyered up?'

That earned a glance from Pavlik, presumably for the TV police jargon. 'Virginia asked for an attorney, yes.'

'She's smart enough to do that but dumb enough to kill her father and leave prints?'

Pavlik shrugged. 'She's young. Kids make mistakes.'

I was thinking. 'So Ginny's greasy prints were in William's office?' When Pavlik didn't confirm or deny, I plunged on. 'I assume your people dusted the oxygen tank?'

'The oxygen tank?' The parrot routine was a favorite of Pavlik's.

'The green tank on the ground next to William's body. I'm thinking it was used to break the window.' Or William's head. 'What did they find on that? Blood evidence? Prints?'

Pavlik shook his head. 'Nothing we wouldn't expect to.'

There was a non-answer for you.

Pavlik pushed the file jacket away and stood up. 'You really don't expect me to lay out what else – if anything – we might have on the girl, do you?'

'I don't expect it but I kind of hoped.' I snagged my purse and stood, too. A change of subject seemed in order. 'Baby Mia's baptism is tomorrow, followed by luncheon served in Christ Christian's basement, probably much to the horror of the Slatterys. Want to come watch?'

'Sounds like fun but I have to work.' He came around the desk and gave me a light kiss on the lips.

'Liar,' I said, staring up into his blue eyes. 'You just don't want to be trapped in a church with me, a crying baby, my ex-husband, his hoity-toity in-laws and assorted gelatin molds.'

'You got that right.'

Eric was still where I'd left him, though Lynne's seat was empty. 'I assume the lawyer showed up?'

'Uh huh.' My son dug my phone out of his jeans pocket and handed it to me. 'Mrs Swope said to say thank you but that we don't have to wait for her.'

'How's she going to get home?' I asked. 'Or they, I should say.' No need to assume that Ginny would be detained.

'Taxicab, she said. Do we have taxicabs in Brookhills?'

'Not so you'd notice. And certainly not like an urban area where you can flag one down this late.' I took the seat next to him. 'You OK?'

'Yeah, but it was kind of surreal at Ginny's house. The police taking her away and all, you know?'

I knew. I gave his shoulder a squeeze. 'The good news is that she has a lawyer now. Who knows, she could be out any—'

The door next to the main desk opened and Ginny emerged. Looking neither left nor right, the girl charged right through the lobby and out the revolving door.

Eric jumped up. 'I'm going after her.'

I nodded and turned to greet the two women trailing behind her.

Lynne smiled, but there was no disguising that she'd been crying. 'Oh, Maggy – thank you. But I told Eric you didn't need to wait.'

'We were happy to stay.' I turned to the fiftyish blonde with her. 'I'm Maggy Thorsen.'

'Kay Spinelli. I would have driven Mrs Swope and Ginny home but I'm sure they're happy to have a friend here.' She handed Lynne a card. 'Take another of these and, remember, you need to have Ginny back here at three tomorrow afternoon.'

'So what's going on?' I asked Lynne as Spinelli left us.

'No charges, thank God. But they want to see Ginny again tomorrow, after the medical examiner gets . . .' Lynne's voice cracked, and she cleared her throat, '. . . done. Did the sheriff tell you anything?'

'I'm afraid not.' I wasn't sure if Lynne meant about Ginny or about the divorce papers, a subject I intended to let Lynne broach with the detectives.

Truth was the sheriff had not only been noticeably weary but markedly closed mouth, telling me little I didn't already know except that Ginny's pepperoni fingerprints had been found in Thorsen Dental.

'The detectives think Ginny lied about being in William's office,' Lynne said, waving for me to go through the revolving door ahead of her.

She didn't say why they thought that, and I wasn't about to tell her about the greasy prints if she didn't already know.

Outside, Eric was walking back toward us from the parking lot. 'Ginny's waiting by the Escape,' he said as Lynne joined us. 'She says she doesn't want to talk.' My son looked miserable.

'That's understandable,' I said. 'She's had a very tough day.'

He shook his head. 'I don't get why they're harassing her. Ginny took me straight home from Uncommon Grounds and then went to the Callahans. I can swear we didn't stop at Dad's office, if it would help.'

Problem was my house was west of Uncommon Grounds and the Callahan home and Thorsen Dental east. If Ginny *had* gone to the office, she most likely would have dropped Eric off first and then done so on the way to her cousin's house.

I didn't think it best to point that out right now. 'I'm sure Ginny told the investigators that.'

'But that's just it,' Lynne said. 'As Eric says, Ginny isn't speaking – not even to defend herself to the detectives.'

'Lawyered up,' Eric said, proving the TV-loving apple didn't fall far from the tree. 'Smart.'

'That's what I thought, too, at first,' Lynne said, accompanying me down the sidewalk toward the parking lot, 'but Ginny won't even talk to our lawyer.'

That didn't seem so smart. 'What about to you, Lynne? Did you have a chance to talk to Ginny alone?'

'For a couple of minutes, but she wouldn't tell me anything either.' She stumbled stepping off the curb.

I put a hand out to steady her. 'Probably worried somebody was listening.'

'So what?' Lynne scraped the back of her hand across her eyes and then held it there against the glare of the parking lot lights. Ginny's lone figure stood next to the Escape. Lynne lowered her voice. 'What is she so afraid they'll hear?'

It was a good question. Approaching the vehicle, I pushed the fob twice to unlock all the doors. 'I'm taking you to Mary's.'

As I swung open the passenger door for Lynne, her daughter finally spoke: 'No.' She got in the back seat.

'Ginny's right,' Lynne said, climbing in herself. 'The last thing she needs right now is to be grilled by my sister.'

'What have you told Mary so far?'

'Only that William apparently committed suicide.'

I closed the passenger door and circled to the driver's side, waiting for Eric to get into the back seat next to Ginny.

Instead he took the keys from my hand.

Taking the hint, I slid in next to Ginny. She didn't look at me.

Her mother was still talking. 'This morning, Mary kept insisting she come, but I told her she'd help me more by going to work.'

I leaned forward. 'I'm getting the impression you and Mary aren't very close.'

Lynne glanced sideways at my face between the seats. She seemed surprised to see me there. 'It's been a little strained at times, I admit. We're just so different.'

That might be true, but weren't siblings supposed to help each other in troubled times?

But then this was coming from the woman who hadn't seen her own brother for two decades. And then he had died.

Ding, ding, ding sounded as Eric turned the key. 'Seat belt, Mom?'

'Sorry.' I sat back and strapped myself in, but continued the conversation with Lynne. 'You and Mary seemed fine at the book club.'

Lynne's shoulders lifted and then fell. 'Oh, we don't argue. We just don't like each other much.'

Presumably their father pronouncing Mary 'the smart one' hadn't done much for the sibling dynamics. 'You truly would prefer Eric drop you off at home?' Then I remembered. 'Oh, we can't drop you off anywhere. Your car is at our house.'

'Mrs Swope and Ginny should just stay with us tonight.' Eric piped up from behind the wheel. 'My room has a king-size bed, if they don't mind sharing, and I'll sleep on the couch.'

I restrained a groan. I'd been trying very hard *not* to assume more responsibility for the Swope family and their problems.

'Oh, we couldn't do that,' Lynne said. 'And we certainly wouldn't be good company.'

I wasn't thinking about them as company. More like . . . baggage to be stowed.

'Oh my God, Mom,' the teenage volcano next to me exploded. 'It's been a long day. Can we please just crash at Eric's for the night and stop *talking*?'

'Well, I *am* exhausted,' Lynne admitted as Eric turned the Escape toward home. 'Though I'm not sure either of us will be able to sleep.'

'Ginny can use my iPad,' Eric offered.

I tapped Lynne on the shoulder. 'Xanax?'

EIGHTEEN

The door to Eric's room was still closed when I passed by the next morning. A snarled blanket and pillow on the couch marked where he'd spent the night and I found Eric, sheepdog by his side and mug of freshly brewed coffee in his hand, in the kitchen.

'Bless you for making coffee.' I opened the dishwasher to retrieve my favorite mug and saw dirty dishes among the clean. 'I completely forgot about Sarah. She must have stuck our dishes from last night in here not realizing it had been run.'

I claimed my clean mug from the top rack anyway and noticed another with brown stains next to it. 'At least she had coffee.'

'There was half a carafe left on the burner.'

'She did turn it off, right?'

Eric grinned. 'Yeah, though it smelled kind of burned. I scrubbed out the pot.'

I was gratified on two counts. My son knew his way around a coffeemaker as well as he did a wine bottle and my partner had drunk half a pot of coffee and then stayed around long enough for the rest of the pot to turn acrid before she turned off the burner and drove home.

Setting the mug on the counter, I filled it from the fresh pot Eric had brewed. 'I didn't think to ask you last night, but was Dad expecting you to sleep at his place?'

'I texted him that you needed me.'

I was touched. 'How'd you sleep?'

'The couch wasn't bad but I'm not used to falling asleep without watching a movie or something on my iPad.'

'It was good of you to offer it to Ginny.' I added a touch of cream to my coffee from the carton on the counter. 'Did you find a book or something to read?'

'Nah, I watched *Jurassic Park* again on that.' He gestured to the phone on the table.

I resisted telling him he'd hurt his eyes staring at the tiny screen. Let's face it: if half my own mother's warnings had come true I'd be walking around with a finger stuck up my nose and Frank as seeing-eye dog.

'I kept thinking about Ginny,' Eric continued. 'Having to go back and all.'

'Me, too.' I brought my coffee to the table and sat across from him.

'It's not like she can tell them anything. At least, I don't think she can.'

So Eric had doubts about our new friends, too? 'How's Ginny been handling the death of her father?'

'Stepfather,' Eric corrected.

'That's right – I'd forgotten. Did they get on OK?'

'I guess so.' He slid the chair back and crossed to the coffeemaker. 'You know she got herself kicked out of Quorum, right?' He held up the pot. 'Refill?'

I glanced down at my two-thirds-full cup. 'Sure.'

As Eric topped me off, I said, 'Mrs Swope did tell me about Ginny's grades. Are you saying she was failing on purpose?'

Eric thought about that as he replaced the pot and returned to the table. 'She said she hated Quorum. That everybody was stuck up.'

It wasn't a direct answer to my question, but then Eric hadn't known Ginny all that much longer than I'd known Lynne. 'Did she tell her folks that?'

'She said her father didn't care if she was miserable. Though, as it turns out, it doesn't matter what he thought.'

'Because he's dead.'

Eric grimaced. 'That's kind of ghoulish, Mom, don't you think?'

Rhetorical question. 'So what *did* she mean?'

'The divorce,' he said, picking up his phone. 'What else?'

I set my mug on the table. 'Ginny knows?'

Eric didn't look up from his phone. 'About what?'

'That her mother and stepfather were getting divorced. Her mom hasn't told her.'

'Well, she knows.' He met my eyes. 'It's not hard to figure out. I knew about you and dad before you said anything.'

Ouch. 'You did?' I reached across the table and touched his

hand. 'I'm so sorry. We should have been honest with you from the beginning.'

Since Eric had been away at school, Ted and I had decided not to say anything to him as we'd tried to work through our 'issues.'

Me, by pleading. Ted, packing.

It wasn't our finest hour, either as spouses or parents.

But our son was shrugging. 'When I came home from school that first semester break I knew things weren't right. It was a relief when you finally told me what was going on.'

'I'm so sorry,' I repeated, tears welling up.

'Don't be. You have a right to be happy.' He went back to his phone.

I sat thinking about divorces and keeping secrets. Then I picked up my own cell.

NINETEEN

'Did we find anything in Doctor Swope's office?' the sheriff repeated. 'If you mean on his phone, we'd need a warrant to examine that.'

I'd taken my own phone into my bedroom to make the call in private. I could hear conversation in the kitchen, meaning one or both of our houseguests was awake.

'No, not on his cell.' I lowered my voice a notch further. 'I meant maybe papers or something that would be a clue as to whether he was anxious or depressed.'

I was doing exactly what Lynne had tried to avoid by asking *me* about the divorce papers rather than the detectives. And it was having exactly the effect she'd feared.

Pavlik knew I was fishing and wanted to know for what. 'Spit it out, Maggy.'

Lynne had been ready to call the detectives and tell them about the divorce when Eric came in with news of Ginny being brought in for questioning the night before. So it wasn't like I was letting the cat out of the bag. Right?

Besides, given that Lynne's divorce lawyer and process server, along with Sarah, me, Ginny and Eric all knew about the divorce, it wasn't much of a secret. Except from the investigators. And they were the very ones who needed to know.

'Lynne had William served with divorce papers that night at the office,' I said into the phone.

Silence at the other end.

'Pavlik?'

A rustling. Then, 'Divorce.' Another stretch of paper shuffling. 'You're sure?'

'Yes. Lynne told me she tried to stop the server.'

'She had changed her mind about the divorce?'

'No, but Ginny came home unexpectedly and her mother didn't want to put her in the middle of it.'

'But Doctor Swope was served with notice that the divorce papers were filed despite his wife's attempt to stop it.'

'Exactly,' I said. 'William accepted the notice as he went into the dental office Friday night. Or so Lynne was told by the server.'

'That's what they were, then.'

'You knew about this?' All my angst was for nothing?

A one-two beat of silence and then, 'We had an anonymous tip that a man approached Doctor Swope near the front door about ten minutes after seven and handed him something. The informant imagined it might be a drug exchange, but . . .' He let it drift off.

With William buying or selling? 'Drugs?' I'd been perched on the edge of my bed and now I slid back and tucked my legs up under me. 'Did the preliminary tox screen show anything?'

'We know that Swope was on painkillers for a back problem.'

I remembered William massaging the small of his back as he'd stood on the porch following his confrontation with Ted. 'Lacrosse injury,' I said.

But Pavlik's mind was elsewhere. 'Don't suppose you have any idea where the process server was from?'

'Brookhills Investigations and Process Serving, I think. Or the other way around. I can't remember.'

'You had it right the first time.' I could hear Pavlik scribbling a note. 'Thank you.'

'You're welcome,' I said. 'I assume this means the divorce papers weren't found?'

'It would be in the file if they had.'

'You might want to check the trash en route to the office,' I said, thinking of what Lynne had said. 'If William was angry or upset he might have tossed them.'

'Thank you again,' Pavlik said. 'We'll handle it from here.'

'Hey, don't shoot the messenger – especially one who called you of her own free will.'

A sigh. 'You're right, and I'm sorry. I appreciate the information.'

'You're welcome,' I said. 'So who—'

A knock on the bedroom door.

'Mom?' Eric's voice called. 'You about ready?'

I put my hand over the phone. 'Ready?'

'Yeah. Church starts in half an hour.'

And that's when I remembered the baptism.

TWENTY

E ric and I left Lynne in the kitchen and Ginny still sleeping and made it to Christ Christian just as the congregation was standing for the first hymn.

Ted had saved us seats at the front but that didn't spare me the dark looks from both my ex-husband and his new in-laws for not getting Eric to the church on time.

The baptism itself went as well as can be expected when you douse a kid with water. I don't know who was more red-faced – Ted or Mia. I do know, though, who smelled worse.

As Rachel's mother claimed the stinky baby to change her, I managed to pull Ted aside in the narthex. 'I was on the phone with Pavlik this morning.'

Using Pavlik's name was intended to make Ted think I had an inside line on information so he'd speak freely. It didn't work. 'Oh, yeah? What did you pry out of him?'

'Not much,' I admitted. Though it wasn't for want of trying on my part.

One thing that did strike me as odd, now that I thought about it: the sheriff had said, 'That's what they were,' as if he suspected that William had been handed papers rather than exchanging cash for drugs, as the witness suspected.

Another kind of notice, perhaps? 'Was William in some kind of legal trouble? Is that why you went off on him Friday night?'

Ted opened his mouth and then closed it again as the church organist passed by. She hesitated, seeming surprised to find us in a huddle, but then kept on going.

'Back in Louisville,' I pressed. 'Something his ex-partner or Rita Pahlke told you about.'

My ex looked after the organist and then turned back to me with a look of resignation. 'You're not going to let me out of here until I tell you what I know, are you?'

'Of course not. How long were we married?'

I could see the answer 'too long' in his eyes but he didn't vocalize it. Instead, he said, 'I'm not sure what to believe from Rita Pahlke's lips, if anything.'

I nodded, encouraged. 'Aliens, tracking devices, something about fluoride.'

'She accused him of everything from alien abduction and mind control to billing fraud and drugs.'

Interesting as well as weird. So was Rita Pahlke the anonymous tipster who called in the 'drug deal' outside the 501 Building? And then there was Bethany's firing back in Louisville for misuse of the nitrous oxide. Could Pahlke also have been the one to blow the whistle on her?

I put my hand on my ex-husband's shoulder. 'And Clay Tartare? I assume you find him more credible.'

Ted shrugged. 'He certainly has more to lose. He told me his office has been accused of upcoding.'

'Upcoding?'

'Doing one procedure but charging the patient or insurance company for another by putting the wrong code on the bill.'

'So like filling a tooth but charging for an extraction?'

'Or things far more expensive, like implants and bone grafts that costs thousands of dollars.'

'And because codes are used to identify the individual dental procedures, people don't notice,' I guessed.

'Or their insurance pays so they don't look.'

'I assume this took place while William was with the practice?'

'According to Tartare,' Ted said. 'First Swope fired their office manager for some trumped-up reason, then he up and moved out of state.'

From what little I knew about current billing practices in dentals offices, the upcoding couldn't have taken place without the office manager's participation or at least knowledge. And that office manager, assuming it was Bethany Wheeler, was not just fired, but dead. Meaning she sure wasn't talking.

'The way Tartare sees it,' Ted continued, 'he's been left holding the bag.'

Between that and Swope stealing his girl twelve years ago, it seemed Clay Tartare had reason to hate William Swope. But kill him? 'Certainly would have ticked me off enough.'

Ted eyed me suspiciously. 'Why'd you say it like that?'

'Like what?'

'It would have ticked you off *enough*. Please don't tell you have some wild theory.'

'My wild theory, I might remind you, was dead right when it came to your wife.'

'I'd appreciate it if you *didn't* remind me. But are you saying the sheriff thinks William didn't jump? That he was pushed? By whom?'

So many questions and even more possible answers. 'I honestly don't know. And the sheriff's office seems to be reserving judgment until the ME's report comes back.'

'So your sources haven't completely dried up.' A grin was hiding just under the surface.

That made me cranky. 'You left Uncommon Grounds at around seven but didn't call to say you were on your way to pick up Mia until nearly ten-thirty.'

'So?'

'So where were you?'

'Now you think *I* killed him?' Ted's raised voice made the

buxom woman passing by with a tray of deviled eggs pause long enough for me to snag one.

As she continued on her way, I said, 'Of course not. But Lynne thought you and William might have gone out for a drink. I doubt that, but I do know your son was at my house for hours waiting for you to call.'

'I went home.' Ted's jaw was set in a stubborn line.

'Alone?'

'No, I had a hooker come over,' he snapped.

'I *meant* was there anybody at your house like a housekeeper who could vouch for you?' I said in a tone meant to shame. In truth, I hadn't completely ruled out a hooker.

'No,' Ted said. 'I was angry so I wanted to work out.'

'And left your son and infant daughter cooling their heels.'

'Give me a break, Maggy. I was stressed and needed some time to myself. You know, do weights, take a swim, chill in the hot tub.'

Sure, I knew. But I had to go to the YMCA to do that, not 'home.' I plopped the deviled egg in my mouth.

Ted stepped aside to let a red-faced man with a steaming buffet pan pass by. 'No need to tell Eric, OK?'

But I was sniffing the air. 'Kielbasa?'

'And sauerkraut.' Ted's smile reminded me of Eric when he was up to something. 'Grandma and Grandpa Slattery wanted to host us at the Arms but I said it was too far away. Then they tried the Morrison but I nixed that, too.'

The Slattery Arms was the family's flagship hotel in downtown Milwaukee. They'd purchased the Morrison about a year ago but hadn't yet gotten around to re-naming it after themselves. 'You thought lunch in the church basement preferable?'

'Depends who you ask.' He gestured across the way to where Mr Slattery, red Solo cup in hand, was pretending to admire a centerpiece that looked like an aluminum foil Christmas tree covered with pink crosses. As we watched, a shell-shocked Mrs Slattery joined him with Mia. Whether it was the contents of the baby's diapers or the circa 1965 'Girls' Room' she'd had to change her in that had traumatized Grandma, I couldn't guess.

I grinned back at my ex. 'And Sarah thinks *I'm* passive-aggressive. I suppose the gospel reading about a camel having more chance of fitting through the eye of a needle than a rich man has of getting into heaven was also your work?'

'Let's just say it was more than a happy coincidence,' Ted said before slipping away to reclaim his daughter.

It was mid-afternoon when I pulled the Escape into the driveway. I'd said goodbye to Eric, who had gone home with his dad and sister after the christening lunch. Since the dental office was closed on Mondays, Ted would drive our son back up to school in the morning.

Ginny presumably wouldn't be returning to Minneapolis any time soon. If at all.

I'd expected the two Swope women to be long gone by the time I got home but Lynne's white Toyota was still parked on the gravel apron next to my garage. As I got out of my Escape I saw Ginny waiting on the porch steps for her mother.

Lynne was trying to pull the door closed behind her without squishing the sheepdog's nose. 'Back up, Frank.'

'I'm home,' I called without thinking.

The sound of my voice made Lynne glance behind her and Frank took the opportunity to make his escape, dodging Ginny on the steps and bounding right past me into the backyard.

Lynne blinked at the door she still held. 'How in the world?' The crack between the edge of the door and the jamb couldn't have been three inches.

Kind of put that whole camel/needle thing in modern-day perspective. 'Are you heading home?'

'I wish,' Ginny answered. The girl looked tired, if resolute. 'Back to Quantico for another round of water-boarding.'

Of course. I'd forgotten she was to return to the sheriff's office this afternoon.

I glanced at the front door of my empty house and then at Frank, who, mission completed, seemed to be torn between sniffing his butt and dragging it along the ground. 'Want reinforcements?'

The offer stemmed more from curiosity than kindness on my part. Given Ted's revelation about the investigation into

William's former practice, I had to wonder how much Lynne knew. Could she possibly be as clueless as she claimed to be about Clay Tartare's business in Brookhills?

'That's nice of you, Maggy,' Lynne said, coming down the steps to join us. 'But—'

'Great idea,' Ginny said, plucking the car keys out of her mother's hand. 'You ride with Mrs Thorsen and I'll drive your car.'

Lynne hesitated but her daughter was already stomping toward the Toyota. By the time I had herded Frank into the house the car was backing down the driveway.

'I suppose she wants to get this over with,' I said, waving Lynne toward the Escape.

'More likely to get away from me.' Lynne pulled the seat belt across and clicked it in. 'And my questions.'

'Has she opened up at all?'

'Not really. She slept until noon, or at least pretended to, then locked herself in the bathroom. I barely had a chance to get ready myself.'

'Not unusual teen behavior, from my experience,' I said as I slipped the car into reverse. 'You did say that Ginny doesn't know that you filed for divorce, correct?'

'Correct.' Lynne swiveled her head toward me.

'And you haven't told her since? Maybe at the sheriff's department last night or after we got home and you two were alone?' It was a long shot, but Ginny could have texted Eric overnight about the break-up.

'Did you *see* my daughter?' Lynne said. 'She's barely speaking to me and she certainly doesn't want to hear anything I have to say. Why?'

'No reason, really,' I said, backing the car down the driveway and out onto the street. 'Sometimes kids have a sixth sense about this sort of thing, though.'

'Why?' she repeated. 'Did Ginny say something to you?'

Lynne's tone sounded a little hurt, presumably at the idea that her daughter would speak to me when she was so obviously freezing out her own mother.

'I've barely exchanged two words with Ginny,' I said, not wanting to betray Eric's confidence. 'But the divorce might explain why she didn't want to talk to the police.'

'You mean Ginny was trying to protect me?'

Sure, that'll work. 'Maybe she didn't want you blamed for William's suicide in the same way you didn't want it on her shoulders.'

'What a sweet thing,' Lynne said, tears in her voice.

I left her to her own thoughts as we drove the rest of the way to the county complex. Spotting the Toyota as I pulled into the parking lot, I parked next to it. 'Ginny must be inside.'

'Then I hope Kay is here, too,' Lynne said, scanning the parking lot as she got out.

'You have told *her* about the divorce, right?'

'No. Do you think I should?' Lynne asked over her shoulder as she hurried to the entrance.

'I do.' Now that Pavlik knew about the filing, even if his detectives hadn't found the papers that William had been served they'd want to talk to Lynne. And here we were, about to walk into their den.

The thought made me hesitate but Lynne had already ducked into the revolving door. I followed and saw Detective Taylor on the other side.

He glanced at me, then said, 'Mrs Swope.'

'I'm here with my daughter, Virginia. Has she already gone up with our lawyer?'

Taylor didn't so much as blink. The man reminded me of a snake, but snakes at least have an excuse. No eyelids. 'She has, but we have a few questions for you as well. If you'd just come with me?'

Lynne looked uncertain. 'Can Maggy come with me?'

Taylor seemed amused. 'If she's your lawyer.'

'Kay Spinelli is but you said she's with Ginny.'

'Would you like Ms Spinelli to be present while we talk?' Taylor, for all his coldness, seemed to be proceeding cautiously.

'Does Mrs Swope *need* a lawyer?' I asked, cutting to the chase.

'That, Ms Thorsen,' Taylor said without so much as looking at me, 'would be up to Mrs Swope.'

TWENTY-ONE

'You said Detective Taylor thought Lynne was hiding something.' I was back in Pavlik's office, sitting in the second guest chair for a change of scenery. 'I assume my telling you about the divorce provided that "something"?'

Pavlik had seemed testy since I'd walked in, maybe because of the stack of case jackets on his desk. 'Lynne Swope is the decedent's wife. I don't have to tell you that we always look at the spouse.'

'But this hasn't been ruled a homicide.'

'Yet until we know otherwise it's investigated as one. I told you that.'

I sighed, still feeling like a snitch. But while I was at it: 'Ted said William's former practice is in trouble for billing fraud. I assume he – or Clay Tartare – told you?'

'Yes.' Pavlik said, not specifying which. 'But there's no criminal investigation. And when and if there is, it won't involve Wisconsin.'

If not criminal then the investigation was probably an internal one by the dental board. For now. 'Though I assume it could have jeopardized William's ability to practice here,' I said. 'And still could Tartare's in Kentucky.'

Pavlik just shrugged.

Not reaping more than I was sowing, information-wise, I switched back to the original reason I was there. 'Taylor is interrogating Lynne; does that mean Hallonquist is grilling Ginny?'

'Detective Hallonquist had a couple more questions for Virginia,' Pavlik said. 'She may even be gone by now. As for Mrs Swope, don't tell me it hasn't occurred to you that she may have had something to do with her husband's death. We talked about it.'

'Of course it occurred to me.' I weighed telling Pavlik that Lynne and Clay dated more than a decade ago, given the sheriff's current mood. 'But I suspect everybody.'

'Tell me about it.' The remark might have been teasing but there was no smile in Pavlik's eyes. 'And, yes. Lynne Swope filing for divorce is a pertinent fact. But it's even more disturbing because she hid it.'

Another twinge of guilt for landing Lynne in the hot seat. Then again, maybe that was where she belonged. 'I suppose Lynne's fingerprints were in William's office?'

'She's his wife.' Pavlik was studying me with an odd expression on his face.

'What?' I asked, swiping at my nose in case something was hanging.

But the sheriff got up from the desk and held out his arms. 'Give me a hug.'

I did, relaxing into his arms. The height difference between us made it possible for me to burrow into his shoulder and for him to rest his chin on top of my head.

'Listen, Maggy,' he said into my hair. 'I know I'm just supposed to smile and accept the fact that you get involved in things like this. You, the scrappy amateur sleuth. Me, the obliging hick sheriff.'

I felt myself stiffen and tried to pull away. He wouldn't let me as he continued, 'But it's not cute anymore.'

I froze. 'What are you saying?'

'I'm saying that you barely know these people. Stay out of this and trust us to do our jobs.'

I felt an 'or else' coming. 'I *do* trust you.'

He put his hands on my shoulders and tilted his head so we were nose tip to nose tip. 'I believe that. And I know you don't mean to undermine me.'

'I've undermined you?' I scarcely recognized my own voice, forced out of a throat that felt on fire. 'Like with Taylor? He's—'

'I know he can be an asshole. But that's why it's important for me to have his respect – or fear, if necessary – to keep him and others like him in line. That's hard to do when they're snickering behind my back.'

'About . . . me?'

Pavlik pulled me toward him again. 'Honestly, my love? Yes, about you.'

'I'm so sorry,' I said against his shoulder. 'I didn't mean—'

'I know you didn't. And you know that it hurts me to say this, but . . .'

I felt myself duck in his arms. The 'else' was coming, without even the attached opportunity of an 'or.'

'. . . I think it would be best if we took a break.'

TWENTY-TWO

'What in the hell is your problem?'

One, I hadn't slept at all. And while that had made it easy to get to Uncommon Grounds at 5 a.m. in preparation for our 6 a.m. opening, the lack of sleep had also caused me to not only brew the wrong coffee of the day – Sumatran, instead of Kenyan AAA, as the sign said – but leave an empty pot on the heating element.

Sarah had arrived, picked up the scent of hot glass and plastic and pulled the thing off the burner to put in the sink. Only problem was when the hot carafe touched the water in the sink the glass exploded, leaving Sarah with a handle and nothing attached to it.

Hence my partner's question.

In answer, I did what you might expect a responsible coffeehouse owner to do in the situation. Burst into tears.

Sarah was not a toucher but she tried her best to give me a hug. Even patted me. Kind of.

'I'm sorry,' I wailed. 'It's just Pavlik. I didn't get any sleep last night.'

Sarah, who'd already moved back and away from me, looked disgusted. 'You're screwing up because you spent the night screwing?'

'No.' The sleigh bells on the door jangled. 'He . . . we . . .' And off I went again.

Sarah's glare could have pinned a butterfly to a mounting board. 'Go in the back and get yourself together, do you understand me? I'll take care of the customers.'

Now who was the responsible one?

I did what I was told, passing the jam-packed storeroom.

'Not to worry,' I told myself in the true spirit of self-flagellation, 'you'll have plenty of time to work on holiday baskets. You have no life. You may as well sleep here.'

Pavlik had dumped me. Eric was with Ted on his way back to school. Sarah I'd nearly maimed with a coffee pot. The only one who loved me was Frank and even he'd had enough of my whimpering, finally jumping off the bed in disgust at around three a.m. this morning.

I sank down at the office desk, head in my hands. 'You shouldn't be so surprised.' I continued my monologue. 'You're not a nice person. Cynical, snarky. Yeah, you keep most of that inside but you're not fooling anybody. Sarah is right – you're passive-aggressive through and through. No wonder Ted left you. And for a criminal. And now Pavlik—'

'What in the hell is wrong with you?' Sarah was at the door rephrasing her earlier question.

I raised my head. 'Pavlik broke up with me.'

To her credit, Sarah looked stricken. 'You're selling the business?'

I sat up straight. 'What? Why would I do that?'

'Because it's what you do.' Sarah took the side chair. 'The last time you were dumped you quit your PR job and opened a coffeehouse.'

'That was subsequently destroyed in a freak snowstorm,' I reminded Sarah.

'Boo-hoo-hoo. Only to be rebuilt in this fabulous train station, owned by your equally fabulous new partner.'

'Fabulous' was not a word I'd ever heard Sarah use, much less attribute to herself, but it served to make me appropriately ashamed.

I put a hand on her arm. 'I'm sorry. You *are* fabulous and I'm very lucky to have you as a partner.'

She shook me off. 'Damn right. Now stop kvetching and tell me what's going on.'

Sarah was not any more Yiddish with her *kvetching* than Eric was Spanish with his *cojones*. America, the linguistic melting pot.

I took a deep breath, trying to pull myself together. 'I told you. I went to Pavlik's office yesterday and he said we should take a break.'

'For how long?'

I closed one eye and thought. 'I'm not sure. I don't think he specified but I kind of blocked everything after that.'

'So maybe he meant for one day,' she said, flinging out a hand. 'You're there morning, noon and night.'

'Just since Saturday,' I protested. 'And sometimes I call instead.'

'Much better.'

'The sarcasm is appreciated,' I said. 'I'll have you know I was in his office just once yesterday and I had a good reason.'

Sarah seemed to bite back another comment, settling for a neutral, 'What was that?'

'I'd gone with Lynne Swope to take Ginny for a follow-up interview with the detectives. When we walked in Pavlik's goons took Lynne in for questioning, too.'

'And the sheriff objected to your calling them goons?'

'But I didn't,' I protested. 'Not even behind their backs.'

'Until now.'

True. 'To be honest, I was feeling responsible for her being detained because I'd told Pavlik about Lynne filing for the divorce. Though she was about to do it herself Saturday night before Eric burst in, so I'm not sure why I—'

'You don't have to justify it to me,' Sarah said. 'I don't have a horse in this race. When did you deliver this tidbit to Pavlik?'

'Yesterday.'

My partner cocked her head. 'The same visit that he told you it was over?'

Over. 'No, in the morning. I called him before the christening.'

'And then went to his office after it.'

I threw up my hands. 'Yes, yes – so, I'm a pest. But I thought I was helping.'

Sarah didn't say anything.

'And Pavlik seemed to think so, too,' I went on, more for my own benefit than my partner's. 'I even remembered the name of the company that served the notice and he thanked me.'

'So what changed?'

I thought about that. 'I'm not sure. He had a stack of folders on his desk and seemed out of sorts.'

'So you made him feel better by demanding to know why the woman you ratted on was being questioned by his goons?'

'I just asked him why. And I told you, not in those words.'

'Yet he didn't seem to appreciate it anyway?'

I frowned. 'At first he didn't seem to mind, or at least not that I picked up on. But then he gave me this big hug and told me the amateur detective thing wasn't cute anymore. That his deputies don't respect him and it's my fault.'

Now Sarah looked shocked. 'He said that?'

'Yes,' I said, hands outstretched in disbelief. 'Can you believe it?'

'Of course. I'm just surprised he'd admit it.'

'So you think he's right?'

'If he feels that way it doesn't matter what I think.'

Lovely. This week's homework assignment from the shrink must be 'validating feelings.'

'It's that damn Taylor,' I said.

'The homicide detective?'

'He's a jerk, but I think what it boils down to is that Pavlik is getting tired of the eye-rolling and knowing looks whenever I'm around.' I sighed. 'I guess I can't blame him. I'm tired of it, too, and I don't have to be around these people every day.'

'And Pavlik is their boss. Isn't there an election coming up?'

'An election?'

'County sheriff is an elected position with a four-year term, remember? Pavlik is, what? Two or three years into it?'

'About,' I said. 'Are you saying he dumped me because I make him unelectable?'

'I wouldn't say that, mostly because I'm not sure it's a real word.' The gentle ribbing seemed like an effort to get me to lighten up.

It didn't work. 'It is, too. Check your dictionary.'

'Nobody has dictionaries anymore. They just do what I do – Google each spelling and use the one that gets the most hits.'

I grimaced. 'OK, you win. I'll stop feeling sorry for myself.'

'No, please. Keep it up. You usually don't allow me to pick on you like this.'

'You pick on me plenty,' I said, standing up.

Sarah remained in her chair. 'So what are you going to do?'

'About Pavlik? I'm not sure.' I retied the strings of my Uncommon Grounds apron as the bells on the door signaled a new customer. 'One thing I do know is I'm staying as far away as I can from the Swopes. I wish I'd never—'

'Mom?' Eric's voice called from the store.

Before I could ask what he was doing in Brookhills rather than on Interstate 94 halfway to Minneapolis, my son continued, 'Ginny and I need your help.'

TWENTY-THREE

'I just don't see what I can do,' I said for the third time.

My normally level-headed son had dug in his heels and refused to let his father take him back up to school. Now Eric and Ginny were across the table from me. Sarah had brought lattes all around and left us to talk privately.

It was uncommonly thoughtful of my partner so I wasn't surprised to hear her puttering just the other side of the service windows.

'What's wrong with you, Mom?' Eric demanded. 'Do you *want* to see Ginny's mom arrested for her stepfather's murder?'

Right at that moment I couldn't have cared less. But I'd spent nearly twenty years trying to be a better person – or at least appear to be – for my son. Why stop now? 'No, of course not. But has Lynne been arrested? My understanding was the investigators were just asking her some questions.'

'They asked me questions, too,' Ginny said. 'For, like, hours.'

I was at the end of my patience. Lynne and Ginny had asked for my help yet they gave me – and the detectives – only the information that suited them. 'Maybe it wouldn't have been "hours" if you'd answered them. What are you hiding?'

The girl didn't flinch. I did notice, though, that the hands on her lap were clenching and unclenching. 'Nothing. I just know from TV you shouldn't answer questions without a lawyer present.'

'But you still refused to talk to them once Ms Spinelli was there,' I pointed out. 'And you didn't answer her questions, either. Or your mother's.'

Ginny kept the string alive, saying nothing. But the hands kept going.

'Your fingerprints were in your father's office,' I said. 'You had to have been there.'

Now she did flush. 'OK, so I was.'

Finally.

'But my dad wasn't *in* the office, so technically I didn't see him at his office.'

I wanted to slap her smug little face. 'If you're practicing your statement to the detectives, don't forget that "*technically*" he also wasn't your father.'

'Mom,' Eric protested. 'Be nice. Ginny's going to tell the truth from now on.'

Sure she would.

'What time did you stop at the dental office?' I was trying to phrase the question precisely so she couldn't weasel her answers.

'Maybe nine forty-five?'

'Are you asking me or telling me?' I knew Eric would think I was bullying his friend but I'd had enough of being manipulated.

And Ginny seemed to sense it. 'I left Caitlin's house at nine-forty.'

'You told the detectives you left around ten and the building was dark.'

She glanced at Eric and then away. 'It was. But I stopped in anyway.'

I frowned. 'Why, when no one was there?'

'Did you see your dad's car, maybe?' Eric asked.

Ginny brightened. 'That's right. I noticed it when I drove by.'

Not likely. Diane had said William's car was in the parking lot when she'd arrived Saturday morning. Not only was that lot not lighted but the arbor vitae blocked it from the road. Why was Ginny lying? Or *still* lying.

'But you must have known they would confirm your story with Caitlin. Did you ask her to lie for you, too?'

'She was messed up enough that I knew she'd have no idea what time I left.'

'Messed up, how?' I asked.

A look of dismay. 'You're not going to tell Aunt Mary, are you?'

'You are way beyond worrying about my tattling to your aunt.' I stopped short of adding, *young lady.*

'Just pot. And beer.'

Lovely. 'Continue.'

'So, like I said, when I saw Dad's car I figured I might as well get it over with.'

'Get what over?'

'Our "talk."' Ginny made a face. 'He'd convinced himself I was like this genius and then I got kicked out of Quorum before the end of my first semester.'

'But you said your dad already knew, right?' Eric seemed puzzled.

'Yeah, right,' Ginny said, nodding. 'I'd texted when it happened so he'd hear it from me first and not the school.'

I shot Eric a look that said, I hoped, please don't break that kind of news to me in a text. I got a little grin in return.

Back to Ginny. 'But you and your father hadn't talked about it by phone or in person?'

Ginny shook her head. 'Uh huh. He just texted me to come home this weekend and bring the car.'

Which is why she'd made the sudden offer to Eric and surprised Lynne with the visit.

'Did he tell your mom you'd been expelled?' I knew Lynne said she hadn't known but I was taking nothing for granted at this point.

'No. He said before we broke the news to Mom he wanted to talk to me and then to the school. See if we could work something out.'

'He thought he might get you reinstated?'

'I suppose so. Maybe make some big contribution or at least find somebody to blame for me getting bounced.'

'Somebody besides you?' I asked.

'Of course,' Ginny said. 'It couldn't be my fault since I'm just a reflection of him.'

'Of your *step*dad?' Eric asked.

'Sure,' Ginny said sulkily. 'He'd adopted badly.'

Sarah had referred sarcastically to the Swopes as a 'happy family.' I was thinking more 'dysfunctional family.'

Though let he who is without one, cast the first stoned sibling.

'What about the Lexus?' I asked. 'Was your father planning on taking it away?'

'Probably, though he liked seeing people's reactions when they realized it was my graduation present.' Ginny shrugged. 'I'm not sure what the big deal was. He bought it used.'

Now it was Eric who had the I-wanna-smack-her look on his face. He'd gotten my cast-off Dodge Caravan with genuine fake wood panels. But I'd thrown in a full tank of gas.

'I know you were very young when your mom married William,' I said. 'Did you two get along OK?'

'Sure, when I was little. When I got older, though, he started to get creepy.'

From the service area came the sound of a piece of flatware hitting the floor, followed by a 'Shit!' Sarah was listening to every word.

'Creepy how?' I asked. 'Did he come on to you?'

Ginny seemed horrified. 'Ick, no. Just . . . he was an old guy and he'd walk around the house with his shirt off and his gut sucked in. Especially when I had girlfriends over. Like he was this Madonnis?'

'Adonis, I think you mean.' When I was Ginny and Eric's age I thought my parents were old, too. Happily – or not – we all eventually get payback in the form of our very own potbellies, thinning hair and saggy skin. 'Back to that night – how did you get into the building?'

'I have keys.'

I blinked. 'Why would you have keys for the dental office?'

Ginny shrugged. 'My dad gave them to me the last time I was here.'

'For just the dental office itself?'

'And the front delivery entrance downstairs. Which was a good thing because the revolving one next to it wouldn't budge.'

Ted would go ape-shit if he knew his partner had been handing out building keys.

Ginny was frowning. 'But when I got to the tenth floor I didn't even need the key. The office door was open.'

'So you went right in?'

'Uh huh. The lights weren't on in the waiting room but the door that leads to the exam rooms was sitting open so I went back.'

'Weren't you kind of spooked?' Eric asked.

'A little. I yelled, like, "Dad? Are you here?"'

'Any answer?' I asked.

'No, but I heard papers rustling.' She seemed unsettled by the memory. 'I thought he must be there after all.'

If Ginny could detect 'papers rustling' at the end of the hall William certainly should have heard her calling for him.

'So even though you didn't get a reply from your dad you went down the corridor to his office?'

'Uh huh, but he wasn't there. There were papers on the floor, blowing around. I didn't get it at first.'

'That the window was broken?'

'Uh huh.' Again, this time with her head bobbing up and down. 'It was the outside air blowing the papers, not the AC or a fan or anything.'

I remembered the wind whistling in one door of Uncommon Grounds and out the other on Friday night. 'What kind of papers?'

The girl shifted uncomfortably. 'I don't know.'

I wasn't buying it and apparently my son already knew better. 'You said you'd tell my mom the truth if she agreed to help us.'

'She hasn't "agreed to help us,"' Ginny snapped.

'And I won't unless you're honest with me.' And maybe not then.

The girl's shoulders slumped, reminding me of her mother.

'I told you,' Eric persisted, 'you have to be upfront with her.'

She took a deep breath. 'OK, so I picked up one of the papers.'

'The divorce notice?' I guessed.

I got another 'Uh huh,' tears pooling in her eyes. 'And there was an envelope on the desk with a lawyer's name on it.'

We'd circle back to that a little later. 'Did you see anything besides the papers on the floor? Glass, maybe?'

Ginny blinked. 'I don't think so.'

'That means the window was busted out, right?' Eric asked.

'Makes sense. I mean, what could have hit it from the outside way up there?' His face changed. 'Unless maybe a bullet?'

'Nobody has said anything about a bullet or that Doctor Swope was shot.' Certainly not Pavlik, though now I wasn't sure he would have told me had he known. I turned back to Ginny. 'Did you look out?'

She nodded and the motion caused the tears to overflow. The girl might have thought her stepdad 'creepy' but the night of his death had affected her.

'What did you see?'

Ginny glanced at Eric before answering. 'My dad on the ground below.'

'So he was already dead,' I said.

'Obviously,' Ginny snapped.

Eric stared her down. 'Tell Mom the rest.'

I looked back and forth between the two young people. 'Do you mean about Ginny taking the divorce papers?'

The girl's mouth fell open. 'How did you know?'

'The process server gave them to your dad when he entered the building. The police didn't find them so somebody had to have taken them. And, besides, Eric said you knew about the divorce even though your mom told me that you didn't.'

'Blabbermouth,' Ginny muttered in the direction of my son.

'Hey, the "blabbermouth" is the *only* reason I'm considering helping you,' I reminded her.

'OK, you're right.' Ginny appeared slightly chastened. 'The divorce papers had blown onto the floor so I gathered them up and put them in the envelope from the lawyer.'

'What did you do with it?' I asked.

'Hid it in my room.'

And who'd find anything in a teenager's room? At least without a search warrant. 'You didn't leave them in the office because you didn't want anybody to know your mom was divorcing your dad?'

Ginny dipped her head.

'Were you afraid the police would believe he jumped because your mom had filed for divorce?' I asked. 'Or that your mom had pushed him?'

If I imagined I was going to shock the girl, I was wrong. 'Wouldn't you?'

Of course. But that was me. 'Is that why you told Detective Taylor after the interview on Saturday morning that you felt responsible for your dad's death?'

Eric's brow furrowed. 'You did?'

'He was going all Doctor Phil about people blaming themselves when somebody commits suicide, remember?' Ginny asked Eric. 'Since they already thought Dad killed himself, I figured me getting kicked out of Quorum would give them another "precipitating event." I mean, if his getting fired by your dad wasn't enough for them.'

Lynne had said she wanted to prove William's death was a homicide so Ginny wouldn't blame herself. Ginny, on the other hand, had been steering the investigation toward suicide to protect her mother.

A cracked mother-daughter *Gift of the Magi*. And it wasn't even Thanksgiving yet.

TWENTY-FOUR

'So which was it?' I asked.

Ginny's jaw jutted out. 'Whaddaya mean?'

'You haven't said whether you think your dad jumped or your mom killed him. Whichever it was, it caused you to steal the divorce papers and then lie to the police about being there.'

Ginny was silent.

I kept going. 'Once your fingerprints were found and you realized your dad's death was being investigated as a homicide, you took it a step further and let them suspect you.'

Eric's mouth opened but I held up a hand to silence him. 'It's a big deal, Ginny. So, again, what *were* you thinking?'

'I thought that my mom pushed him out the window,' she burst out. 'Is that what you want me to say?'

Honestly, yes. 'Of course not—'

But Ginny wasn't done. 'And you know what? I wouldn't have blamed her. The pervert was cheating on her.'

Hadn't Ginny just said she'd kind of liked William? Seemed like quite a leap from there to thanks for killing the pervert, Mom. 'So you knew about the divorce before you saw the papers that night?'

'No, but that doesn't mean I was clueless about the affair. I just didn't realize Mom had gotten up the guts to divorce him.'

'Your mom told you about Bethany?' I was surprised. Lynne protected her daughter from the divorce but not the seamy reason for it?

'I was home when she came to the door. She was like five years older than me, if that,' Ginny said. 'He might as *well* have been sticking it to my friends.'

There was a lot of anger there. 'Did your mother ask you to keep it a secret?'

'Of course. She was mad and hurt and . . . well, I was the only one she could talk to.'

I understood, unfortunately. If Eric hadn't just left for school when Ted dropped the bomb about Rachel I might have confided in him, too, in the heat of the moment. Though the alternative – trying to keep it from him – hadn't worked either.

'So you think your mom confronted your dad Friday night,' I said, 'with the divorce papers.'

Ginny held her head very still and then nodded just once.

'Have you told your lawyer any of this?'

'No. I didn't want her to think my mom did it.'

Since Kay Spinelli seemed to be representing both Lynne and Ginny, there was also a conflict of interest just waiting to happen.

A thought came – so elementary a light bulb should have gone on over my head. 'What time did you say you stopped by the office?'

'About quarter to ten?'

'And after seeing him and gathering up the papers, you went home?'

'Uh huh. Mom was on the phone with you when I got there, remember?'

'Then you must have heard her tell me she'd gone past the building but hadn't stopped in.'

'Of course. I figured she was lying.'

'Your mom said she left Uncommon Grounds around nine-fifteen?' Eric asked.

'Uh huh,' Ginny confirmed. 'She texted me right around that time saying she was leaving.'

I didn't recall Ginny telling the detectives that last part.

'What time exactly was the text?' My son seemed to have taken over the interrogation.

Ginny pulled out her phone and punched up her messages. 'Nine-sixteen.'

'Did you reply?' I wasn't sure if I was the good cop or bad cop in this scenario.

'No. My mom texts like all the time. It's annoying.'

A reassuringly teenage thing to say. 'Your mom sounded frantic when she called me looking for your dad. Yet you said nothing?'

Ginny's eyes were big under her fringe of bangs. 'What was I supposed to do? Either she already knew where he was or I'd have to admit I'd left him dead and lying in the rain.'

'You honestly thought your mom was putting on an act?'

Ginny shrugged. '*I* was, wasn't I?'

There was that. 'When you picked up the divorce papers and the envelope did you open any desk drawers?'

'It wasn't like I was robbing the place or something.' A defensive tone had crept in.

Why now? 'I'm just wondering where your fingerprints might be.'

'I'm not sure,' Ginny said, cocking her head.

'Because you weren't thinking straight?'

'I hadn't had that much beer.'

'I wasn't thinking about beer.'

Ginny didn't answer and Eric jumped back in before I could pursue it. 'What about the elevator buttons? Did you touch those?'

'Oh, yeah.' She seemed grateful for the change of subject. 'I must have.'

'No big deal,' Eric said. 'If they know you were on the tenth floor they'd also know you took the elevator.'

'True,' Ginny said. 'And there must be a ton of prints on those buttons.'

I decided nothing would be gained by circling back to what Ginny might – or might not – have been on that night. 'Where did you park?'

'On Silver Maple.'

'And you didn't hear or see anything?'

'You mean like hear glass breaking or see my dad's body falling? No. But I was on the sidewalk so I couldn't see him behind the bushes, even if it hadn't been dark.'

'And when you went back down you didn't check your dad's body. Maybe to see if he was dead?'

'No.' Ginny shuddered. 'I could tell he was dead, even from upstairs. His eyes were open and he was just, like . . . staring.'

That didn't add up. 'You couldn't have.'

'I did, too.'

'What my mom means, Gin,' Eric said, 'is that your dad was on his stomach when we found him.'

She threw out her hands. 'I can't help that! You wanted me to tell the truth and I'm telling it.'

'Good,' I said. 'And you're going to have to do it again to the detectives. They'll want to know why you didn't say anything earlier.' Hadn't I just given this very speech to her mother?

'I was protecting my mom.' The 'duh' was implied. 'And who said I'm talking to the storm troopers again?'

'That's why we need you, Mom,' Eric said. 'The sheriff will listen to you.'

'Pavlik and I have decided we're not seeing each other anymore. He wants me to stay out of this, so I'm not sure what I can do.'

Something passed through my son's eyes. Concern, certainly, and maybe disappointment. 'But I told Ginny she needs to straighten this all out. That you would help.'

'My "helping" is what broke Pavlik and me up in the first place.' I felt like I was the kid in the room.

And Ginny confirmed it. 'You're going to let some guy tell you what you can do?'

'Yeah, Mom.'

They were ganging up on me. Taking what we'd taught them about being their own people and tossing it back at us. At me.

I took a deep breath. 'No,' I said. 'I'm not.'

This time the entire rack of silverware hit the tiles.

TWENTY-FIVE

'What's Pavlik going to do?' I asked Sarah as I put the silverware that she'd dropped into the dishwasher. My partner could have done it herself, of course, but she'd been too busy listening. 'Stop dating me again?'

'Dating,' Sarah said, handing me a fork. 'There should be a better word for it at your age.'

'"My age" is younger than your age,' I reminded her.

'Hey, I'm not the one "dating."'

The one relationship Sarah had been in since I'd known her had ended badly, which you might expect when you hold a gun on someone.

'But the point is,' my partner continued, 'why should you get any more involved than you already have? Which is plenty.'

'Because Eric asked me to,' I said. 'He feels sorry for the girl. Ginny's stepfather is dead and she's worried that telling what she knows is going to land her mother in jail for his murder.'

And for good reason. As far as I could see, Lynne was still a viable suspect unless she could prove she went straight home from Uncommon Grounds. The twenty-nine minutes between the 9:16 p.m. text and 9:45 p.m. when Ginny said she arrived at the dental office would have given Lynne plenty of time to drive there and push William out the window.

'So is the kid scared,' Sarah asked, 'or a pathological liar? Take your pick, from what I heard.'

'Yes, and thank you so much for eavesdropping.' I flipped up the dishwasher door and pulled the lever to lock it.

'You want privacy, don't hold your conversation in my train station.'

Since it *was* her building, I didn't have a rebuttal. 'I agree with you that Ginny is hiding something.'

'Has it occurred to you that she might be using you?'

'You mean to influence the investigation? Of course. That's

why before I go near Pavlik with this I'm going to do some nosing around of my own.'

'Which he'll love.'

'Who cares?' I hit the start switch. 'He and his minions already think I'm a busybody. I might as well live up to my reputation.'

'You're doing the time, might as well do the crime. Or continue doing the crime, huh?'

'Exactly.' Two years ago, I'd used my knowledge of Brookhills to help the then new county sheriff solve a murder.

Granted, I'd been suspected of that murder, but the fact remained I *had* helped.

And I'd done it again and again since then, most recently in South Florida a week ago. Faced down wild animals, heroically held the fort, took down the perp – all those sidekicky kind of things.

And now, suddenly, I was a liability? Had Green Hornet dumped Kato? Batman ditched Robin? Hans Solo *gone* solo?

I think not.

But if that's what Pavlik wanted, I'd respect his decision and do my best to stay out of his way and not ask questions. You wouldn't catch me approaching the sheriff with a timid please, sir, I want some more information?

Sarah was studying me. 'You're imagining old movie scenarios again, aren't you?'

'Of course not,' I lied. Film classics were my comfort food and the unfortunately punctuated *Oliver!* was part of the rotation. 'I'm just trying to figure out what my next step is.'

'Other than going to Pavlik,' Sarah said.

'Other than going to Pavlik.' I dumped a scoop of freshly ground beans into a paper filter. 'First thing I need to do is confirm exactly what time Lynne left here Friday night. Who knows? She may have texted Ginny and then waited to hear back from her.'

'That's easy enough to find out. When Amy gets in at three ask her if she saw Lynne leave.'

'I intend to.' Seating the filter on top of an empty carafe, I slipped the whole thing below a brewer. 'If Lynne was here until quarter to ten or even nine-thirty on Friday night then as far as I can see she's in the clear.'

'Only if you believe darling daughter about when *she* was there. And what's to say that Ginny isn't the one who killed Daddy Dearest?'

It did alliterate better than Mommy Dearest. 'Honestly? Nothing. For all I know Ginny and her mother are both pathological liars, as you say. I'm starting to think I should pay more attention to what they're *not* saying than what they are.'

'And don't forget you have other leads and suspects beyond Thelma and Louise.'

And *I* was the one with old movies on the brain?

'The former partner, for one, and your picketer,' Sarah continued. 'Maybe she's another of Swope's conquests.'

'You heard what Lynne said about William's taste in women. Rita Pahlke doesn't fit the profile.'

'Which is young, I know.' Sarah stopped. 'Maybe that's why Ginny stopped by. Maybe they were doing it Woody and Soon-Yi-style.'

Ugh. 'You have to stop saying whatever comes into your head,' I scolded. 'People are going to think you mean it.'

'So if I just think them, it's OK?'

'It's . . . better.' Or it would be, until my partner – without her mouth as a safety valve – exploded into a million pieces like the carafe this morning. 'Or maybe just say them to me.'

'Which I just did.' She waved her hand. 'Let's move on.'

Scary thing was that Sarah often said the things I only thought. So maybe she was *my* safety valve, as well. 'The possibility that Ginny was being sexually abused by William had occurred to me.'

'So I overheard.'

'What did you make of it?'

'You mean his preening shirtless in front of teenage girls? Giving his stepdaughter a Lexus and sending her to an expensive school so *he'd* look good? The multiple affairs. I'd say he's a casebook narcissist and now that he's getting older, he – like Avis – is trying harder.'

She waited until I digested all that and then added, 'So to speak.'

Double ugh. Blessedly a timer on a pot of coffee went off, signaling it had been sitting for twenty minutes and was past prime drinkability. I dumped the old coffee into the sink and, setting the carafe aside next to two other empties, pushed 'brew' for the pot I'd just set up.

'I forgot to tell you,' I said when I'd finished. 'I got some interesting information from Ted at the christening. William's former practice is under investigation for billing irregularities.'

Sarah had started to rinse out the pot I'd just emptied but stopped and half-turned. 'That's a fun new wrinkle. How could you "forget" that?'

'I really haven't had a lot of time to digest it, to be honest. Ted told me this at the christening and, when I got home, Lynne and Ginny were leaving for the sheriff's department so I tagged along. Then Lynne was detained for questioning. Pavlik broke up with me. This morning—'

Sarah held up a soapy hand. 'I'll stipulate that you've been distracted. But something like this? Truly?'

She was right. I was off my game. 'I know. I'm sorry I didn't tell you.'

'And you wonder why I eavesdrop. Is that why Ted was so hot? Swope didn't tell him?'

I nodded. 'But Clay Tartare did. That's the reason Tartare followed him here.'

Sarah cocked her head. 'Tartare wasn't involved?'

'He claims he had no idea what was going on. That William fired their office manager and then took off himself.'

'Now there's a motive for murder.' A wrinkle formed between Sarah's brows. 'Is the office manager we're talking about this Bethany slut? I thought she was fired for this nitrous stuff. Did I waste all that time hazing Lynne for nothing?'

'Only if you call your own amusement "nothing." But you bring up a good question. William told Lynne that Bethany had been fired for misusing the nitrous. If he'd fired her for cooking the books why wouldn't he tell his wife?'

'Or his partner.' My own partner was fully engaged, pots forgotten. 'So the delightful Doctor Swope was screwing the partner – in a business sense – in addition to Bethany in a more deeply personal one.'

'That's what I'm thinking.' Though not in quite so colorful

terms. 'And when he got wind that somebody was on to them he let Bethany go and took off himself.'

'And now Bethany is dead. My murder/suicide theory isn't looking that far-fetched anymore, is it?'

'It's still a long stretch of time between the murder and the suicide. And we have no reason to believe Bethany Wheeler's drowning wasn't an accident.'

'We have no reason to suspect it was. An accident, I mean.' Sarah had turned to the sink and added over her shoulder, 'Now there's something you should look into.'

'In Kentucky? There's enough we don't know right here in Wisconsin. For example, why did Ginny decide to stop by the office when by all accounts the lights were clearly off?'

'Is that why you asked if she'd been in the desk? You really think she was robbing the place? Of what?' Sarah put the carafe she'd been washing into the dish drainer and picked up another.

'Prescription pads, maybe? I'd love to know what crime scene found—' I stopped.

'What?'

'I was just thinking about when I asked Pavlik if Lynne's fingerprints were found in William's office.'

Sarah pulled a dry dish towel out of the drawer. 'What did he say?'

'That Lynne was William's wife so of course she'd been in his office. And then he broke up with me.'

'One too many stupid question?'

'Maybe so.' I chewed on that for a minute. 'I didn't know he'd set a limit.'

Sarah snapped me with the towel. 'Lighten up. Your stupid questions often bag you information you haven't even asked for. It's your method.'

'Thank you. But the reason I brought up Lynne being William's wife is that the divorce and the billing fraud may be two separate motives for getting rid of William but they dovetail nicely.'

'But motives for who? Lynne was the one divorcing the dead guy and Clay Tartare is the one he duped. Ohhhh . . .'

'Exactly,' I said, nodding. 'Lynne and Clay are supposedly former lovers, but we just have Lynne's word—'

'That it's so "former."' Sarah was warming to the theory. 'So

William gets old and trophy wife decides she's made a mistake. She and the boyfriend kill hubby, netting them both the cost basis *and* each other.'

'Maybe they even set William up for the billing fraud,' I suggested. 'Think about it: if Clay is vindicated he gets to keep his practice and any ill-gotten gains he may have pocketed.'

'With no one alive to testify otherwise,' Sarah said. 'I like it. Feels like one of those movies where the jury is hung because there's equal evidence against both suspects.'

'Except there's no evidence against either in this case.'

'There has to be something,' my partner persisted, leaning against the sink. 'What did crime scene come up with?'

'I don't know. But since Pavlik's not an option Ted is our next best bet. It's his office, after all.'

'I'll let you beard that lion since you were married to it,' Sarah said. 'And what about Rita Pahlke? How does she figure in all this?'

It was a good question. 'She may suffer from some kind of mental illness. Ted said she was babbling about everything from "alien abduction to billing fraud and drugs."'

Sarah straightened up. 'Meaning maybe the whack job isn't so wacky. She knew what was going on.'

I chewed on my lip. 'When neither Tartare or Lynne Swope supposedly did. But how could she?'

The bells out front jangled and Sarah looked past me out the service window.

'Well, well, well,' she said, lifting one eyebrow. 'Here's your chance to ask Alien Invasion yourself.'

TWENTY-SIX

'Don't get too close,' Sarah said in my ear as she followed me to the service window. 'Remember that *Twilight Zone* episode?'

Benevolent aliens arrive on earth, supposedly wanting to serve man. Turns out it's for dinner. Yum.

I smiled and then tamped it down for our customer. 'What can I get you?' '

'Oh,' Rita Pahlke said, seeming startled by the sight of me. 'You're just, just . . . everywhere, aren't you?'

'Here more than anywhere,' I said, wondering if the woman had lost it. Or more of it. 'This is my coffeehouse, remember?'

Sarah came up behind me. 'And the dental office where I hear you peed on the dead man belongs to Maggy's ex-husband. That makes you practically family. Welcome.'

Pahlke frowned. 'I didn't exactly pee on him. It kind of ran downhill.'

'Leading to the life lesson: don't spit into the wind or pee upstream of a corpse,' Sarah said cheerily. 'So what can I get you?'

'A good cup of coffee, I hope. The hotel's is awful.' She set her bag on the counter and unfastened her coat.

I resisted the urge to inform her that the bottom of the average woman's purse has more bacteria than a toilet seat. 'So you'll be staying with us in Brookhills for a while longer?'

Even to my own ears I sounded phony and a little arch. A lot arch.

'Just until tomorrow,' Pahlke said. 'The sheriff said I could go then if I provided my contact information.'

Sarah took the pot I'd just brewed off the warmer. 'Good-looking, isn't he?'

My partner subscribed to the 'rub a bruise and it'll stop hurting faster' school of tortured thought. Never mind that it was my bruise she was rubbing.

Rita Pahlke's face was puzzled. 'Each to their own, I suppose. But I prefer hair on men. I'm sure he's very nice, though.'

Pavlik had hair. Dark, thick, tousled – hair that just begged for you to run your fingers through it. 'I think you're talking about Detective Taylor not Sheriff Pavlik. And he's not.'

'Not what?' She was digging through her bag for money.

Nice, I'd meant, but I didn't pursue it. 'The sheriff did tell me that you've been very helpful.'

'I just answered his questions – or the detective's, I guess – as best I could.'

'Had you been at the building very long before we saw you Friday morning?'

'Less than two hours. I waited around until the restaurant opened at seven, which was irritating. Sunrise was six-forty.'

'So?' Sarah asked, sliding the to-go cup across the counter to our customer.

'So it doesn't do any good to picket, does it? If no one can see you?'

Made sense. In a crazy kind of way. 'You had breakfast at seven—'

'Oh, no – I just picked up a large coffee to bring along. By the time I saw you I'd drunk the whole awful cup. I swear they'd reheated the coffee left over from the night before in the microwave.' She went to the condiment cart to tip cream into her cup.

'Why aren't you out there today?' I asked.

Pahlke was perusing books on the shelves next to the condiment cart. 'With Doctor Swope dead there's really nothing to be gained.'

'Gained how?' Maybe William hadn't merely laughed, as Lynne had put it, at Pahlke's extortion demands.

'Yeah, exactly what *is* your deal?' Sarah had elbowed me aside and was leaning on the counter with a 'you can trust me' expression. Either she wanted Pahlke to confide in her or buy a used car.

'My deal?' Rita repeated, slipping a book back onto the shelf. 'What do you mean?'

'I'm asking,' Sarah pressed, 'what did you have on Swope?'

'Shouldn't you ask what they have on us?' Pahlke's eyes were wide.

I glanced uneasily at my partner and then back. 'By "they" you mean . . .'

'The man, of course.' Pahlke still hadn't blinked.

'Better than little green *men*,' Sarah said out of the corner of her mouth before raising her voice to address our visitor. 'You think Swope was in cahoots with the government somehow?'

'Can you possibly be that naïve?' Pahlke asked incredulously. 'Just search "government conspiracy" and "dentist." You'll find it all.'

And anything else you might want. 'But why William Swope in particular?'

The woman's eyes shifted. 'I hang around. I hear things. See things.'

'Like what?' Sarah asked.

Pahlke didn't answer.

'For what it's worth,' I said, 'William Swope *is* being investigated.'

'Drugs.' She said it like it was yesterday's news.

Assuming Pahlke been the source of the anonymous tip, apparently nobody had told her that it hadn't panned out. At least not in the way she'd expected. 'You saw the . . . deal?'

'Uh huh.' She dug a fifty-dollar bill out of her purse. 'Guy in a suit stopped him on his way into the building. Handed him an envelope.'

I frowned as I put her change on the counter. 'Did Doctor Swope give him anything in return?'

'I couldn't tell from where I was, but he turned and went right into the building without opening the envelope. I've seen enough deals going down to see the signs, believe me.'

Oddly enough, I did.

TWENTY-SEVEN

'Rita Pahlke may be a lunatic,' I said to Sarah as the door closed behind the woman. 'But she's an observant one.'

'Who looks like a street person but pays for coffee with a fifty-dollar bill,' Sarah said. 'How does that work?'

'*And*, according to Pavlik, she's staying at the Morrison. That's not cheap.'

'You've got a connection there. Maybe you can charm Stephen Slattery into letting you search her room.'

Rachel's brother, Stephen, was managing the Morrison's transition to a Slattery Hotel.

'Now that Pavlik's a non-starter,' Sarah continued, 'you might want to re-establish relations with him.'

'There never were any relations. A dinner, that's all.' Though it was true Stephen Slattery was a good-looking guy with meltingly chocolate-brown eyes. And seemingly a decent human being, despite his uppity parents and jailbird sister. Which meant, 'He's not going to let me into a guest's room.'

Not that my partner was listening. 'Check and see if Clay Tartare is at the Morrison, too. Maybe you can get a two-fer.'

I ignored that. 'Lynne said William didn't take Rita's demand for money to keep quiet seriously.'

'Think she's lying?'

'God knows,' I said. 'Or maybe William lied to Lynne. Either way, Rita seems to have money to flash around.'

'Though if it is hush money from Swope she has to be bummed. Not only was the goose laying the golden egg about to be busted but so was his neck.' She let her head flop unnaturally to one side.

My partner did have a knack for painting the picture.

The door jangled, saving me.

Amy was a full fifteen minutes early for her three p.m. shift, bless the goody-goody.

'I'll handle things out front,' Sarah said with a significant look toward Amy's back as she disappeared down the hall. 'You grill the barista about wifey's whereabouts.'

So many suspects, so little time. I shifted gears and obeyed, stopping to snag a bottle of water from the refrigerator on the way to the office.

'Do you have a second?' I asked as she hung her jacket on a hook.

'Of course. What's up?'

'I'm just wondering about Friday night.'

'The night of the book club meeting.' Amy tilted her head, sending the multiple hoops on her ear tinkling. 'Helping the sheriff?'

'I wish.' I sat down at the desk and gestured that she should take the side chair. 'Pavlik and I are taking a break.'

Amy's eyes filled with tears. 'Oh, Maggy, I'm so sorry.'

'So you just assume that he dumped me?' I asked. 'Maybe I decided to end it. Maybe he was getting too serious.'

'But why would you do that? You're crazy about him.'

And totally transparent, apparently. 'Yeah, OK – he dumped me. Says I'm making him look bad in front of his deputies.'

Amy sat back. 'That's terrible.'

'I didn't mean to.'

'No, I meant that it's terrible that he cares more about what they think than he does about you.'

'It's important that he maintains their respect.' Why did I continue to argue Pavlik's case? Against myself?

But Amy was too busy empathizing to argue back. 'I'm just so, so sorry. The sheriff is a smart man, though, and he'll realize what he's lost soon enough.'

Who goes looking for a pain in the butt they've misplaced? 'Thank you.'

'You were asking about the book club?' Amy reminded me.

'Yes, thanks. I was wondering what time Lynne Swope left that night.'

The barista rested one elbow on the desk. 'Lynne killed her husband?'

I'd been trying to twist the stubborn cap off the water and stopped. 'Why do you say "killed"?'

'I thought you knew. The medical examiner ruled out suicide. I just got a news alert on my phone.'

See, Maggy? With a news app who needs Pavlik? 'Did the report say anything more? Like what the findings were based on?'

'Something about a head wound. Blunt force, I think.' As she spoke, Amy took the water from me and twisted off the cap before handing it back.

I took it, thinking. The head wound would be the blow I'd seen to William's forehead. Both Pavlik and Sarah suggested it could have been caused by him hitting the ground. The ME apparently thought otherwise. 'Lynne's daughter Ginny asked me to try to help. Given Pavlik has cut me loose, though, I'm not sure how much I can do.'

'But you're great at this stuff, Maggy. You don't need Pavlik.'

Maybe not, but I sure wanted him. 'Do you remember what time Lynne left the meeting? From what I've been able to piece together, William was dead by nine forty-five.'

As I said it, I realized the sheriff didn't have that information. And wouldn't, unless Ginny decided to speak up. So I was one up on the sheriff's department on that, at least.

'About nine-fifteen, maybe? Lynne was one of the first to leave, and I cleaned up and was out of there myself by nine-thirty.'

'Do you remember if her car had gone? It's a white Toyota.'

Amy wrinkled her brow. 'I can't say for sure. I didn't notice it in the lot but she probably walked over, don't you think?'

I hadn't thought about it at all but it made sense that Lynne had left the Toyota wherever she parked it for work. Meaning that after the meeting she could have gone up to her office or just sat in the car for a while, waiting for a reply from her text to Ginny.

The financial planner hadn't mentioned doing either, but that was par for the course with the Swope women, with whom I seemed to be on a 'need to know' basis.

'Does that help?' Amy asked after a moment.

'It answers my question but still gives Lynne half an hour to drive the five minutes to her husband's office.'

'And push him out of a window? Why would she do that?'

'Exterminating a louse?' Sarah was leaning against the door jamb.

'But as Lynne keeps pointing out, she was in the process of divorcing the louse,' I argued for the defense. 'She didn't have to kill him.'

Sarah came farther into the room. 'Even our black widow admits death is cheaper than divorce. Especially when you add in the cost basis thing.'

'Cost basis?' Amy asked.

'When you sell something,' I said, willing to share what little I knew, 'you have to pay tax on your profit. That profit is the difference between what you spent for the property, called the cost basis, and what you got when you sold it.'

'Minus improvements,' Sarah, the former real estate broker injected. 'But forget about that for now. What's important is that if you inherit property the basis isn't what was originally paid for it but what it was worth when the owner died.'

'Even a spouse?' Amy asked, her face lighting up.

'Bingo.' It seemed as though Sarah had been doing her research. 'And I'm betting Lynne Swope was already calculating just how much she'll save on taxes next year when she brought it up on Friday.'

'But Lynne was talking about my brother at the time,' I reminded my partner.

'Whose stash was cash. Don't you get it?' Sarah was now leaning, both hands on the desk. 'It was in Swope's head at the time because she'd been thinking about doing away with hubby instead of divorcing him. She had it planned the whole while.'

'But the news said the Swopes *were* "in the midst of a divorce,"' Amy said. 'So she had filed.'

I really had to ask Amy what news app she used. 'Exactly. Why even start divorce proceedings if you planned on killing the guy?'

'It *is* kind of a red flag,' Sarah admitted.

'Red flag for who?' Amy asked.

'The detectives,' I said. 'They always suspect the spouse, so Sarah means why would Lynne give them even more reason? Why not just pretend everything was fine in the marriage and then kill him?'

My partner wasn't willing to discard a perfectly good theory yet. 'Because Swope didn't have a history of depression or any other condition that suggested he'd do himself in. If Lynne wanted it to look like a suicide she had to provide a reason.'

'And divorce did that,' Amy said, nodding.

I was mulling it over. 'Ted's kicking William out of the practice might have sufficed but Lynne wouldn't have been able to predict that was going to happen.'

'Exactly,' Sarah said. 'Maybe that's why she tried to stop the papers from being served. A viable reason for the guy to take the final leap dropped into her lap. No reason to dirty everything up with divorce.'

Did Sarah have a point? Could Lynne have been upset about Ginny's coming home not because of the divorce notice but because she was planning to kill William that night and didn't want her daughter in the middle of it? Only problem was: 'Lynne was on the phone trying to call off the server when we walked into her office that afternoon. *Before* Ted went ballistic.'

'We only have her word for that,' Sarah said. 'The woman could have been ordering pizza for all we know.'

True. Just because Lynne said it didn't necessarily make

it true. I already was going in circles, so thought I might as well take a drive.

TWENTY-EIGHT

My shift might be over but I had no intention of going home. First stop, the Morrison.

Stephen Slattery was outside on the circle drive, supervising the placement of a bronze plaque.

'The Morrison by Slattery,' I read.

He turned. 'Maggy! Great to see you.'

'Same here,' I said, returning his hug. 'I'm glad to see you're keeping the name.'

'The Morrison has been a destination for visitors for nearly a hundred years. You don't mess with that if you're smart.'

'And you're smart.' I stepped back to get a better view of where workers were setting up scaffolding on the east side of the stone building. 'Though it's been looking shabby for the last ten.'

'The upkeep of a building like this is nonstop. The owner got behind when money got tight and once that happens it's nearly impossible to catch up.'

'Without a huge injection of cash,' I added. 'Which the Slatterys have.'

Stephen grinned, his dark eyes sparkling. 'Don't hate the money, Maggy. Love what can be done with it.'

I laughed. 'Is that your new mantra? When we last spoke you weren't quite so philosophical.' Stephen's relationship with his parents could be tense.

'Keeps me sane,' he said. 'That and being here instead of at the Arms in downtown Milwaukee.'

'Your folks don't often make the fifteen-mile trip west?'

Stephen indicated I should go ahead of him through the heavy double doors. 'They're east-siders. To them, going to Brookhills is—'

'Slumming?'

'More like unnecessary. They do appreciate the grand dame, though.' He swept his arms wide as he stepped into the lobby.

Though the burgundy and gold rugs had faded and the flocked wallpaper was loosening a bit, the three-story lobby of the Morrison was still awe-inspiring. '"Grand dame" is the perfect term for this place. Are all hotels women?'

Another grin. 'Only the good ones. So what brings you here today?'

'Being nosy. What else?'

'I was hoping you'd missed me.' The eyes were intent on mine now. 'Still seeing the sheriff, I take it?'

The glow I'd felt at the first sentence – at least *somebody* was attracted by me – was dampened by the second.

Stephen must have seen it on my face. 'Did I say something—'

I waved it off. 'No, it's not you. Pavlik and I broke up and it's still kind of fresh.'

'How fresh?'

'Like twenty-four hours fresh.'

'Ouch.' He put his hand on my shoulder. 'I'm sorry. You want to sit down? Have coffee or something?' He gestured toward the café in the back corner of the lobby.

'Thanks, but a raincheck, maybe?' Though judging by Rita Pahlke's opinion of the Morrison's coffee we'd best do it at Uncommon Grounds. 'I need to run by Ted's office this afternoon too.'

'OK.' He still looked penitent.

I liked that in a man. 'But can you do me a favor and confirm that a couple guests are staying here?'

Apparently he wasn't penitent enough. 'That's not really what we do, you know. Privacy and all?'

'Would it help if I said they're both possible suspects in a homicide investigation?'

'Does that mean we can expect the sheriff?' He held up his hands. 'Not that he's not a perfectly nice guy.'

'Hey, I don't want to see him anymore than you do.' I wasn't above using my break-up with Pavlik to get what I wanted. 'So if you can just confirm that Rita Pahlke and Clay Tartare are staying here, I can be on my way. Maybe even head off the sheriff's deputies.'

It was a bald-faced lie but Stephen bought it. He really *was* too good for me. 'They are both guests, though separately, if that's what you're getting at.'

It wasn't, but it was good to know. 'So two rooms. Could you check to see when they arrived and for how long?'

'The same day, I think – Friday.' He sat down at the concierge desk and tapped the computer. 'Actually, I'm wrong. Ms Pahlke arrived on Thursday and Mr Tartare on Friday for just one night.' Another couple of key taps. 'Though he extended that.'

'So Clay is still here?'

Stephen nodded. 'Until tomorrow. Both of them.'

'I'd like to talk to Clay Tartare.' I gestured at the red phone on the desk. 'Is that a house phone?'

'It is,' Stephen said. 'Do you want—' He interrupted himself. 'There's Mr Tartare now.'

I turned and saw the tall man getting off the elevator. I gave Stephen a quick kiss on the cheek. 'Thank you and call me, OK? For coffee?'

He smiled. 'Better yet, wine. Which I recall is your beverage of choice.'

'Amen to that.' I hurried away and caught Tartare at the front door. 'Clay?'

He turned. 'Maggy, right?'

'Right.' I stuck out my hand. 'I'm sorry we didn't get a chance to talk on Friday. I know Ted is very grateful that you let him know what was going on.'

He shook my hand. 'Going on?'

With William and your office and all.' Admittedly, it was a little weak. 'Can I buy you a cup of coffee?'

Tartare hesitated, then, 'Sure – why not?'

Why not, indeed.

The coffee, when we were finally waited on, was as awful as I'd been led to believe.

I stirred the second of two creamers into the murky brew. 'I assume you've heard that William's death wasn't suicide?'

'Detective Taylor called to tell me.'

That, in itself, was interesting. I'd been one of the first to find William but nobody had told me anything. 'Are you a suspect?'

'I hope not, though obviously I had reason to be angry with William.'

'But his death isn't going to end the investigation – which I assume is being done by the dental board?'

'Correct on both counts.'

'So you could lose your license.'

Tartare met my eyes. 'Overbilling and suspected prescription drug abuse. It doesn't get much worse.'

He had that right. 'Ted told me about the upcoding. What kind of prescription drugs are we talking about?'

'Painkillers that we prescribed in the office – things like Vicodin and Percocet.'

I'd been the wife of a dentist long enough to know that drug abuse is a real problem among dentists and medical professionals in general. 'William was on painkillers for his back. Was he prescribing for himself?'

'Too risky,' Tartare said. 'From what I've been told these were real patients and legitimate prescriptions. Swope would send the script to the pharmacy in our building to be filled while he finished up with the patient.'

'Your pharmacy was dirty, too?'

'I don't think so. But William arranged to have the pills delivered to the office for the patients to pick up at the front desk as they left.'

'The medication you prescribed as well?'

'Unfortunately. He had me convinced it was providing a service to our clients. All very convenient until the supposed narcotic painkiller wasn't as effective as simple acetaminophen or ibuprofen.'

'He switched them out?'

'That's my theory. There were also some forged prescriptions but I think that was his daughter's work. William wouldn't have been that stupid.'

'Ginny.' It fit with my theory she'd been up to no good in the dark dental office.

'Whole damn family is nuts,' Tartare said, staring into his untouched coffee.

'Including Lynne?' I asked.

'Especially Lynne. And I'm not just saying that because she

dumped me, which I'm sure you know all about.' Now Tartare was looking me straight in the eyes.

I could feel my color rise. 'Yeah, well, maybe I heard something.'

'And it's true.' He stood. 'But I realized very quickly that I was the lucky one.'

'Lucky?'

'Sure,' he said, picking up the coffee-spotted check. 'I'm still alive, aren't I?'

TWENTY-NINE

C lay Tartare's trashing of Lynne had been a surprise. But by the time I got to Ted's office I realized that Tartare had said exactly what you'd expect if he and Lynne were involved. Far smarter, of course, than declaring undying love for the widow.

While Thorsen Dental wasn't open, the rest of the building was and the parking lot was half full. Parking next to Ted's Miata, I waved to the worker mowing the lawn and rounded the corner on the sidewalk before detouring onto the grass. The spot where William's body had lain was newly mown, only the knotted remains of yellow tape and a few small pieces of glass marking the scene.

Continuing to the front entrance, I took the elevators up to ten. Thorsen Dental was dark beyond the rippled frosted glass sidelights, the door closed and locked.

I didn't expect an answer when I rapped and I wasn't disappointed. Pulling out my phone, I punched up Ted's number and waited.

A click. 'He didn't want to go to school. What was I supposed to do, tie him up and throw him in the trunk?'

'Nice greeting,' I said into the phone. 'And I'm not here to scold you.'

'Here where?'

'Outside the office door. Open up.'

Getting no immediate answer, I realized Ted was weighing his options.

'I parked next to your car,' I told him. 'No use pretending you're somewhere else.'

A clunk from inside the office was followed by an expletive.

Finally, Ted opened up. He was rubbing his knee.

'You might want to turn the lights on.' I pushed the switch by the door and nothing happened.

'Diane turns the main power off when she leaves.'

'And you can't turn it back on?' I reached through the reception window to the main switch and flipped it.

Ted blinked against the light. 'I didn't want visitors. For all the good it did me.'

'Sorry. But your son and your deceased partner's daughter showed up at *my* workplace wanting me to help prove that my financial advisor didn't kill said deceased partner.'

Ted sighed and in apparent surrender waved for me to follow him back to his office.

'Convoluted but right up your dark alley, I would think.' He sat.

I followed suit. 'I'm trying to quit getting sucked into these things. For all the good that's doing me so far.'

'What? No more stumbling over bodies, no more sleuthing?' Ted pulled a patient file toward him and flopped it open, no doubt in an effort to appear too busy to talk.

The gesture reminded me of Pavlik the last couple of times I'd been in his office. 'Not if I can help it. I don't see a way out of this one, though, so stop acting like you have better things to do and help me.'

'Why do you need *my* help?' He slapped the file folder closed. 'The sheriff must have told you Swope's death wasn't a suicide. You couldn't have warned me an apparent homicide took place in my building?'

Since I wasn't about to tell him about my break with the sheriff, I just said, 'I didn't know either until an hour ago. Are your building tenants freaking?'

'People want to feel safe. Somebody being pushed out a window is bad on two counts: one,' Ted held up an index finger, 'whoever did it is still out there. And two,' his middle finger joined in, 'the glass must break pretty damn easily.' He shot a wary glance toward the big pane in his own office.

'I'm not sure it was that easily,' I said. 'There was an oxygen tank on the ground near William's body. If his death *had* been a suicide, I'd assume he used it to break the glass before he jumped. Now I'm thinking it was the murder weapon, or at least what sent William out of the window to break his neck ten stories below.'

Ted chewed on that. 'The tank *was* from the nitrous cart we found in his office.'

I was picturing the thing: two cylinders on a cart with tubing that connected to the piece that goes over the patient's nose. One tank – the oxygen – would be green. The nitrous oxide tank was blue. 'Why would it be in an office? It's used in the treatment rooms, isn't it?'

'That's what I told the investigators when they asked.' Ted was eyeing me suspiciously. 'What's going on? Why are you brainstorming with me?'

'It happened here in your building. I think you have a stake in all this and should be involved.'

We might be divorced but I'd been married to the man for nearly twenty years. Ted wasn't buying it. 'Right.'

I surrendered. 'Pavlik and I aren't seeing each other anymore.'

To his credit, my ex didn't gloat. He even seemed to feel bad for me. 'I'm sorry, Maggy. I know you cared for him.'

'Thank you.' I was trying to be as mature as Ted. 'We had . . . professional differences.'

A moment of puzzlement. 'I see.'

'So anyway,' I continued, 'why do *you* think the cart was in William's office?'

'If I had to guess I'd say he was out of prescription drugs to abuse and taking the edge off with the nitrous.'

'So you knew he was an addict?'

Ted shrugged. 'It fits. The back pain he'd bring up sporadically but always using the same words—'

'College lacrosse injury.'

'Exactly. He said it to you?'

I nodded. 'That night on the porch when he got up from the chair.'

'Yet he asked me to help him move his new desk and didn't seem to feel a twinge. And then there were his eyes.'

'What about them?'

'I knew he was on painkillers so it wasn't surprising his pupils were nearly pinpoints, especially with all the light in here.' He swept his hand toward the window. 'But it seemed constant. And then there was the B12.'

'A vitamin?' It seemed like a reach.

But Ted surprised me. 'Regular nitrous oxide use – or abuse – lowers your body's ability to utilize B12 so abusers often take a supplement. Wisely, I might add.'

'Is nitrous oxide dangerous otherwise?' I asked. 'Beyond the vitamin deficiency, I mean?'

'It can be. For our use with patients, it's combined with oxygen. That's why there are two tanks on the nitrous cart. But kids get hold of it in whippets—'

'What's that?' I interrupted.

'The small canisters used to charge whipped cream and stuff in professional kitchens. Nitrous' effect is short, so you have to inhale repeatedly. Without the oxygen mix the brain can be deprived of oxygen.'

That didn't sound good.

'And the B12 deficiency isn't insignificant,' Ted continued. 'It can cause nerve damage in the upper and lower extremities, like numbness in fingers and toes.'

'I noticed when William picked up his mug Friday night that he didn't seem to realize the coffee was hot until he sipped it.'

'An oral surgeon with nerve damage in his fingers,' Ted said. 'Do I know how to pick 'em or what?'

'What,' I confirmed, but I was thinking about Ginny. 'Did you notice anything missing Friday night? Prescription pads from William's office, maybe?'

'I honestly don't know,' Ted said. 'Why?'

'Because Clay Tartare thinks Ginny forged prescriptions. I'm wondering if she planned to continue the habit in her father's new practice.'

'But she wasn't here that night.' His eyes narrowed as he rocked forward in his chair. 'Or was she?'

I hesitated and then nodded. 'She stopped by around quarter to ten. William was already dead, or so she says.'

'And you think she was there looking for prescription pads?'

I shrugged. 'She'd flunked out of school – any normal kid would be avoiding her parents, not stopping in to say hi. But she also admitted there were no lights on in the building.'

'So she should have assumed her father was gone.'

'Exactly,' I said. 'And the office empty.'

'Then how did she get in?'

'She says William gave her keys.'

'For the building? That son of—'

I held up my hands. 'I know how you feel about handing out keys to people but I'm wondering whether William actually gave them to Ginny.'

'She stole them?'

'Or borrowed them sometime over the summer and had copies made.'

'All in preparation for raiding the office Friday night?'

'Or whenever the chance presented itself.'

'Swope told me that Ginny had been in trouble for drinking and drugs. It was one of the reasons he gave for making the move from Louisville, though he asked me to keep it quiet.'

'And you did?' I asked. 'Our son drove home three hundred miles with somebody you knew was a druggie?'

Ted winced. 'He said she was clean now.'

Of course he did. 'Except for the beer and marijuana at her cousin's house. Not to mention whatever she was after here. You said you didn't know if any prescription pads were missing. What about the drug cabinet? If Ginny had keys for the office maybe she also had them for the cabinet.'

But Ted was shaking his head. 'Those keys don't leave this office.'

'Where do you keep them?'

'In the file cabinet.'

I followed him to the office behind the reception desk and a tall metal file cabinet. Ted pulled out the second drawer of the cabinet, toppling one of the framed photos on top.

'At least you'd know if somebody had been in here,' I commented, righting a framed version of the picture Diane had shown me of her twins.

'Diane calls it her "tin-can" burglar alarm. Says it's better than nothing.' He jangled a set of keys. 'See? Still here.'

'You file the keys under K?'

'Like I told Diane, nobody can tell what they open,' he said defensively as he dropped the keys back in.

I assumed the office manager had to choose her battles in bringing the office up to her standards – and the twenty-first century – so I left it to her. 'What about prescription pads? Are they under P?'

'They're printed from the computer as we need them now.' Ted shoved the drawer closed, sending two photos tumbling this time.

I gave up and trailed Ted back to his office. 'So Ginny couldn't have stolen them from William's desk.'

'Not unless he had old pads from his former practice tucked away,' Ted said, settling into his chair. 'Or Ginny hoped he did.'

'What did you say when you confronted William on the porch?'

'Why ask me? You were hovering by the door, weren't you?'

Sometimes it felt good to talk to somebody who knows you so well. Sometimes not. 'People were chattering so I missed most of it.'

Ted sat back in the chair hard enough to make it squeal. 'I think I called him a bastard—'

'Son of a bitch,' I corrected and then reined myself in. 'At least that's what you said inside the shop. You may have called him a bastard *out*side.'

'Maybe. I remember getting increasingly irritated as Swope took his good-natured time pulling a chair away from the building and sitting down. He even held up a hand for me to wait so he could take a sip of his coffee.'

I could imagine the scene and Ted as a ticking time bomb.

'Finally,' Ted continued, 'he set the cup down and asked what the problem was. I said Clay Tartare had called and told me about the board's investigation.' Ted had closed his eyes in an effort to remember and now they popped open. 'That's right – that's when I called him a bastard, because he laughed.'

'At what?'

'I told him he had a lot of nerve playing disapproving parent to Ginny when it was obvious he was hooked on drugs himself.' He looked up at me. 'I assume Clay told you that, too.'

I nodded. 'I expect the investigators checked the drug cabinet?'

'They did. Nothing missing. But then that wasn't his MO.'

Stealing drug samples would be traceable. William Swope had been smarter than that. 'Switching out the patients' pills once they'd been prescribed. It's hard to believe he got away with it.'

'Swope was smooth, which is probably why I didn't check him out as well as I should have. He had me fooled.'

'And a lot of other people, from the sounds of it.' But not Rita Pahlke. Had she been one of the patients whose drugs were stolen? Maybe that's why her teeth were in such bad shape. Once burned she'd been twice shy. Of both dentists and their tracking devices.

On the off-chance William kept old patient files, I asked, 'Can I get into his office?'

'Nope,' Ted said. 'The detectives still have it off limits.'

I stuck my head into the corridor and saw that the door at the end of the hallway was closed and sealed with tape so any tampering would be noticed.

Not that I had any intention of tampering, noticeably or not. 'Did they say for how long?'

'Nobody has told me but one of your main suspects called to say she'd been given the OK to come by tomorrow and pack up his desk.'

'Lynne? When'd she call?'

'About an hour ago, maybe?' Ted lifted up his cell. 'Thanks for giving her my number, by the way.'

'You're welcome.' Assuming Lynne Swope hadn't used her one phone call to discuss housekeeping with Ted, she hadn't been charged. 'Was she calling from home?'

'How would I know?' Ted asked. 'She just said she'd be in to box up his desk in the morning.'

Interesting how everybody seemed to be packing up to leave. 'How did she sound?'

'Sound? OK, I guess. I have the phone number she called me from.' He slid his phone across the desk to me.

I pulled mine out and compared. The digits matched Lynne's call the night of William's death. I punched it up and hit the send button.

'What are you doing?'

'Calling her, of course,' I said, getting to my feet.

'Can't you do that somewhere else? I'm—'

Busy. Right. 'Lynne?' I said into the phone, waving for my ex to shush. 'Are you OK?'

'Oh, Maggy. I'm so glad you called.'

'How did it go at the station yesterday?' I was walking toward the door.

'Wait!' Ted said.

I put my hand over the phone and mouthed, *What?*

Ted looked sheepish and cupped his hand behind his ear, indicating he wanted to hear.

I rolled my eyes and hit speaker. '. . . Talked to the process server, apparently.'

'So they found out about the divorce,' I said, not coming right out and admitting I'd been the stoolie who told them. 'Did they give you any detail on the medical examiner's report?'

'Just that he'd determined that William's death wasn't a suicide.'

'A homicide then?'

'That's what I assume, since I was obviously being questioned in connection with it. Once I realized that, though, I asked for my lawyer.'

'Kay Spinelli?'

'Seemed the most expedient. She finished with Ginny and then came to the interrogation room. Which reminds me, Ginny texted that she's with Eric. He didn't go back to school?'

'No. He was worried about you and Ginny and decided to stay home an extra day.' I glanced at Ted. 'Or two.'

'That's sweet,' Lynne said. 'Are you sure—'

'Yes, I'm sure he's gay,' I said. 'He's just a nice, caring guy.' And probably didn't mind missing a few classes in exchange for being in on the excitement. 'Listen, would you mind if I stopped over?'

A hesitation.

'I have a nice bottle of wine I can bring,' I offered.

'Sure, come on over.'

THIRTY

Ted seemed genuinely disappointed when I left but I promised to keep him informed. Not only did my ex control the crime scene but he had provided a good amount of information, something I'd need in this post-Pavlik era.

Lynne's colonial was on Brookhill Road, just our side of the dreaded traffic circle. She greeted me at the door and took the wine to open while I went into the living room.

'Sorry for the clutter,' she called from the kitchen. 'Our house in Louisville was quite a bit larger.'

While not nearly as small as my front room, this one seemed even more claustrophobic. No sheepdog, admittedly, but boxes, still unpacked, and furniture meant for a much bigger house.

'Have a seat,' she said, indicating a white armchair upholstered in what appeared to be raw silk. She handed me a glass of wine.

I sat frozen, holding the delicate stemmed glass out away from my body and, more importantly, the chair. 'Are you sure we should be drinking red wine?'

'Oh, sure,' she said from the matching couch. 'I hate this stuff anyway. William thought it was impressive.'

'Well, it is that,' I said, not quite relaxing. How long were you questioned for yesterday?'

'A couple of hours, maybe? I got home about six or so last night.'

'That's not too bad.' I leaned forward over my knees to take a careful sip. 'I was worried when I didn't hear from you.'

In truth, I hadn't given Lynne a thought the night before, despite being awake most of it. Wallowing in self-pity takes a lot of dedicated time and energy.

'I'm so sorry,' Lynne said. 'I should have called you.'

'Not a problem.' I'd succeeded in making her feel guilty – or making her act like she felt guilty. Hard to tell with the Swopes. 'What were the detectives asking?'

'To be honest, almost exactly what you warned me.' She set

her goblet on the carved wood table between us. 'You know, why I didn't tell them about the divorce, et cetera, et cetera.'

Glad I helped prepare the witness for testimony. 'And you told them the truth?'

'Just like you said. That I didn't want to say anything in front of Ginny.'

I started to put down my glass and hesitated. 'Do you have a coaster? I don't want to mar your tabletop.'

'Oh, don't worry,' Lynne said, smiling. 'I'm not keeping the tables, either. My taste in furniture runs toward more clean lines. Contemporary or modern.'

The widow seemed awfully merry. Or merrily redecorating. 'Lynne, did you know William was abusing drugs?'

'Nitrous oxide?' Lynne asked. 'I'm not sure I'd call it "drugs" or "abuse." Nitrous isn't a federally controlled substance and it's perfectly legal to inhale in medical or dental settings.'

'Yet William fired Bethany Wheeler for doing just that.'

'I said it was an excuse. She'd become a romantic liability.'

I left the pills aside and stuck with the inhalants. 'So you wouldn't be surprised if he was using it in his office Friday night.'

'Before he died?' She squinted, thinking. 'No, not really. He was under a considerable amount of stress.'

And then somebody killed him when he was nice and relaxed. 'I don't know if you remember but there was a green oxygen tank on the ground near William's body.'

'I do, vaguely. Though I have to tell you a lot of that morning is a blur.' Lynne took a sip of wine and held up a hand while she swallowed. The gesture reminded me of the delaying tactic Ted said William used on the porch Friday night. 'This is *so* good.'

Apparently she hadn't looked at the label when she opened the bottle. My cabinet at home was empty so I'd stopped at the gas station for a bottle. The wine selection suffered in comparison to the hanging air freshener scents. I'd chosen pine. And a merlot.

'Glad you like it,' I said politely and then returned to the subject. 'At first I thought William might have used the tank to break the window.'

'In order to jump?' Lynne waved toward the flat-screen television which she'd switched off when I came in. 'I was watching the news and they said the wound to William's head was "ante-mortem"?'

'Before he died.'

'I'm not stupid,' Lynne snapped.

No, but you *are* an ungrateful bitch. 'My point is that William may have been hit—'

The front door cracked open and Ginny stuck her own head in. 'Hello?'

Lynne got up to greet her daughter. 'You were up and out early this morning.'

'It only seems that way because you slept late.' Ginny picked up Lynne's wine glass and took a sip. 'Ugh.'

Either the girl didn't like wine, or didn't like crappy wine. I was betting on the latter. 'Eric isn't with you?'

'He just dropped me off.' She settled on the couch next to Lynne and sat facing me. 'So what have you found out?'

'What has Maggy found out?' Lynne rotated her head toward me now. 'I thought you were reluctant to get involved, given your relationship with the sheriff.'

If the last three days were Lynne's idea of *un*-involvement, then . . .

'Oh, that relationship is over,' Ginny said, washing her words down with another sip of cheap wine. 'And Maggy's not somebody who lets a man tell her what to do, anyway. Right, Maggy?'

Why did I feel like I was being handled?

Because I was. But if Ginny could lay all my cards out on the table, I could do the same with hers. 'Right. But first things first: tell your mother what you told me.'

Ginny frowned.

'OK, I'll get us started.' I turned to Lynne. 'You know that Ginny was brought in for questioning because her fingerprints were found in William's office.'

'I do, though I still can't understand how they got there.'

I slid a quick glance Ginny's way. 'It seems that—'

'Oh my God,' the girl exploded. 'I'll tell her, OK?'

'OK by me.' I settled back in the chair.

'So I went by Dad's office that night about a half hour after you texted me that you were going home.'

'You did? Why?'

'I wanted to talk to him alone. About school.'

Lynne looked a little hurt but she didn't let it derail Ginny's recounting of that night. 'Did you see him?'

'Uh huh.'

Since Eric wasn't there to do it, I said, 'Tell her everything, Ginny.'

She reached for the wine glass and I slapped her hand. 'Now.'

'Have it your way.' The girl sat back sullenly and folded her arms. 'I went to the office Friday night. The window was broken and I looked out and saw Dad on the ground.'

Lynne looked stricken at this succinct summary. 'Dead?'

Ginny seemed to suppress a sarcastic remark. 'Yes.'

I took a sip of my own wine. It sucked, but not as much as Ginny's attitude. 'The rest?'

'I don't know what you mean.'

'I mean *why* you went there.'

'I already told you. I went to talk to my dad.'

'Despite the fact that there were no lights on in the building.'

'I told you – I saw his car in the parking lot.'

I set down my glass. 'You couldn't have – the lot is hidden from the street.'

'I—' Ginny slapped her mouth shut.

Leaning forward, I said, 'You had your dad's keys duplicated the last time you were home and when you saw nobody was in the office you thought the coast was clear. What were you looking for? Drugs? Prescription pads?'

A hesitation and then a bratty shrug. 'Whatever I could find.'

'Ginny!' The rebuke seemed automatic.

The girl turned to her mother. 'You have a whole lot more to get upset about than this. I didn't take anything.'

'Except the divorce papers,' I pointed out.

'That's why nobody found them,' Lynne said slowly. 'But why would you do that?'

Druggie or not, 'She didn't want you implicated.'

'Implicated.' Lynne's nose wrinkled as she thought. 'Ginny, you thought I killed your dad?'

The girl squirmed. 'I knew he'd been fooling around. When I saw the divorce papers I figured you'd brought them and you and Dad had had a fight.'

Lynne waggled her head, not seeming to know how to respond. Then she pulled out her phone and held it up. 'I texted you I was going straight home.'

A shrug. 'I figured you lied.'

Couldn't blame the kid. There seemed a lot of that going on, which reminded me that I wanted to confirm a chunk of information her mother had fed me. 'Lynne, while you have your phone out, could you check the exact time of the call you made from your office on Friday afternoon?'

She looked surprised. 'Friday afternoon?'

I nodded. 'To the lawyer to try to stop the papers from being served.'

'Oh, sure.' She tapped the phone. 'If you think it will help.'

'I'm trying to put together a timeline.'

'Here it is,' she said, showing me. 'Three fifty-eight.'

I squinted at the screen. Sure enough, an outgoing call to a law office at 3:58 p.m. on Friday – just before our meeting.

'Don't you want to write it down?' Lynne asked.

'I'll just type a note into my own phone,' I said hastily. Truth was I had no use for the information, other than confirming that Lynne had tried to stop the server, as she'd said.

I punched in the note and raised my head. 'How about the text to Ginny saying that you were leaving the book club?'

Lynne punched and then scrolled. 'Nine-sixteen?'

'I told you that,' the girl said.

'I know – I'm just confirming.' I'd remember this timeline excuse for next time. Although, I reminded myself, there should be no next time.

Now to leverage the information. 'Amy also confirmed that you left around nine-fifteen, Lynne. But you didn't call me until after ten.'

Her face flamed. 'You think I killed William, too? Thanks, both of you.'

You're welcome.

'Oh my God, Mom. I'd think you'd be grateful I was willing to take the heat for you.' Ginny stood and flounced out of the room.

Lynne started to go after her but I put my hand on her arm. 'You can deal with her later but we need to talk. Where were you?'

'Where was I when?' A door slammed somewhere in the house.

'Between leaving Uncommon Grounds and calling me nearly an hour later.'

'Could it have been that long?' Lynne asked, reflecting. 'I know that after texting Ginny I walked to my car.'

'In the depot lot?'

'No, I park behind my building.'

Just as Amy had thought. 'Did you go up to your office?'

'No. I waited for a while in the car, I know, and when I still didn't have a reply from Ginny I gave up and drove home.'

'To get here you must have driven right past the 501 Building. Did you see lights?'

'Just the exit signs in the lobby. The ones they have to keep on.' Lynne had been frowning and now she brightened. 'I remember now where all that time went. I was pulling into my driveway when I realized I'd left *Gone Girl* at your shop. It was a library book so I drove back to get it before somebody walked off with it.'

'And?'

'Uncommon Grounds was dark, too, and locked up.'

'According to my timeline,' I said, glancing down at my phone, 'Amy left at about nine-thirty.'

'It was after that, then. When I got home again I realized William's car wasn't in the garage so I tried his cell and office numbers, like I told you.'

'Lynne, William never' – I searched for the word and settled for a phrase – 'came on to Ginny, did he?'

'Heaven's, no!' Now Lynne did jump up. 'I would never have allowed him to touch my daughter.'

I put up my hands. 'I'm sorry. I thought it might be one of the reasons you filed for divorce.' And give Ginny or Lynne – or both of them – a reason for killing William. 'Ginny said he'd been getting "creepy" – her word, not mine – strutting around in front of her friends shirtless.'

'William had a hard time admitting he was getting older,' Lynne said, sinking back onto the couch. 'Somehow he believed that he was still twenty years old and, of course, people wanted to see his six-pack. Whatever remaining cans he had of it.' She picked up her glass and seemed to register for the first time that a good portion was missing.

'Was this new behavior on his part?'

She shrugged. 'More of the same, I'd say. Along with the women. I'm sure they shored up his aging ego.'

'But William couldn't have been more than in his late forties.'

'He was sixty,' she said. 'He dyed his hair, leaving just the right amount of gray.'

Sixty and Lynne couldn't be more than forty herself. But then she'd been 'the younger woman' at one time. 'He looked good.'

Lynne glared at me. 'And how is this helping Ginny and me?'

Not for the first time, I wondered *why* I was helping Ginny and her.

'What about Clay Tartare?'

'What about him?' Lynne's arms were folded like her daughter's had been earlier.

'Were you starting to regret dumping him for the older – and now even older – man?'

'Of course not.' She didn't look at me.

'I don't believe you.' I picked up my wine glass. 'You were divorcing William. People stay in unhappy marriages for years. It's only after they have somebody or someplace to go to that they make the leap.' I cringed internally at the poor word choice.

'William was the one cheating on me. And not just once. The man was a serial adulterer.'

'So why not cheat on him? Seems only fair.'

'Did I ever think about it? Damn right I did.' Now she raised her head, lips pulled back to show teeth like a rabid dog's. 'But *I* didn't do it. Not once.'

I slid back on my chair, no longer cognizant of the wine. 'OK, OK. I'm sorry.'

When she didn't answer me I set the glass down. 'Listen, Ted said the police gave you permission to clean out William's office tomorrow morning. Can I go with you?'

Lynne stood, dismissing me like Pavlik had. 'Ten o'clock sharp.'

I got the message. 'Ten it is,' I said, going to the door.

But Lynne was already helping herself to the rest of the gas station wine.

THIRTY-ONE

'So let's make a list.'

It was the next day – Tuesday – after our commuter rush and before my ten o'clock meeting with Lynne at Ted's office.

Uncommon Grounds was fairly quiet with only Sophie Daystrom out front, immersed in her e-reader. Likely some shade of grey or whatever had taken its place on her reading list. I'd suggest that our favorite octogenarian join the book club but I wasn't sure it was racy enough for her.

I filled Sarah in on my conversations with Ted and Lynne as we finished inventorying the storeroom. Amy had been working on prototype gift baskets and two sat on the shelf – one for the coffee-lover, the other for the tea aficionado. The fact the baskets looked beautiful didn't surprise me.

Sarah's suggestion did. 'You're going to help me? Didn't you say my getting involved was a bad idea in the first place?'

'As reluctant sidekick, that's my job. And my opinion has never stopped you before.' She slipped into the office and returned with a pad of paper and a pen. Balancing the pad on the wire storeroom shelf, she was poised to write. 'So what do we know?'

I guessed I should be grateful I had a sidekick of my own – reluctant or not. 'One: William Swope exited the tenth-floor window.' Just because Pavlik had dumped me didn't mean I had to abandon what I'd learned from him.

Sarah rolled her eyes and wrote down, 'William exited.'

'Maybe you should type this into your phone,' I suggested. 'Then you can send it to me.'

Not surprisingly, my partner ignored me. 'According to the kid he was on his back, but—'

I interrupted, excited that something, at least, made sense. '*That's* why the back of William's shirt was dry – it was to the ground when it started to rain around ten p.m.'

'But the next morning you found him face up. Any chance he wasn't dead?'

'And rolled himself over? I doubt it, given the dent in his head and the broken neck.'

'The kid didn't check? That's kind of cold.'

'Ginny? She was already where she had no right to be. Besides, drunk on beer and probably high on pot—'

'What about the laughing gas?' Sarah interrupted. 'From what you said it was sitting right there. Wouldn't she have thought "party!" and taken a few drags?'

My partner was a smoker – or ex-smoker, depending on the day – not a huffer. But she had a point.

'If for no other reason than to calm herself down, I suppose. But the oxygen – which Ted said should be mixed with the nitrous – was already out the window.'

'But he also told you that addicts go straight nitrous despite the whole depriving the brain of oxygen thing, right? Huff those things that sound like the dogs?'

'Whippets.' Which was a breed of canines, if I remembered my Westminster Dog Show facts. 'Which reminds me, do you think we should tell Mary about Caitlin's stash of pot?'

Sarah was circling and re-circling something on her pad. 'What time did you say the rain stopped?'

'Three in the morning.' It took me a second but then it registered. 'Whoever turned him over had to do it after three a.m. in order for his shirt to be dry.' Or dryish.

'I suppose the Swope girls alibi each other for the entire night.'

'No time like the present to find out.' I punched up Lynne's cell number and put the phone on speaker. 'Lynne? Sorry to bother you when you're probably getting ready to go to William's office, but I had a quick question. Did you or Ginny get up Friday night? Maybe notice when the rain stopped?'

There was a thud and Lynne sounded distant, which was to be expected given our conversation of the night before. 'I was worried about William, as you can imagine, so I didn't fall asleep until very late. In fact, I remember waking up around four or so, surprised that I'd even been able to nod off. It didn't seem to be raining then, though I didn't stick my head out.'

'And Ginny?'

'The girl sleeps like a log. Why?'

'Just wanted to get it into the timeline before I met you.' I held up a finger to Sarah. 'See you at the office in about half an hour.'

'You have a timeline?' Sarah asked when I ended the call.

'No, but I'm sure going to get one. They're very useful, I've found.'

My partner seemed about to inquire further and then think better of it. 'So the Swope women deny leaving the house. For what that's worth.'

'Yup. I know Ginny got home about ten fifteen because I was on the phone with Lynne. And *she* . . . Hang on a second.'

Leaving Sarah in the storeroom, I went out to our bookcase and returned waving a novel.

'You've had a sudden urge to read?' Sarah guessed.

'This must have been Lynne's copy of *Gone Girl*. It has the Brookhills County Library stamp inside it.'

'The library only has a single copy of a book that popular? Even if it *is* kind of yesterday.'

'They probably do have multiples,' I admitted. 'But the presence of this one backs Lynne's version of what happened Friday night. She told me she left it behind and when she came back to retrieve it Amy was already gone. I thought Lynne might be making it up to account for the time when William was killed, but here it is. I shelved it myself the next day but had completely forgotten about it.'

Sarah remained unimpressed. 'Maybe she left it here to give herself an alibi. Who knows if she even came back?'

'She's a reader. You'd think she'd be able to distinguish between fact and fiction.' I laid the book on the shelf between two gift baskets.

'I'm sure she knows the difference,' Sarah said. 'She just doesn't want to let us in on it. Her *and* her kid.'

'Lynne said she isn't having an affair with Tartare and he corroborates it,' I said.

'So it's the one truth to throw us off. Personally I think it's Lynne and Ginny who are in cahoots. Step-daddy is gone and they get to live happily ever after with their new cost basis.'

'Do you honestly think that would be worth killing somebody?'

'Added to the other bennies of death versus divorce. Normal people like you and me don't think anything is worth killing another human being for, Maggy, but—'

'I'd kill for Eric,' I admitted.

'Good for you, mama bear.'

'Mama lion,' I corrected her. 'Mama bear is the one in Goldilocks.'

'Oh, that's right,' Sarah said. 'And as I recall, she didn't kill Goldilocks for trespassing. Though in places with castle laws she'd have been within her rights.'

I was very glad Sam and Courtney had come to live with Sarah as teenagers, not toddlers. Something told me story time in the Kingston house wouldn't have been pretty.

'*Anyway*,' I said, removing my apron, 'I'd best go meet Lynne.'

'Make sure you ask whether her husband and daughter are both addicts.'

'I will,' I said, shrugging into my jacket. 'But I'd also like to know why, six months after moving here, the family has barely unpacked.'

THIRTY-TWO

I t was a gray Tuesday morning but Thorsen Dental's lights were on and Diane was behind the reception counter.

'Morning,' I said to her back.

'Oh, Maggy,' she said, turning a framed photo in hand. 'Sorry I didn't hear you come in. The police must have been in here overnight and knocked over my pictures.'

I held up a hand. 'I'm afraid that might have been us.'

'You?' A frown line appeared on her forehead.

'Mostly Ted,' I said, lest she think I was nosing around myself for the drug cabinet key. 'He closed the drawer kind of . . . hard.'

'I guess he did,' she said, holding up the photo. 'Knocked my babies right off their feet. This is my Jamie now,' she said proudly, exchanging the photo for another one.

'Big guy. Did he play football in school?'

'He did,' she said, taking the photo back. 'Defensive line.'

'All my pictures of Eric are digital.' I pulled my phone out intending to show her a few but noticed it was after ten. 'Lynne Swope was supposed to meet me at ten. I probably should call—'

'Oh, she's here,' Diane said brightly and then lowered her voice. 'Seems to be in an awful hurry, I must say. The deputy barely had time to take the tape down before she hustled in there.'

I had to wonder if Lynne purposely told me to come late. Thanking Diane, I started down the corridor toward William's office.

In one exam room, Ted's back was hunkered over a patient and across the hall his hygienist was supervising some rinsing and spitting. She looked up and waved as I passed by. I found Lynne in the last office, hefting one box off the top of a mahogany desk and replacing it with an empty one.

The room itself was a mirror image of Ted's office at the opposite end of the hall but the furniture was noticeably more expensive and a plush Oriental rug covered the floor. One expanse of floor-to-ceiling window was boarded over with plywood, though, dimming the morning light and blocking the view of the city in the distance.

'Am I late?' I wasn't but it sure seemed that Lynne was finishing up.

'No. I couldn't sleep so I got here a little early.' She opened a desk drawer. 'The sheriff's deputies were just unsealing the room.'

I wondered if she'd already been here working when she'd answered my call to her cell phone. 'Did they tell you anything?'

'Oh, it wasn't anybody I knew so I just stayed in the background until they were gone. Seems like every time I see one of the detectives something bad happens.' Pulling out a stack of manila folders, she stuffed them into the new box without bothering to look at the tabs.

But I did. Mostly new folders and some apparently empty, but a few were dog-eared, as if they'd come from his old practice. No 'Pahlke,' though, from what I could see. 'Aren't you going to look through these?'

'Why?' She pulled out another stack. 'No matter what led up to it the end result is the same. William is dead. Oh, by the way.' She slid a thin black notebook across the desk to me. 'Here's this year's calendar. Maybe it'll help with your timeline.'

Bless my non-existent timeline. I flipped open the calendar and turned a few pages, my enthusiasm waning. 'This is empty.'

'I guess that makes sense. William wanted a fresh start here. He must have bought a new planner.'

'Have you come across the old ones?' I asked, peeking over her shoulder.

'No.'

Would she tell me if she had? Or *anything* that really mattered? 'Lynne, was William stealing patients' drugs and sending out fraudulent bills?'

She turned to face me, her hands balled into fists resting on her hips. 'You can't honestly believe that woman. I told you she's crazy. And a blackmailer.'

Actually she'd said extortionist, though blackmail was a form of extortion.

'The Louisville practice is being investigated. Do you deny the allegations?'

The word 'allegations' seemed to calm her some. 'I don't give them any credence. And I certainly wouldn't repeat them.'

The last was said in an accusatory tone.

'It can't hurt William's practice now,' I pointed out.

'That's a low blow, Maggy. And from someone I've come to consider a friend.'

'But true, all the same.' I held up the front page of the calendar, which showed the entire year, each month in its own little square. 'You said you moved here just after tax time, right?'

She seemed thrown off balance by the change of subject. 'Yes. Why?'

'So the end of April?'

'May the first. Again, why do you ask?'

The woman routinely didn't answer my questions; she had a lot of nerve demanding I answer hers. 'That's one, two, three, four, five.' I touched each month as I counted. 'November the first was six months.'

'So?'

'So you filed for divorce a little more than six months after the move.'

Now she saw where I was going, though it didn't seem to bother her. 'Wisconsin law says you have to be a resident of the state for six months in order to file here.'

'And you said the divorce laws were more advantageous in this state.'

'Kentucky is an equitable distribution state when it comes to property division, as is Minnesota. Wisconsin, though, is a community property state.' She smiled. 'You'd be surprised what a difference it can make.'

'Which explains why you moved to Brookhills rather than to Minneapolis where Ginny was going to school.' Though she didn't plan to stay long, given she hadn't unpacked or furnished her office beyond the essentials.

'I am a planner, after all,' Lynne said. 'William wanted to escape his past and I wanted to escape him. I'm just the one who chose the route.'

'Is that why you kept your mouth shut about the "allegations"? If William's practice came tumbling down your property settlement might be worth a whole lot less.'

A nod. 'I wasn't the one romancing young women into cheating and stealing for him. I shouldn't have to pay for his crimes.'

'Do you have any idea who went to the board?'

'Probably that idiot Clay at the urging of his new office manager.'

'I suppose an office manager would be in a position to catch it.'

'Or to do it.' Lynne Swope turned back to her work.

'Like Bethany Wheeler.' I circled the desk so I could see Lynne's face. 'She was overcharging patients and switching out drugs. All for William. Did she tell you about it when she came to see you that day?'

Lynne smacked the desk with the palms of both hands and leaned forward on them. 'Yes, she did – is that what you want to hear? She told me everything she'd,' finger quotes, '"done for him." The over-billing, the drug scam, the after-hours sex fueled by nitrous and painkillers.'

'So you killed her?'

'Me?' Lynne straightened, appearing genuinely surprised. 'Why would I do that?'

'Because she was about to blow the whistle on William and you needed the time to divorce him.'

It was a good theory but Lynne was shaking her head. 'I needed the time but Bethany wouldn't have gone to the police. I'm certain of that.'

'Why?'

'Because the little fool loved him. She still hoped I'd divorce William and he'd marry her.'

'You call Bethany a fool but the same scheme had worked for you. William's first wife found out about your affair and divorced him.'

'And paid for it, financially.'

'Not that you cared. You were the young office manager back then, cheating with the married doctor. Were you also scamming clients for him, too?'

'No. Apparently that was a new trick the old dog was teaching.'

For whatever reason, I believed her. 'But how could they get away with it without his partner knowing?'

'Clay's not the brightest bulb, believe me.' The financial planner shifted the box. 'Now can you hand me the files in that drawer?'

I gathered them, taking the time to digest what Lynne had just told me. Was the woman a killer – perhaps even a two-time killer? I had no idea. I didn't even know exactly how Bethany had died, beyond that she'd drowned somehow. A boating accident or—'

'Please.' Lynne was holding the folders already in the box upright expectantly, waiting for mine.

I handed her the stack and reached for another. As I did, I noticed the top one was tagged *Staffing-L'ville*. Keeping that, I passed the rest to Lynne.

'What's that?' she asked.

I flipped it open. 'Looks like job applications.'

'So?' She said it as a sigh, almost as if she were bored of the subject of William. As she probably was.

But I was paging through the applications and résumés and finding them fascinating. 'I assume these are William's notes. "Pretty but a little horsey through the hips." Each application has a photo attached to it.'

Now I'd caught her attention. 'Strawberry blonde,' she read over my shoulder. 'Flat-chested. Smart.'

'Did William consider "smart" a negative or positive?'

'Oh, positive,' Lynne said. 'My husband did like a challenge.'

'"Not sure – gorgeous but naïve,"' I read on the next cover sheet and then squinted at the picture. 'She looks familiar.'

'She should.' Lynne took it. 'And I'll be damned if he didn't have her nailed in more ways than one.'

'What do you mean?'

'William should have trusted his instincts.' She held up the photo. 'This is Bethany – naïve enough to think he cared about her. What a . . .'

She went on but I wasn't listening anymore. I was looking at the picture of a young blonde woman with a pronounced widow's peak.

THIRTY-THREE

'Can I use your laptop?' I had burst into the dental exam room and now two sets of eyes turned my way.

One set hovered above a mouth held open by cotton wads and clamps; the other was glaring at me from below a miner's head lamp. 'What for?'

I held up a hand to shield my eyes from Ted's light. 'I need to Google something. Privately.' Lynne was gone but there was no computer in William's office. And this certainly wasn't something I could do at the front desk with Diane over my shoulder.

'In my office.' Ted gestured something that could be read as 'get out' or 'go ahead.'

I did both.

Slipping into his desk chair, I cracked open the top and touched a key. Nothing happened.

Argh. The man probably shut down his computer every night. And didn't fire it up the next morning. And why should he? He had 'people.'

I hit the power button and waited.

When the search engine came up I typed the words Bethany Wheeler obit, figuring that should about cover it.

It did. *Bethany Wheeler. Died at the age of 24 on April 2.*

No maiden name. And the photo was different than the snapshot attached to her file. In this one Bethany wore what Lynne had called 'Reese Witherspoon bangs' covering her high forehead, but she was recognizable all the same as the woman in the personnel file.

I studied the heart-shaped face, wishing I dared retrieve the framed photo from the file cabinet for comparison. But I was almost sure I saw traces of the little girl with the widow's peak, holding her brother – Jamie's – hand.

I scrolled lower in the obituary.

'Preceded in death by her husband, Victor Wheeler, Bethany is survived by her mother, Diane Laudon . . .'

And just like that, I had the confirmation I was looking for. Bethany Wheeler was, indeed, Diane Laudon's daughter.

But if Diane had come to Brookhills to avenge her daughter, would she use her own name? Not that the average widow and foster mother – assuming those parts of her story were true – would know how to get the fake identification and social security number she would need to get a job.

And I could attest that Diane's credentials and experience were impeccable since I'd done the search. I thought about that. Bethany died April 2 and Diane had started here toward the end of April. April 24, to be exact. William, not until May 1. So, somehow, she'd known he was making the move to Thorsen Dental.

I clicked back to Google and entered William's name, searching for anything posted in April. And found it. Just a line in the 'New to Town' column of the April 11 *Brookhills Observer* – William's name and the date he was joining Thorsen Dental – but it was enough. Diane could easily have come up with it as well. A little research on Thorsen Dental and she'd have found the job opening. It must have seemed like fate.

Once hired, Diane would have no worries that William would notice a family resemblance. Bethany was adopted. It did explain, though, why the office manager didn't have an adult photo of her daughter on display but there was one of her son. The fact that she even displayed the younger photo made me wonder whether Diane was playing with Swope. Daring him to notice the woman he'd bedded in the face of the little girl she'd been.

So how had Diane felt when William walked past those family photos every day for six months, probably not even noticing them? Was she angry?

Then there was Lynne. She said she'd read Bethany's death notice, but that was before the Swopes moved to Brookhills. Even if Lynne had read far enough down to see Diane's name, there was no reason for her to have remembered it and put it together with the office manager in her husband's new office.

Fact was, Bethany just didn't matter that much. To anybody, that is, but her mother.

I switched back to the obituary and clicked print. As I did, I caught the bottom line: The family suggests memorials to the Drug-Free Foundation.

My assumption when a family suggests memorials to the American Cancer Society, for example, is that the person died of cancer. Had drugs – an overdose, maybe – killed Bethany? If so she'd probably had a habit far worse than making free with the nitrous oxide. Or was I reading too much into the wording of the obituary?

No printing noises, so I hit print again and considered the nitrous cart. Ted had told Diane to cancel William's appointments and that William would leave his keys on her desk. Had she waited for William and – realizing that it was her last chance – beaned him with the oxygen cylinder, sending him flying out the window?

Pavlik said they'd found nothing they didn't expect to find

on the tank. That might include blood and the like, of course, but the officer manager's fingerprints wouldn't raise any red flags.

Diane had the keys and was accustomed to being the last one in the dental suite and closing up. William wasn't. Which made me wonder – he certainly wouldn't have packed up his desk in the dark but the lights were off both when Lynne had driven past and when Ginny had stopped by and seen William's body. Had Diane automatically flipped off the power when she—

The computer screen went black.

THIRTY-FOUR

As I feared, the reception desk was empty when I raced out. No sign of Diane and the only light came from the windows. I saw a paper in the printer's tray and picked it up.

'What the hell?' Ted's head came around the corner. 'I'm in the middle of a procedure. What happened to the power?'

'Your office manager is a woman of habit. She switched it off as she left. Just like Friday night.' I waved the obituary in my hand. 'I know you have document sharing, but you also share a printer?'

Ted nodded. 'A top-of-the-line laser printer is expensive.'

Twenty years ago maybe, but I wasn't going to debate it with my cheapskate ex-husband. 'Call Pavlik and tell him I think Diane Laudon is William's killer. She's taken off but I'm going to see if I can follow her.'

'Diane? I—'

I didn't wait to hear the rest.

I reached the parking lot just as Diane was swinging open the door of a blue Hyundai Accent just two cars away from my Escape.

'Diane!'

The office manager turned, keys in her hand. 'Oh, hi, Maggy.

Will you tell Doctor Thorsen I wasn't feeling well and needed to leave? That I'll see him tomorrow?'

'You saw the obituary I sent to the printer,' I said.

A quick uptake of breath followed by a slow shake of the head. 'You have a child. You understand.'

My child, thankfully, was still alive. 'Bethany died of a drug overdose?'

The adopted mother shoved a curl of gray hair off her forehead. 'Suicide, overdose. I've found it's pretty much the same thing when you're dealing with an addict.'

'Had Bethany had a problem with drugs before?'

'Before William Swope, you mean? No, though her mother was a junkie. That's why Bethany and Jamie came to me in the first place.'

'How old was she then?' I was hoping I could stall Diane long enough for Pavlik and his troops to get there.

'Four.' She swung her purse across the driver's seat and let go so it landed on the passenger one. 'Beautiful little girl already showing signs of an attachment disorder. That's why I couldn't have her separated from her brother, you see?'

I did see, unfortunately. In a lot of ways, I was in utter sympathy to what Diane had done. In others ways, not so much. 'Attachment disorder. You mean she had trouble bonding?'

'With some people. Others she was inappropriately affectionate with. The poor baby was starved for human interaction – she didn't . . . well, she didn't quite know how to handle it. She could be inappropriate, especially with older men. Looking for a father figure, I suppose. My husband, he did the best he could with her. But—' She shook her head.

'William must have been thirty, thirty-five years older than Bethany.'

'Her first husband was even older. Victor died of cancer and Bethany nursed him right through to the end.'

'She sounds kind.'

'To a fault. Their junkie mother tracked the twins down a couple years back, probably looking for a handout. Jamie told her to go to hell but Bethany gave her a chance.'

'She went into your field – medical office management.'

Diane nodded. 'And more's the shame. If she hadn't she

wouldn't have gone to work for Swope after Victor died. She was still mourning and I think that's why she fell so hard. She would have followed Swope to hell and back.' A grim laugh. 'I guess she did, in a way.'

'William Swope told his wife that Bethany drowned.'

'He'd be right about that.' She slid into the driver's seat. 'When Bethany was fired she came home to me. She was a mess – trembling and crying when she got off the plane. I put her to bed and stroked her hair, told her I'd call her brother and we'd get her into treatment in the morning. To just rest and that every-thing would be all right.'

'But it wasn't?' It came out as a hoarse whisper.

'That night she swallowed every pill she'd brought with her, climbed into the bathtub and went to sleep. The next morning I found her slipped down under the water.'

My stomach rose into my throat. 'I'm so, so sorry,' I said again.

'I'll never know . . .' She ran her hand over her face and started over. 'I mean, they say you'll never know what's in their heads. But . . . I think Bethany was afraid I would put her in rehab and go after Swope.'

It's something I might have done.

'As it turned out, she was right. Though I didn't know it that night.'

'What changed?'

'Me.' She was looking past me into the distance. 'When some-body you love kills themselves it opens this door you never even knew was there.'

'Suicide.'

'Yes.' She met my eyes. 'Here one second, gone the next. So . . . easy.'

And irreversible. 'But look at the misery left behind.'

'And questions – lots and lots of questions.'

With no answers, as Taylor had said.

'So anyway,' Diane said, taking up the story again, 'I decided if life was ever going to make sense again I needed to do some-thing about Swope. I like to think that Bethany would have wanted that. She just . . . couldn't stay to see it happen.'

'But what about Jamie?' I asked.

'Jamie is why I made it through. But I still had to do something. Something for Bethany.'

Diane put the key into the ignition. 'You printed out Bethany's death notice. I assume you saw my name?'

'Yes.' I stayed where I was so she couldn't swing the door closed. 'It confirmed what I'd suspected, looking at Bethany's picture and the one of the twins on your file cabinet.'

She'd started to turn the key and now her hand dropped. 'You recognized her from two photos. He knew Bethany – slept with Bethany – and had no idea she was the girl in that photo. Hell,' a dry laugh, 'I'm not sure he ever noticed it.'

'I'm a mom,' I said. 'Maybe—'

'Don't make excuses for him,' she snapped. 'Swope knocked that frame down every time he opened the drawer to get keys for the drug cabinet. Not only did he never look at it, he never set it back up again.' She was staring out the windshield toward the building facade but, I thought, seeing something very different.

'What happened that night?' My voice came out a whisper.

She looked at me. 'That night?'

'Friday.' When she didn't answer, I said, 'I can understand how desperate you must have been. All this work – getting hired in the first place and suddenly you were down to one night to do what you'd come to do. You knew William would be back to pack up his desk so you just waited for him with the oxygen tank.'

'You think we came to Brookhills to kill him?' She cocked her head and thought about it. 'I guess that's true at its core. But no, I didn't set out to hit him with the tank. He came in, full of himself as usual. Rolled the nitrogen-oxide cart right out of my office where I was replacing the oxygen cartridge. I told him to wait until I finished but he didn't listen. Must have needed his fix.'

I didn't miss the fact that Diane had said 'we.' Filing that away for now, I tried to stay on track. 'So you followed William into his office?'

'*Only* to replace the tank,' she said, like a teacher correcting a student. She was gazing straight out the windshield. 'Oh, don't get me wrong. I wanted my moment. I wanted to tell William Swope exactly who I was and what I thought of him. That he had destroyed the kindest soul on this earth.'

Diane swiveled her head toward me. 'But do you know what he was doing when I got there?'

I shook my head.

Diane Laudon met my eyes. 'Crying.'

'Crying?'

'Can you believe that?' She shook her head back and forth as if she still couldn't believe it herself. 'He was standing at the window reading some papers and sobbing like a baby.'

'Did you see what the papers were?'

'I pulled them away so I could take a look. I was hoping a subpoena or something that meant he'd finally been caught. But no, it was notice of "dissolution of marriage."'

'Divorce.'

'Everything he'd destroyed,' Diane said, 'and he's crying because *his* nice comfortable world is falling down around him.'

I knew that my mouth had fallen open so I closed it. And then opened it again. 'Are you telling me William Swope *did* commit suicide?'

'Hell, no,' she said, turning the key, 'I swung that tank for all my might. Sent him straight through that pane of glass.'

At least I had the satisfaction, if you could call it that, of being right. 'The oxygen went with him?'

'I threw that out after. Figured it would look like he busted out the window with it and jumped. And it worked, for a while.'

'Is that why you flipped the body? To make it look like the head wound was from hitting the ground?'

She tilted her head. 'That wasn't my idea. But it was a damned good one, to give credit where credit is due. And to clean the blood off the oxygen tank, too.'

I was still trying to work through everything and didn't catch the meaning of her words at first. 'Wait, whose idea was it then? Your son's?'

'Jamie? You don't think I'd involve him in this, do you? I protect my children.'

'Then who?'

'Why, the woman who owed it to Bethany for all the hurt she'd caused her in the first place. Her mother.'

'The junkie?' I was thinking furiously.

'This was all her idea in the first place. Bethany told her all about Swope's shenanigans. She came to see me after the funeral and I decided that, junkie or not, she was right. Swope owed us.'

Then I had it. The same hairline but on a brunette.

'Rita Pahlke is the twins' mother.' I stepped back a half-step. 'So you didn't just meet her at Uncommon Grounds that morning. It was all an act to—'

But Diane suddenly floored the accelerator and off she went, propelling the Accent up over the parking barrier.

I jumped into the Escape and followed, wondering where the hell the cavalry was. I'd done my part, first keeping Diane Laudon talking and now tailing her. I could tell you one thing: Pavlik's people would be on their own snagging Rita Pahlke. Assuming Bethany's birth mother was still in town.

The Accent turned right onto Silver Maple and then left onto Brookhill Road.

My phone was on the seat next to me and now it rang. Pavlik, thank the Lord. 'I'm on Brookhill Road heading east following Diane Laudon's blue Accent,' I said without preamble. 'I didn't get the license number but I think she might be heading for the freeway.'

'You're driving?' While it wasn't technically illegal to talk on a cell phone while behind the wheel in Wisconsin, it was frowned upon. Especially by Pavlik.

'I'm being careful, but if she gets onto the highway we're going to lose her. Oops.' Cut off a Honda.

'Oops, wha—' Pavlik started to say. Then, 'I won't ask what this woman said and why she's running now. I'm sending squads. Once you hear them, back off. What cross street are you passing?'

'I'm approaching Highway 108, and you need to pick up Rita Pahlke, too.'

'Pahlke? Why?'

'I'll explain late—' I broke off. 'Oh, dear Lord.'

'What? What?' Pavlik was sounding a little panicked.

'The traffic circle,' I said. 'I hate traffic circles.'

'Why—' Again the sheriff broke off. 'Put the phone down and pay attention to your driving.'

Roger. The Accent was approaching the roundabout now, Diane Laudon forced to come nearly to a stop behind a red car yielding to traffic. As I closed in the Accent plunged into the circle, my Escape almost on her bumper. In the distance I could hear sirens, but 'in the distance' wasn't good enough. Once out of the circle Diane would be at the freeway ramp.

As the red car ahead of the Accent shifted to the center lane of the roundabout I made my move, accelerating and veering to the left, just clipping the Accent on the rear bumper.

The car swerved right and from my higher vantage point in my little SUV I could see Diane fighting the wheel. She brought it back into the lane and accelerated, tires squealing. I stayed close. We were going too fast, I thought, to risk the abrupt change of direction needed to exit onto one of the four arterials that fanned off the roundabout. Too fast to do anything, in fact, but keep the wheel cranked and go round and round.

Oh, and pray. I was praying.

We passed first the one turn-off, then the second. A silver Toyota just nosing out slammed on its brakes as I sailed by. I hunched against the driver's door as if my body weight was the difference between the Escape flipping or not. I could imagine my higher, boxier vehicle doing cartwheels until it came to rest on one of the surrounding lawns, while Diane's ground-hugging Accent continued on its merry way.

As we passed the spot we'd entered the circle, I realized I had to make a move before we gained much more speed. Taking a deep breath, I stepped on the gas pedal. The Escape surged forward and this time it caught the Accent squarely on its left taillight. The blue car went abruptly to the right, according to plan. I went left, which wasn't so much the plan. Yanking the wheel to avoid the center island, I saw the Accent hit the opposite curb.

Diane screamed as the car went airborne.

THIRTY-FIVE

The Accent landed halfway up the flat front lawn of a two-story colonial.

Me, I continued around the circle one last time, my foot trembling on the gas pedal.

Tremulous victory lap complete, I pulled my Escape up on the grass next to Diane's. Ramming cars and running them off the road wasn't in my usual repertoire and now I struggled with an act as simple as putting the SUV into park and turning off the ignition. As an afterthought, I pulled the handbrake. Then I sat, trying to slow my breathing.

The door of the Accent cracked open.

Goddammit. Fumbling to undo my seat belt, I yanked open the door and launched myself after Diane, who was already sprinting toward the house.

My first thought was damn, she's fast for a fifty-something. My second was where did she think she was going?

Then I saw the black car parked on the garage apron. A newly washed Mercedes, water beads still glistening and the engine running. If the owner was stupid enough to leave that car out here with the engine on and door unlocked, I had half a mind to let Diane steal it.

But no. I'd come this far, triumphed over the traffic circle – used its centrifugal force to take out the Accent, in fact – and I was going to see this through.

Besides, the woman was at least a decade older than I was.

Pride spurring me on, I dredged up my last trace of adrenaline to close the distance between us and throw myself at the back of the office manager's knees. The inspiration for the takedown was my success with the bump from behind on the traffic circle, but I had to admit it was a lot more painful without the cars.

Diane landed hard on the cobblestone driveway, me just short of her. Pushing myself up, hands bleeding, I—

Splurt.

What the hell? I looked around to see a thirty-something in khaki shorts wielding a super-sized garden nozzle. He was hosing us down like we were two strays in a dog fight.

'Wait,' I sputtered. 'I'm—'

'I don't care who you are,' he said, blasting me again. 'You destroyed my lawn and you're going to wait right here. Listen.' He pointed skyward as if the sirens were coming from above.

In reality, they were circling. And as I sank back down next to a soggy, silent Diane, the wheeled cavalry finally arrived.

'So you have Diane Laudon in custody, but is there any sign of Rita Pahlke?' If sitting in Pavlik's office was always a little awkward, today was downright painful. And not just because my palms and knees were starting to scab over.

'Not yet. As it turns out, Pahlke's a petty criminal who's been on the streets and in and out of the system for years. The woman knows how to be invisible.'

'Like acting nuts, so everybody looks the other way.' I shifted in the guest chair. 'While according to Diane this whole thing was Rita's idea. She's even the one who flipped the body and cleaned off the oxygen tank early Friday morning to make William's death look like a suicide.'

'Sadly for them, our medical examiners aren't stupid. The blow was obviously ante-mortem and there were still traces of blood on the canister. Even with the rain.' His tone said, 'Amateurs.'

I hid a smile. 'You have to admit that Rita was crafty, right down to being back at the hotel to buy coffee at seven. That way she could be seen picketing for a while before discovering the body at nine with Eric and me as witnesses.'

'Oh, she was crafty, all right. Unless Laudon can prove Pahlke was the mastermind, the only thing we may be able to charge her with is tampering with evidence.'

The birth mother covering up a crime the adopted mother committed at the birth mother's suggestion. Made one's head spin.

'On the other hand,' Pavlik continued, 'Lynne Swope claims Pahlke was blackmailing her husband. Maybe the DA here or in Louisville can make that stick.'

'Diane said Bethany confided in her birth mother.' Probably another attempt on the girl's part to bond with somebody. Anybody. Everybody. 'Rita must have decided to leverage what she knew to squeeze William, using the crazy act as cover.'

'From all reports, the "crazy" wasn't an act.'

Meaning a possible insanity plea. I wouldn't put it past the woman. 'But what about Diane? What'll happen to her?'

'Her attorney will probably argue that William Swope accidentally tripped and fell against the window during their argument. That she did nothing worse than panic and try to cover it up. In my mind, though, it's premeditated murder.'

'She told me she swung at him in a moment of rage.'

'After stalking the man and getting herself hired at his place of employment.'

Fair argument. But, 'Diane wasn't in her right mind. She believed that William turned Bethany into a junkie like her mother and then dumped her.'

'You realize you're defending the woman you ran off the road and then captured.'

'Not according to the guy with the hose. You should have heard the hero on last night's news.'

Pavlik's lips twitched. 'So I'll tell the DA to call him instead of you as a witness for the prosecution.'

'I don't want to be a witness for anybody. Especially the Swope women. As it turns out, Lynne really wasn't at the office that night and Ginny arrived after William was dead just like they said. Not that you'd know that from all the lies and half-truths they told. Any chance there'll still be a criminal investigation into what was truly going on in the Louisville office?'

'That's up to law enforcement there. But with William Swope and Bethany Wheeler dead . . .' Pavlik shrugged.

So maybe Lynne would get her wish and all this – or at least any fall-out from William's role in the fraud – would go away. She, Ginny and their cost basis could live happily ever after. Far, far away, I hoped. 'Poor Clay Tartare is still left holding the bag.'

'He is.' Pavlik stood, the interview apparently at an end. 'You were right about the back of Swope's shirt being dry, you know. And the lividity indicating the body had been moved. In fact, you were right about a lot of things.' The sheriff didn't look happy about it.

'I'll try not to continue the streak.' I expected – hoped for – a wisp of a grin.

When I didn't get it I got to my feet, too. 'Well, I'd better get home. Ted is driving Eric back to school tomorrow morning and we have one last frozen pizza to eat before he goes. And a movie to watch. He ate all the ice cream.' I knew I was babbling so I stuck out my hand.

Pavlik, who'd come around the desk, didn't take it. 'I do love you, you know.'

I started to say that I did know but the truth was, 'No, I didn't know.'

'I'm sorry, Maggy.' He shook his head. 'This has been eating at me for a while.'

Don't cry, Maggy. But I did want to understand. 'Are you sorry because you love me? Or because you don't want to see me anymore?'

The sheriff opened his mouth but I held up one of my scraped hands, suddenly afraid of the answer. 'It's who I am, Pavlik. I would die for my son and maybe even my big, smelly sheepdog. I stick my nose where it doesn't belong. And I'm not nearly as nice as people think I am – which, admittedly, is saying some-thing.' I shrugged. 'But it's part of the package.' I stood on tiptoe and kissed him on the cheek. 'And I'm sorry, too.'

As I turned to leave the sheriff touched my shoulder. 'When you followed me into the Everglades I realized something.'

'That I have a future in law enforcement?' I wanted to see him smile.

But his eyes got even darker. 'I *realized* that I did love you.'

Did. We were very close and the sheriff smelled of Dial soap and aftershave. It was unfair of him to do this to me only to say goodbye, and I didn't know what else there was to say.

I settled on, 'Thank you.'

A tiny grin slipped away. 'I have plans to run for a second term as sheriff.'

'And I'm a political liability,' I finished for him.

'You're a pain in the butt is what I was going to say.'

Now I was the one who smiled.

'Ever since I was a little boy,' Pavlik said, 'I've never been sure of what I wanted until I didn't have it anymore.'

'By then it's too late.'

'Exactly.'

I shook my head. 'I don't understand.'

'I don't want it to be too late. But . . . I needed to figure things out.'

We were going around in circles. 'Which is what you said.'

'And almost immediately realized it was the very last thing that I wanted.'

'What was?'

'To be without you.'

What? I pushed back from him, forgetting my smarting palms. 'You couldn't have told me? I've been miserable these last few days.'

'It's been thirty-six hours.'

Truly? 'Well, it feels longer.'

'For me, too.' He pulled me close again.

'But what about Taylor?' I murmured into his chest after a moment. 'And the rest of them. Losing their respect, I mean.'

'The way I see it, respect me, respect my wife.'

I went very still. 'What?'

Pavlik placed his finger under my chin and tipped my face up to his. There were silver flecks in his blue eyes.

'Maggy Thorsen, will you marry me?'